Muriélle

MURIÉLLE

Muriélle

The Story of a Model,
a Painting,
and the Artistry of
John William Waterhouse

James Kaye

Copyright © 2004 by James Kaye.

Cover Illustration: *La Belle Dame sans Merci*, by J.W. Waterhouse, Hessisches Landesmuseum Darmstadt.

Title Page: Detail from sketch for *Hylas and the Nymphs*, by J.W. Waterhouse, Ashmolean Museum of Art, Oxford.

Page No 241: Engraving of an original water nymph painted by Henrietta Rae. Engraver and location unknown.

Library of Congress Number: 2002095365
ISBN: Hardcover 1-4010-7944-X
Softcover 1-4010-7943-1

All rights reserved. No part of this book may be reproduced or transmitted in any form or by any means, electronic or mechanical, including photocopying, recording, or by any information storage and retrieval system, without permission in writing from the copyright owner.

This is a work of fiction. Names, characters, places and incidents either are the product of the author's imagination or are used fictitiously, and any resemblance to any actual persons, living or dead, events, or locales is entirely coincidental.

This book was printed in the United States of America.

To order additional copies of this book, contact:
Xlibris Corporation
1-888-795-4274
www.Xlibris.com
Orders@Xlibris.com
16852

Contents

PROLOGUE 9
CHAPTER ONE
    THE INTERVIEW 15
CHAPTER TWO
    THE LETTER 43
CHAPTER THREE
    THE TEAROOM AND THE GARDENS 56
CHAPTER FOUR
    THE TURNING POINT 80
CHAPTER FIVE
    THE METAMORPHOSIS 94
CHAPTER SIX
    THE ARMOUR AND THE KNIGHT 109
CHAPTER SEVEN
    MURIEL'S MODEL FRIENDS 126
CHAPTER EIGHT
    THE PLAY AND THE QUEEN 136
CHAPTER NINE
    THE LAKE AND THE WILLOW 167
CHAPTER TEN
    ON WANDERING KNIGHTS
    OUR SPELLS WE CAST 193
"LA BELLE DAME SANS MERCI"
    COMMENTARIES ON THE POEM, THE POET,
    AND THE PAINTER 227

REFERENCES 249
EPILOGUE 251
ACKNOWLEDGMENTS 253
PROVENANCE 255

FOR MY WIFE AND ALL READERS WHO ENJOY
THE ART OF J. W. WATERHOUSE.

PROLOGUE

Muriélle is a novel that takes readers into the mind, heart, and life of an unforgettable young woman when coming of age; intelligent, free-willed, engaging to know, and lovable. Her heartfelt story is fictional, inspired by the life and art of John William Waterhouse during the first months of a relationship with a newly found model, Miss Muriel Foster (Muriélle), the principal character.

Principal events take place in the Primrose Hill Studios, London, where the story begins on a spring day in 1893, then the Royal Academy of Arts, Waterloo train station, Maids of Honour tearoom, Royal Botanic Gardens, Theatre Royal, and lastly The Serpentine, a lake in Hyde Park where the story ends on a day in summer.

Muriel Foster lived in England during the 1890s when seeds of feminism were sprouting into new attitudes, life styles, and behavior of young women different from their mothers and adult expectations, often unacceptable. Young girls were expected to live at home until married, but in the changing times of the period marriage wasn't inevitable. Living single was an option.

Muriel exercised that option to make a new life for herself as a model in an artist community known as Primrose Hill Studios north of London's Regent's Park. There, she became a sitter chosen for her long hair and statuesque beauty. It was there that she entered into the unconventional life styles of older neighbors and friends including interactions with other young models who influenced her life. In her fast-changing new world, Muriel faced conflicts between her youthful naïvety, strict upbringing, and the requirements of sitting as a figure model in an era of Victorian morality.

While much is known of the professional life of her employer and mentor—John William Waterhouse R.A. (1849-1917)—little is known of him privately. There are no children, contemporaries, or memoirs to speak of him, and while a large collection of his works remained with his wife long after he died, and were later sold at auction, no library, diaries, journals, files of papers, or collections of letters are known to exist. There are no institutional records to research except for a handful of sketchbooks and a few letters in museum and private collections. In the latter are also a few mementos.

What happened to the bulk of Waterhouse's personal estate that should have been preserved for posterity, and could have been a wealth of information on the life of the man, remain a mystery. Researchers of Waterhouse can only assume it was disposed of after his death; but how and for what reason?

Anonymity may have been as Waterhouse wanted, for he is described by biographers as retiring and unassuming, and not especially a figure of society or a man in pursuit of honors. He was a private individual and he seemed content to paint quietly in the privacy of his studio homes; first in Primrose Hill and then in St. John's Wood. He was, however, a respected member of the Royal Academy of Arts where he became an associate in 1885 and a full Academician in 1895. There, he exhibited most of his now famous paintings including his 1901 Diploma picture, *A Mermaid*, still on display in the Academy where it has been viewed for more than a century.

Like *A Mermaid*, Waterhouse masterpieces are admired for the beauty of their female subjects of mythology, history, and literature modeled for by young and wistful beauties. He valued above all else the visual appeal of the female figure, draped or undraped, and to this day seductive images of his young models haunt male imagination. Aside from paintings, Waterhouse also sketched heads of young women in chalk and pencil.

He was, accordingly, an accomplished portrait painter of young and beautiful patrons including adolescent girls; always attractive. One of many portraits was of an especially pretty young girl, age about ten, with long red hair worn partly in waist-length braids. Attracted to her beauty, Waterhouse sought permission from her parents to paint her. The portrait on display in the Royal Academy of Arts during a 1914 exhibit drew praise of Waterhouse's portraiture talents but, perhaps, as much for the visual appeal of the lovely young girl.

Waterhouse is not known for portraits of men, or of older women. It is unquestionable that he was a romanticist, a dreamer, and an admirer of young beauty. With brushes and paints instead of swords and lances Waterhouse was a "knight errant" in pursuit of damsels in his artistic adventures.

He was, moreover, a naturalist and a keen observer of the natural scene to give meticulous attention to landscape, plant, and animal details. Much of the English flora and fauna depicted in Waterhouse paintings are identifiable down to genus and species, such as house martins, *Delichon urbica*, in Waterhouse's 1888 *The Lady of Shalott* and 1889 *Ophelia*; and ravens, *Corvus corax*, in *The Magic Circle*.

A yellow iris, *Iris pseudacorus*, is prominent in Waterhouse's *Echo and Narcissus*. Pink wild roses, *Rosa canina*, and white water-lilies, *Nymphaea alba*, are identifiable in *Nymphs finding the Head of Orpheus*, and 1894 *Ophelia*. In the latter is a white willow, *Salix alba*. A yellow water-lily, *Nuphar lutea*, is depicted in *Hylas and the Nymphs*. A foxglove, *Digitalis purpurea*, is seen in *The Lady Clare*, and wild cherry trees, *Prunus avium*, are prominent in Waterhouse's *Windflowers* and *Boreas*.

Butterflies of the family Nymphalidae are seen in Waterhouse's *Summer*, and domesticated pigeons, family Columbidae, appear in numerous paintings such as *St. Eulalia*. Domesticated guinea fowl, family Numididae, are shown in Waterhouse's *The Favourites of the Emperor Honorius*, and scattered through other paintings are goats, leopards, swine, fish, snakes, and toads. In *The Lady Clare* and *The Mystic Wood* is a deer. Waterhouse was prolific and accurate in the depiction of plants and animals.

Waterhouse was a masterful storyteller on canvas, and his interpretation of the John Keats poem of the same name reveals much about the thinking of the painter, and the poet (see "La Belle Dame sans Merci" Commentaries).

It has been written that in no other painting is his desire as strongly present as in *La Belle Dame sans Merci*. The knight is, the biographer believed, Waterhouse himself captivated by his model. His desire for her is betrayed symbolically by the manner in which he grips his lance. In turn, mutual desire is depicted symbolically by a heart upon the model's sleeve, and her noose of luxuriant hair looped around the knight's neck is the obvious start of a seduction, overtly depicted and suggested. She pulls him down to her for an invited kiss, and the finish of the story rests in viewer imagination. In Keats's poem, the knight and his lady "slumber on the moss."

A similar, recurring scene of enticement with a knight reappears in Waterhouse's 1905 *Lamia* based on Greek mythology and another John Keats poem of the same name. The touch of the model's hand and her long gaze are again acts of seduction. The name, "Miss Muriel Foster," is inscribed on a preliminary sketch of Lamia's profile.

Another scene of seduction is cast in *Hylas and the Nymphs* wherein Hylas is believed symbolic of Waterhouse, and the model is the nymph again with long, auburn hair and seductive gaze pulling him down to her.

It's said the Victorian era was "littered with liaisons between artists and models," and that they were "companions, mistresses, and possessions." They were provided housing, finery and allowances. Artists made their models central parts of their work, and affection for favorite models inspired artists to great heights. An important source of information on models of the Victorian era and their relationships with artists is *The Artist's Model from Etty to Spencer* by Martin Postle and William Vaughan. Other inspiration came from writings more than I can name. But for information on the changing morality of young women of the times—a theme in this story—I am indebted especially to Sally

Mitchell's *The New Girl*, and Charles Booth's *London*; both of which investigate morality, life, and behavior of English youth at the end of the nineteenth century.

To bridge the linguistic gulf between American and British English ("TransAtlanticisms") this novel is written for readers on both sides of the Atlantic, compromising grammar, punctuation, spelling, and terminology.

The following story is fictional. It is the story of a young model coming of age while sitting for one of John William Waterhouse's most popular works of art, *La Belle sans Merci*, 1893 (front cover) inspired by his model and based on the poem by Keats. For purposes of the narration, some chronological facts are altered but it all begins on a spring day in 1893 with a knock on a door.

James Kaye
Second Edition
2004

CHAPTER ONE

THE INTERVIEW

"I met a Lady full beautiful, a faery's child;
Her hair was long."

Excerpted from *La Belle Dame sans Merci,*
Keats 1819

A sign on the carriage gate into a quadrangle of twelve artist residences north of London's Regent's Park read "Primrose Hill Studios." A statuesque young woman with blue-grey eyes, and auburn hair rolled up beneath a flat straw hat, stood outside looking in.

Neatly manicured grounds about the residences were bright with garden flowers but despite the sunny day and warm colours of pink and red roses, rhododendrons, and azaleas, and maroon and yellow carnations, the 1893 mid-morning March air was crisp. The young woman pulled her thread-bare woolen shawl closer around her shoulders. House martins flying north in spring migration swooped low over rooftops. She watched them dart about.

A lady in fashionable attire strolling through the gardens came near the gate walking an Aberdeen terrier tugging on its leash. "Excuse me ma'am," the young woman called out. "I'm sorry to bother you but could you let me in? The gate is locked." The startled Aberdeen barked at the sound of a stranger's voice.

"Who do you wish to see?"

"Mr Waterhouse, the artist."

"Is he expecting you?"

"I think so. Mr Pickersgill of the Royal Academy spoke to him about me several days ago, and said I would be here at ten this morning for a sitter interview. I arrived on the hour but the gate was locked and it's now half-past," the young woman said concerned as she looked at her watch. "Mr Waterhouse hasn't come to let me in and I'm afraid he's forgotten."

The lady removed a key from a coat pocket and opened the lock. The heavy wrought-iron gate groaned on rusty hinges as it swung inward. The Aberdeen wagged its tail in a friendly greeting and sniffed the hem of the girl's ankle-length dress.

"I am Mrs Greiffenhagen," the lady said in introduction. "Please enter. Mr Waterhouse lives in number six . . . over there in the left corner of the quadrangle." She pointed in its direction. "Nino may have overslept this morning. I noticed his lights on late last night." The young woman looked puzzled.

"You called him 'Nino' but Mr Pickersgill told me to see a 'John William Waterhouse.' Do I have the right Waterhouse?"

"Oh yes! His name is 'John William' but his friends and family know him as 'Nino,'" Mrs Greiffenhagen explained. "He was born in Italy, and 'Nino' became a nickname when he was a young boy."

"I see . . . but if Mr Waterhouse has forgotten my appointment I'll need to come back another time," the young lady said, disappointed not to have met him as scheduled.

"Don't go just yet! Moments ago Mrs Waterhouse was out on her patio cutting roses. He may be up by now."

"Then I should hurry along. I don't want to be any later for my interview than I am already. Thank you, ma'am, for letting me in."

The young lady bent down to pat the terrier 'good-bye.' The Aberdeen licked a friendly hand then wagged its tail and whimpered as she walked away.

"I'll leave the gate open," Mrs Greiffenhagen called out. "Close it again when you leave."

The young lady acknowledged the request then continued apace to the blue front door of Studio six where she stopped to brush some hair in place before rapping the door knocker. There was no reply. She rapped again. A long moment later the latch clicked and the door creaked open.

"May I help you?" Mrs Waterhouse looked out and asked, puzzled by an unexpected stranger at her door.

"Yes ma'am," the young lady replied, anxiously. "My name is Muriel Foster, ma'am . . . and I'm here to see Mr Waterhouse for an interview."

"An interview, Miss Foster?" Mrs Waterhouse asked, inquisitively.

"Yes ma'am . . . for a position as a sitter. My appointment was for ten this morning. I'm sorry I'm late."

"I am Esther Waterhouse. Please come in. My husband is just getting up. I don't think he expected you. Was the gate unlocked?" Esther asked, as she took Muriel's shawl and hung it on a hall tree hook.

"No ma'am . . . but your neighbour, Mrs Greiffenhagen, saw me standing outside. She let me in."

Muriel straightened her hat in the hall tree mirror and brushed a wisp of hair in place. Esther took notice of its auburn colour and the girl's tall and slender beauty.

"Do you live around here?"

"No ma'am. I live south of the river."

"Well then, you had a long way to come. Did you have any trouble finding the studios?"

"No ma'am. I was told Primrose Hill can be seen from Regent's Park and I knew where the park is. I've been to the zoo before."

Mrs Waterhouse ushered Muriel down a hallway into a studio to a grouping of Chippendale chairs around a coffee-table in front of an open fireplace. Coal embers from a late night fire glowed faintly and a hint of smoke permeated the room.

"Please be seated. I'll inform my husband you are here. He is usually up by this hour and painting but he overslept this morning. Would you like some coffee?"

"Yes ma'am. That would be very kind, thank you."

"The coffee is brewing so it won't take more than a few more minutes. Mr Waterhouse will be in shortly."

"Would you mind if I look about? I've never been inside a studio. It all looks so interesting."

"Then you've never been a model, Miss Foster?"

"No ma'am . . . but I would like to be."

"Then feel free to look about . . . but please try not to disturb anything. Mr Waterhouse is fussy that way. I'll be back shortly with the coffee."

A blue and white vase of aromatic red and pink roses decorated the rectangular coffee-table in front of Muriel. Stacked on top were issues of *The Studio*, *The Magazine of Art*, and *The Art Journal*. Propped between marble bookends stood copies of Sandby's *History of the Royal Academy of Arts*, Cook's three-volume set of *Art and Artists of Our Time*, and a cover-worn copy of William Smith's *A Classical Dictionary of Mythology*.

A cuckoo clock chimed the three-quarter hour. Muriel checked her watch, then stood and walked about the studio cluttered with easels, stools, and dusty tables littered with paints, brushes, and stacks of sketchbooks. A roll of canvas hung from a wall, and lengths of wood for making stretch-frames stood upright in a corner. Framed canvases leaned against a wall.

Pencil and chalk sketches in black and sanguine dotted the walls. Muriel put her hand to her bosom disconcerted to see one of a nude young woman. "How embarrassing," she thought to herself.

On an easel in the centre of the room stood a painting draped with canvas. "Dare I peek?" Muriel asked herself. "Best not to disturb it," she decided.

A portrait of Mrs Waterhouse hung above the fireplace mantle. In a far back corner of the large studio was a recently slept-on sofa bed with a rumpled pillow and covers tossed aside; the just arisen Mr Waterhouse awakened by her knock she feared.

Bookcases stood against another wall filled with sources of reference on art, poetry, history, literature, biology, and mythology.

Clay sculptures with 'JW Waterhouse' etched on bases stood atop the bookcases. Adjacent was a bank of mismatched file cabinets stacked with papers on top, next to an opened, cluttered, roll-top desk with pigeon-holes crammed. A Remington typewriter sat on the desk with an unfinished letter rolled part-way through. Curiosity got the best of Muriel. The letter was addressed to an art gallery in South Australia. "Hmmm," she wondered. "Dear Sirs," it started.

A large, north-facing skylight in the cathedral ceiling and double glass-paned doors to a patio lit the studio with indirect sunlight. A black-painted floor prevented reflection.

Muriel looked out over a garden bright with roses and azaleas enclosed by a high, ivied fence. Up higher on nearby roof tops, native woodpigeons sat perched on chimney tops and a gathering of domesticated pigeons walked about on the patio. Muriel took her seat watching the antics of an amorous cock bob its head, and with tail feathers spread strut in pirouettes before a hen preening feathers, obviously disinterested. Muriel smiled, watching, and looked again about the studio and at the drawing on the wall. "How can girls pose nude like that?" she wondered. It was nothing she could ever do.

Mrs Waterhouse returned with a silver tray and a blue and white service. She sat facing her guest and poured cups of steaming coffee for Muriel and herself. Muriel smiled, thanked her, and took a careful sip to savour the flavour and aroma. "Hmmm," she hummed to herself.

"How delicious," she remarked to Mrs Waterhouse. "What kind is it?"

"It's an imported 'Bourbon Santos' from Brazil, my husband's favourite . . . the best of the Santos varieties grown in the highlands of Sao Paulo. The higher grown the richer the flavor he claims."

"Well it's delicious, but Bourbon is a funny name for coffee. Isn't that a kind of liquor?"

"Not in this case," Esther laughed, breaking an otherwise dour expression. "The coffee name comes from the island of

Bourbon in the Indian Ocean. It was from there, my husband tells me, that the beans went to Brazil where they are now grown and exported already roasted around the world. They come by sea to Liverpool and then by train down here to London."

"I see."

"Mr Waterhouse grinds the beans himself, and he delights in morning coffee and afternoon tea."

"Well I like his coffee . . . and your lovely vase of roses," Muriel said, as she leaned close to sniff a red one. "They smell so nice," she remarked.

"Mr Waterhouse and I enjoy garden flowers . . . and wildflowers when we visit the countryside. Most of my husband's canvases are sprinkled with flowers, and two of his earliest paintings as you might know are of flower markets."

"No ma'am, I didn't know, but I love flowers myself. I work as a flower girl in the Waterloo train station."

At that moment Mr Waterhouse entered, and in knowing his renown as one of England's well known figure painters Muriel arose to curtsy in polite respect.

"Good morning Mr Waterhouse," she said in a cheery voice.

"And good morning to you, but please . . . please be seated." Waterhouse studied the very pretty woman as she took her seat. She was not anyone he knew or remembered meeting.

"This is Miss Foster," Esther said in introduction. "She's here for an interview."

Esther then dutifully excused herself to leave her husband and the prospective model to themselves; knowing that when models are about she was not to interfere needlessly in her husband's painting or his business.

"May I pour you another cup of coffee, Miss Foster?"

"Yes sir, thank you . . . it's most delicious."

Waterhouse sat opposite and poured steaming cups for both of them, trying his best to remember where and when he might have met the young lady, or had he ever. He didn't want to embarrass them both by having forgotten. He knew he had lapses of memory at times.

"Morning coffee I think is an elixir for life," Waterhouse said, as he took a long first sip, "certainly to get one's day started . . . and believe me I need a start this morning," he chuckled. "I was up late last night."

"Yes sir, I know," impish Muriel remarked nonchalantly, looking down into her cup to avoid eye contact.

Waterhouse looked startled by her comment. "How could you have known I was up late?"

"Your neighbour, Mrs Greiffenhagen, let me in through the gate. She told me. She said your lights were on late last night."

"I should have known. Mrs Greiffenhagen seems to know all of everything that goes on around Primrose Hill."

Muriel laughed, then took another sip of coffee, savoured the flavour and remarked casually in jest: "It tastes Brazilian." Waterhouse looked surprised she should know such a thing, but Muriel continued before he could comment.

"It tastes rather like a Santos variety I think . . . maybe a Bourbon Santos . . . and from the rich flavor the beans must have come from the higher elevations of Sao Paulo."

Muriel commented matter-of-factly in pretense she knew about coffees when in fact she knew nothing. She then took another sip looking down into her cup again. Waterhouse sat puzzled.

"Now don't tell me Mrs Greiffenhagen told you the kind of coffee I enjoy. I know she seems to know everything about everybody around here but___"

"No no sir!" Muriel interrupted with a giggle. "I'm only joshing, and I wish to apologize, but I have moments when something funny catches my fancy. I never heard of Bourbon Santos from Sao Paulo, but the name sounded funny. Mrs Waterhouse told me when she served it."

"Well of course," he chuckled, "The Mrs told you, but you had me going for a minute. I couldn't imagine."

Waterhouse sat amused by the young woman's delightful humour and charming personality. He had an immediate liking for her.

There came a lull in the conversation however and with

joshing aside Muriel now felt a bit uncomfortable sitting before one of England's most distinguished painters to whom she hadn't yet been formally introduced, and carrying on an inane conversation about something of which she knew nothing.

Moreover, it occurred to her since Mrs Waterhouse departed that she was alone with a man contrary to proper etiquette for a young unmarried woman. With a quick glance, Muriel smiled nervously at Waterhouse then looked about the room; again at the drawing of a young woman who obviously *had* been alone with him.

Waterhouse's jovial demeanour turned sober. He raised his cup with both hands and sipped while gazing intently over its steaming brim at the pretty lady seated in front of him, admiring her youthful beauty but struggling to remember what previous arrangements if any had been made for an interview.

"I'm sorry Miss Foster," Waterhouse finally apologized, "but to save my soul I don't remember an appointment for this morning. But Mrs Waterhouse said you are here for an interview." Muriel felt embarrassed he had no knowledge.

"Yes sir . . . for a position as a sitter. My being here was to have been arranged by someone else. I'm sorry you weren't informed." Waterhouse felt relieved he hadn't forgotten but disappointed he hadn't known she was coming.

"I'm known to forget things," he said to help ease her mind, "sometimes badly, but had you and I discussed an interview I would have remembered someone as lovely as you." Waterhouse smiled and Muriel lowered her eyes blushing at his flattery.

Waterhouse extended his hand to introduce himself. "I am John Waterhouse. Now tell me how we came to have this appointment."

"Sir, my name is Muriel . . . Muriel Foster. This interview was to have been arranged by Mr Pickersgill of the Royal Academy. He told me a week ago he would speak to you on this matter."

"So, Pickersgill was in on this. I should have known. We talked not long ago about my need for a red-haired sitter and he offered to help find one through the Academy . . . but how do you know Fred Pickersgill?"

"I work as a flower girl in the Waterloo train station and Mr Pickersgill came in last week on his way into London from the Isle of Wight, where he said he lived. He bought a boutonniere from me and when I pinned it to his lapel for him he asked if I had done any modeling. I told him 'no,' but that I wanted to be a model . . . and maybe an actress."

"Well you *are* pretty . . . I should say beautiful . . . and your hair is a lovely auburn, the colour I'm looking for in a model. On those attributes alone you have potential, and if your hair is long enough for my needs I could use you as a sitter, providing of course you can sit still," Waterhouse chuckled.

With another blush at another compliment and a smile at Waterhouse's humour about sitting still—unknowing he meant it seriously—Muriel continued.

"Mr Pickersgill said you were searching for a sitter my age with auburn hair, and he suggested that I meet you this morning at ten. He gave me your address and said he would make the arrangements."

"Well that explains this morning, and the time. I'm usually up and painting by this hour, but I haven't seen Pickersgill since he returned to the city, and I don't have a telephone for him to get in touch with me. I heard, however, he left London for a week the day after his arrival. That would explain why I didn't hear from him . . . but it was good he sent you to see me. I do need a sitter with long, auburn hair."

"Maybe you would consider me. My hair is quite long."

"I must say I like the colour of it. The model who usually sits for me is dark-haired and dark-eyed, but she took a part in a play which takes up too much of her time now to model. Incidentally, that is her on the wall." Muriel fidgeted. Had he noticed her looking?

Waterhouse reached for a copy of *The Magazine of Art* and opened it to a bookmark. "This is a painting of her I did last year of *Circe offering the Cup to Ulysses* which now hangs in the Oldham Art Gallery up near Manchester."

Muriel laid the magazine in her lap for illumination from the overhead skylight, and while studying the model's revealing diaphanous attire, hiding little of her breasts and limbs, Waterhouse studied her.

He was a classical painter—a romanticist painter—giving to his oils interpretations of mythological characters and personages from medieval tales as well as from poetry and literature. Waterhouse was a masterful figure painter and a story-teller in paints. Also a portraitist, he painted a model beautiful whether her portrayals were of personages innocent and angelic or wicked and tragic. An aura of modesty and personality was of importance equal to beauty and sexuality.

As the young model-hopeful sat before him with eyes lowered, Waterhouse studied her briefly but critically. She was youthful in appearance, perhaps in her late teens, but quite adult in her demeanour. Her tall, willowy form with good posture was excellent. Her perfect face with unblemished skin and lustrous blue-grey eyes was most becoming. Her hair rolled up on the back of her head suggested tresses of quite some length. She was out-going, witty, humorous, and articulate with no faults of speech. She had a seductive, captivating smile, and what good fortune for him that she knocked on his door. Waterhouse liked her at once.

"Would you remove your hat and take down your hair? I need to see the length of it."

Muriel looked up from the Journal taken aback by his unexpected request; one she hadn't anticipated. A man doesn't ask an unmarried woman to take down her hair without the reason being romantic or less than gentlemanly.

Muriel replied however with a soft, apprehensive "yes sir," fearful his request to remove her hat and take down her hair was preliminary to asking her to undress. She glanced again at the nude drawing on the wall.

Muriel placed the magazine atop the coffee-table but kept her eyes lowered as she removed her hat and took down her hair.

Waterhouse watched her raise her arms to pull the pins which lifted and accentuated the curvatures of her youthful bosom beneath a tightly buttoned bodice.

With an artist's eye for female beauty Waterhouse studied Muriel's graceful hands with slender fingers as she removed a comb from a purse and combed out her hair well beyond arm's length; long, lustrous, auburn hair resplendent in its sheen in the light through the skylight. Muriel ran her fingers up under her hair back of her slender neck then raked it out and let it drop behind her.

"Please stand Miss Foster. Let your arms dangle at your sides and turn twice slowly, very slowly, all the way around."

Muriel stood, and her luxuriant hair fell to her knees. Waterhouse marveled at its length. Some twenty years before he painted a model with hair the same length for his *Flora*, his first painting exhibited; and *Undine*, his second, but Muriel's hair was more attractive by its colour.

Muriel rotated twice slowly. The ends of her lengthy tresses trailed behind as she turned to face him again.

"Now hold your hair behind your neck so it doesn't drape the sides of your face, and keep your elbows up and back. Turn your head to your right, and then to your left . . . then face straight ahead and look down, then up, but hold each pose until I tell you. I need time to study your form and profiles."

"Yes sir," Muriel replied in a soft, almost inaudible voice, embarrassed that he wanted to study her 'form.'

"How tall are you?"

Caught again by a question not anticipated, Muriel answered softly, "I'm five foot eight, sir."

"And what is your weight?" Another question not anticipated. Muriel hesitated to answer fearful Waterhouse would think her thin.

"About eight stone sir, or a little more. I haven't weighed for awhile, but I hope you won't think me too thin to be a model."

"Heaven's no! Eight stone or so for a young woman of your age and stature is fine. It's desirable!"

"People always tell me I need to gain weight."

"Well, don't listen to them! I would describe you as slender . . . not thin. Being slender is an asset for a sitter . . . and that lovely hair of yours is an artistic plus. Tall, graceful, slender, red-haired models like you with blue eyes are preferred by painters of beautiful women." Muriel blushed, but she smiled within at the compliment.

"Thank you for the flattery sir, but I think I'm thin . . . and then there is this problem about my hair."

"How, pray tell, could you consider your hair a problem? It's long and lovely. Every girl should be so fortunate."

"It's not the length of my hair, if you are thinking of length, sir, but look at the colour of it. Some think red-haired people have fiery tempers . . . definitely not a plus for anyone. But I want to assure you sir that I never lose my temper . . . well almost never . . . although boys who pull on my hair could tell you some horrid tales. Most are quite true I'm afraid to say . . . if that makes you think me temperamental."

"Not at all! Miss Foster," Waterhouse replied, smiling to himself. Her candour and delightful prattle amused him, and as she talked and turned, Waterhouse gazed with an artist's scrutiny at Muriel's lovely profiles. He studied her forehead and eyebrows and bright eyes, and eyelids with lengthy lashes; slightly upturned nose; sensual lines of mouth, lips, chin, and throat; the fairness of unblemished skin; and that wonderful knee-length auburn hair. He gazed into her eyes to study flecks of grey in with the blue until she lowered them embarrassed from the intensity of his looking. The modest young woman standing before him radiated an aura of youthful beauty, and her rose-scented perfume was intoxicating.

"Oh my!" Waterhouse exclaimed to himself, and quoted from Keats: "Full beautiful / A faery's child / Her hair was long."

"Now Miss Foster, please close your eyes and keep them closed. Keep your elbows up and back and rotate slowly . . . very slowly . . . twice around again, then stand in place."

Muriel complied, and with eyes closed Waterhouse gazed

mesmerized by her countenance as if gazing into the angelic face of a goddess—a St. Cecilia—or the mythical Ariadne, both in peaceful sleep as he imagined he could paint them.

With her blue eyes closed, Waterhouse studied Muriel's shapely form and posture; the straightness of her back and shoulders; the flatness of her abdomen; the suggestion of ample curves beneath her bodice; and the roundness of full hips made more so behind by a bustle. She had an appealing hour-glass figure accentuated by a belt drawn tightly around her narrow waist.

Waterhouse sat enamoured with the artistry of Muriel's statuesque form; the symmetry of her features, proportions, and balance; features of which he could with brushes and paints transfer onto tightly stretched canvases as any of the many women of myth and literature he wanted to paint. Her appearance promised superb modeling potential. He wanted her.

"Thank you," he said. "You may lower your arms and open your eyes . . . and please be seated. You may redo your hair."

Muriel sat and once again combed out her lengthy tresses still embarrassed having let her hair down in front of a man. Only girls of questionable repute do that. She rolled her hair onto the back of her head and pinned it in place, keeping her eyes lowered to avoid seeing Waterhouse watch her every move.

"Is that all, sir?" Muriel asked, hopefully, fearing he would now want to see her nude. A refusal would cost her a sitting opportunity. Muriel glanced again at the sketch on the wall.

"Yes, that's all. I don't need to see anything more." Muriel heaved a sigh of relief. "You have the qualities of a good model. Your profiles, stature, and form are excellent, and the length of your hair is perfect for my needs. I want you to sit for me starting a week from today."

Muriel beamed, caught by surprise that his decision to employ her as a sitter came so quickly and without being asked to undress; but Muriel was the model Waterhouse sought for months. She was the ideal painters want in sitters and seldom find, but her beauty would be trapped forever in any of his paintings for the world to see and admire.

Just as conductors can read and interpret scores of composers without hearing them played, Waterhouse saw Muriel's potential without sketches for portrayals of the classical women of the poets, playwrights, and myths.

She was foremost his vision of the beautiful Psyche—more beautiful than Venus—the love enchantress of Cupid and the personification of the soul. Waterhouse marveled to himself. Muriel *was* the Psyche he long wanted in a model. She was his Venus, Flora, Echo, and any one of the Danaïdes with a water jug. He sat transfixed by her beauty then broke from his fancies.

"Forgive me my distractions," he said, thinking back to Muriel's telling about Fred Pickersgill. "Pickersgill was my instructor and mentor when I studied art in the Royal Academy Schools."

"He didn't tell me that."

"Well I was a student not only of his methods, but of his interests in mythology and history. And he does, as you mentioned, now live on the Isle of Wight but returns to the city on occasion. Have you ever modeled before?"

"No sir . . . but I would like to."

"Well," Waterhouse said, stroking his bearded chin, "I can say you have the features of a good model, but there are other requirements you will need to consider."

"What, sir?" Muriel asked anxiously, hoping she could meet them except posing nude should the question be asked.

"For one thing, you must have a great deal of patience to hold a pose, sometimes in awkward and uncomfortable positions. Surprising as it may seem, sitting still is hard work. Your back will ache. Your muscles will cramp and your extremities will grow heavy. Your derriere will grow numb when sitting and you will want to squirm. You will need to look in one direction but you will get bored and want to look around. Your head will nod and you will fall asleep. And sitters can get light-headed and faint. But despite all of that, you can't be a sitter if you can't sit still. It's that simple!"

"Even so, what's so hard about sitting still?"

"Because sitting . . . or standing . . . in one position constantly works the same sets of muscles. That's tiring, and there is nothing more exasperating to an artist than a sitter who can't sit still."

"But I won't move," Muriel responded assuredly.

"But you've never modeled. It takes practice and experience to hold a pose. A good model must have self control not to scratch or squirm when an itch or an ache demands it, and not chatter to the distraction of the artist."

"How long would I have to sit still and not talk?"

As the devilish character Waterhouse can be when whimsy moves him, he looked askance at Muriel and answered in a voice as gruff as the sternest of taskmasters.

"All day long if I need you to young lady . . . and by gosh and by golly when I say sit still and be quiet I mean sit still and be quiet, and don't you dare scratch, squirm, yawn, cough, sneeze, hiccup . . . or breathe." Nino smiled to himself.

But before Muriel could react to Waterhouse's harsh demands, his expression softened and he grinned and winked at her. On to his wit and humour, Muriel smiled back. "A kindred josher," she thought to herself.

"Importantly Miss Foster, your hours must be flexible with your work to model when I need you . . . and I won't tolerate tardiness or absenteeism. I can't paint you if you're not here, *on* time, to sit for me, and I will expect you here between ten and two when the light is best any day you are scheduled for sitting. Do those conditions of employment present a problem?"

"No sir. My work requires I be on time in the mornings to buy flowers before the carts depart, so I know I can be on time . . . and my work is on my own schedule. We buy flowers from growers who cart them in from gardens and greenhouses but after that we wander through the station to sell them. Our time is our own."

"So, if you sit for me you could miss work for a day, or several days?"

"Yes sir . . . but I still need an income. How much will I earn? Will it be more than what I make selling flowers?"

"Well how much do you earn?"

"I sell bouquets of violets and rosebud boutonnieres at sixpence each and I make a thrippence profit. On good days with the gratuities gentlemen sometime give me I make up to three or four shillings a day. One day I made five."

"How much do you pay for transportation?"

"Nothing, sir. I don't use transportation. I live by the railroad tracks not far from the station, so I walk them every day right into Waterloo and home again. If the weather is bad I just don't go to work."

"But to work here you *will* need transportation. Is there any available from where you live?"

"Yes sir. I can take an omnibus up Westminster Road and over the Waterloo Bridge to Piccadilly, and then take another to Regent's Park at the zoo . . . just like I did today."

"So if I pay your transportation expenses plus three shillings to start for any four-hour day you sit would that be acceptable? You would make about the same as selling flowers but in half the time."

"Yes sir . . . that would be acceptable." Muriel beamed by the offer.

"And if you continue through the first painting I will pay you a bonus of one guinea when finished. Beyond that if I find you can hold a pose to my satisfaction I will put you on a modeling rate of a shilling an hour with a guarantee of at least four shillings a day for any day you sit." Muriel beamed still more.

"Also, I will pay you a guinea bonus for *every* painting finished with you as the sitter . . . and I will put you on a retainer of ten shillings a week for times between paintings when you don't sit. And please understand Miss Foster that by accepting a retainer you agree not to sit for another artist. I will want you available any day I need you . . . but you can still work as a flower girl for extra money when not sitting."

"Yes sir, I understand." Muriel just radiated. She couldn't believe her good fortune to find such a well paying job.

"There is another requirement to consider."

"What, sir," Muriel asked with apprehension of the coming question; the one she feared.

"For some paintings I will need you to pose without your clothes. Is that acceptable?"

Muriel caught her breath, flushed, and stiffened at the question she had worried might be asked. She glanced again at the drawing on the wall and fidgeted. She had been offered the best income ever but now faced losing it. Muriel paused, hesitant to answer the question although she knew already her reply.

"Sir . . . I'm sorry, but that is not acceptable. I could never sit for you out of my clothes. That would be too embarrassing for me and not proper to my upbringing. My mother and my morals would never allow it."

Waterhouse understood the young girl's reluctance in the age of Victorian morality. He didn't want to offend her virtuous proprieties. He faced inhibitions himself at times from the morality of his own up-bringing and from mores of the times.

He had on occasions been driven to the brink of breaking the shackles of ethical and honourable constraints—in other words to sin—to be a man but not a gentleman. But he sat frustrated for the moment by, perhaps, a misunderstanding on Muriel's part of his well-meant intentions and the sincerity of her desires to be a model.

"My relationships with models are honourable and professional," Waterhouse said to assure her.

"I don't doubt that sir but I can't sit for you without my clothes. I could never do that."

"Understand that you will pose here in the privacy of the studio. The door will be closed. There will be no one else than the two of us . . . not even Mrs Waterhouse. And for rest-breaks you will of course wear a robe when not on the model-throne."

"Nevertheless, I can't pose for you like you've suggested. When I thought of modeling for you after talking with Mr Pickersgill I remembered your painting *St. Eulalia* my mother and I saw not long ago in the Tate. It's a tragic painting one can't forget in the way you painted her dead and half naked, and before coming for this interview I knew I couldn't pose for you like a St. Eulalia if you asked. I just wouldn't."

"Well, I do ask that you think about it . . . but if you are reluctant to pose nude you can support your decision knowing that your image . . . however I paint it . . . will be seen on exhibit in the Royal Academy, and in galleries and museums by all of London and much of Britain."

Waterhouse couldn't help but smile seeing Muriel catch her breath with a hand to her bosom, not realizing a painting of her would be seen so widespread and by so many.

"I truly want to sit for you sir but only if clothed, and my decision stands, But regardless, I will need to discuss this matter with my mother although I'm afraid I know already what she will say."

"And what will she say?"

"She will say 'no' to any modeling at all even if you paint me in full-length gowns."

"Then why are you here? Didn't you come for a sitter position?" Waterhouse asked, perplexed.

"Yes sir . . . but not to pose nude. And to be truthful about being here I came on my own. My mother doesn't know. She would disapprove if she knew about this interview and coming alone to a man's home without a chaperone. But I hoped that if you engaged me as a sitter for more than I earn selling flowers my mother could be convinced to let me be a model. We need the extra money . . . but sir, *only* in costume."

"My first painting of you *will* be in costume . . . or draped as we say . . . but I have paintings in mind requiring a sitter nude for water nymphs and mermaids. So think about it. But before you leave, let me pour you another cup of coffee, and please tell me about your mother and your family. You live at home I presume."

"Yes sir. I live with my mother in a small three-room upstairs flat on a dirt alley by the railway tracks just south of Waterloo station. Before that we lived in the port area of Greenwich where my father worked as an assistant for a marine insurance company, but after he died my mother and my brother and I moved from the waterfront overcrowded with dock workers, drunken sailors, and all the brothels. It was no place for a widowed mother with young children to live, I can assure you, but the tenements and back-alley flat where I live now is little better."

"What happened to your brother?"

"Thomas left home a year ago to live on his own because my mother is so devoutly religious and domineering at home in her strict rules of discipline. Men have freedoms to move away that women don't. Girls are expected to live at home until they marry, and mama would never let me live on my own."

"Well someday perhaps when you're older," Waterhouse said in sympathy to her plight. "Where were you born?" he asked to change the subject.

"In Blackheath, near Greenwich, sir."

"I've been to Greenwich a number of times. It's an interesting old part of London, but as for me I was born in a much older city . . . in Rome . . . and lived there as a young boy."

"Yes sir, I know . . . and your nickname is 'Nino,'" impish Muriel remarked, looking down again into her coffee cup.

"How in the world did you know that? Pickersgill must have told you." But before Muriel could answer to the contrary, Waterhouse slapped his knee to his own question. "Ah! It was Mrs Greiffenhagen, wasn't it?"

"Yes sir," Muriel giggled. "When I asked where you lived, she let slip your nickname, then explained it because you were born in Italy."

"I guess that's innocent enough," Waterhouse chuckled.

"I've never been to Italy, or outside of London," Muriel lamented. "Maybe someday when I'm rich and famous I can travel the world," she said jokingly. "Do you ever go back to Italy Mr Waterhouse?"

"I go on occasion to visit and paint. *L'Italia è uno dei più bei paesi d'Europa.*" Muriel responded with a puzzled look.

"*Mi capisce?*" Nino asked.

Muriel looked more puzzled.

"I guess you don't," Waterhouse commented.

"Don't what, sir?"

"I said Italy is one of the most beautiful countries in Europe . . . and then I asked if you understood me."

"I'm sorry sir but I don't speak Italian. I tried teaching myself French one time but never got very far." Nino smiled. He knew some French from travels to art expositions but didn't want to test her, perhaps to her embarrassment.

"How do you happen to sell flowers?"

"Because I have no apprentice training for other work, so I sell flowers. But I like my work. It's a good job," Muriel hastened to add.

"I am my own employer. I can do what I want. My time is my own. I sell flowers or not sell flowers, and go home early if I want when shop apprentices and factory workers work twelve to fourteen hours a day and earn no more than I do in less time."

"I never thought of the advantages of selling flowers. Then you *are* your own business woman, aren't you?"

"Yes sir, and there's more to the benefits of my job. In the worst of weather, or if I'm sick, I don't go to work at all. Not many girls my age have those privileges, so I like selling flowers . . . and I meet interesting people like Mr Pickersgill."

"I rather imagine some men buy your flowers just to make your acquaintance and carry on with you."

"Yes sir, but I don't . . . I can't . . . encourage them when they do. Mama is so obsessed with sin she doesn't want me tempted by men. Besides, mama says I'm not old enough to be courted. Well I *am* despite what she says. She just wants to keep me at home."

"Young women of your age *do* go out, and they go chaperoned so they can."

"I know. I have friends who do . . . and mama would never let *me* go anywhere not chaperoned . . . but I don't go anywhere anyway. She says to tell men 'no' if they ask to call on me."

Wanting to get off the subject of her home life and now embarrassed for the first time by her dress and shoes when Waterhouse sat smartly attired in a suit with waistcoat and tie. Muriel looked about and commented on Waterhouse's lovely home and studio. "I would love to live in a home like this in Primrose Hill."

Waterhouse had never been poor, and with income from his paintings he lived well-to-do, but his compassionate heart ached from knowledge of Muriel's circumstances. Out of her travail, however, Muriel matured as an unabashed young woman with wit and humour and open and honest in everything discussed. She expressed herself with a vocabulary and a level of intelligence and maturity exceeding most other young women of her status and age. Waterhouse had to believe something more important than being a flower girl awaited her in life.

Muriel turned her attention to the patio where pigeons still billed and cooed. "May I look at them sir?"

"Of course!" Waterhouse remained seated watching Muriel walk to the patio doors, studying her form and the graceful way she moved, almost tip-toeing not to scare the pigeons. She stood fascinated watching the cock strut about, and then turned to look back at Waterhouse. "What kind are they sir?" He arose to join her.

"They are barbs. Note the short bills and large eyes. Barbs come in different colours but the ones around here are mostly white. I think these escaped from a nearby cote since barbs are caged primarily as exhibition pigeons."

"I don't know much about pigeons but they are fun to watch. They fly around inside the train station, sometimes right over people's heads. I've heard them called 'street pigeons,' not meant to be nice I guess. Floor sweepers call them names less nice for reasons you might imagine, but I've never heard of barbs."

"Well, the barb was one of the pigeons Charles Darwin studied here in London when he wrote *The Origin of Species*, a very good account of things. He concluded that all of the many varieties of domesticated pigeons are descendants from a single wild species . . . the rock dove. Barbs are the oldest of the domesticated pigeons in Europe, and are the first mentioned in English literature.

"Shakespeare wrote about them in his play *As You Like It*, written about 1600, only he called them 'Barbary' pigeons as they were known back then. It was thought they came from the Barbary Coast of Africa." Waterhouse walked to his bookcase and pulled out a volume of Shakespeare comedies.

"Let's see now," he said as he flipped through the pages. "I seem to remember the reference is somewhere about here . . . in Act Four, Scene One I believe it was. Aha!" he exclaimed when he found it. "Now this is Rosalind, the daughter of a French duke speaking to her love Orlando. 'I will be more jealous of thee than a Barbary cock-pigeon over his hen.'" Muriel laughed.

"You seem to know everything about pigeons Mr Waterhouse, and about Shakespeare. Have you read all his plays?"

"I've read all of them . . . and more than once. I study them for ideas to paint Shakespeare characters, and I have in mind Ophelia in *Hamlet*; Beatrice in *Much Ado About Nothing*; Miranda in *The Tempest*; and Juliet from *Romeo and Juliet*."

"I liked Romeo, and especially Juliet. I read the play one time and saw a traveling troupe perform for our school. They acted the masquerade dance and balcony scenes when Romeo met Juliet. The girl who played Juliet was so pretty and talented. She didn't miss a line, and everybody applauded her performance. That's when I decided I wanted to be an actress someday. It would be fun to wear costumes and play-act."

"Well, you would make a good model for the Juliet I want to paint. You're as lovely and as angelic as Shakespeare wrote of her."

"I am?" Muriel replied, amused that Waterhouse thought her 'angelic.' "My brother always called me a 'little imp,' and a 'mischief-maker,' but I don't rightly remember he ever called me a 'little angel.'" Muriel laughed.

"Do you think Juliet was impish like me?"

"Little Julia . . . that's what 'Juliet' means . . . had her moments like you I have to imagine," Waterhouse grinned. "Juliet was fourteen when she fell in love with Romeo, and Juliet was love herself. Shakespeare made her so. The love he made so pure in Portia . . . so sweet in Perdita . . . so playful in

Rosalind . . . so intense in Helen . . . and so tender in Viola is each and all of those woven into Juliet.

"Sweet, lovely Juliet, was the daughter and heir to Lord Capulet in Verona. She was a child of wealth. That is how I would paint you as Juliet . . . standing angelic in profile with a necklace of blue sapphires around your neck."

Muriel smiled at Waterhouse's desire to paint her as one of Shakespeare's best known characters, but she was still hesitant to model if he wanted her nude. She glanced again at the sketch on the wall. "Will you paint Juliet nude?"

"Oh no! I would never paint Shakespeare women nude. They weren't that way in his plays. The only nudes I want to paint are mermaids, sirens, and nymphs . . . the women of myths who wore no clothes. I only painted St. Eulalia nude because the Romans left her that way after she was crucified. I have in mind painting Juliet in a flowing white dress with sleeves trimmed in mauve . . . or maybe red."

"How pretty! Mauve is so popular these days. All the girls are wearing purples. Are you painting anything now I can see?" Muriel asked, still curious about the covered painting on the easel and how the model might be draped.

Waterhouse arose and walked to the easel. "Come . . . come look."

Muriel watched with interest as he unveiled a nearly finished painting still wet with oils of a woman with bare feet and shoulders and otherwise scantily clad pouring a green liquid into the sea.

"She is frightfully beautiful," Muriel remarked, noticing also her revealing attire, "but she looks wicked. Who is she?"

"This is the witch Circe, the same mythological character and sitter you saw in my other Circe pictured in the Journal . . . and you *are* observant. Circe *is* wicked, but I paint models beautiful to see no matter their character, evil or not.

"Muriel," Waterhouse smiled, "meet Circe."

"How are you, Circe?" Muriel asked, smiling at the humour of meeting a witch and talking to a canvas, then remarked to Waterhouse, "You do like mythology don't you."

"I have ever since I was a young boy. I love reading the ancient old stories such as about Circe who turned people she didn't like into animals. The sea-god Glaucus once asked Circe for a love potion to make the beautiful sea-nymph Scylla fall in love with him. But Circe fell in love with Glaucus herself and in her jealousy turned Scylla into a sea monster by pouring a potion . . . green as I've painted it . . . into the sea where Scylla lived. After Scylla metamorphosed she attacked ships and devoured sailors."

"That's terrible!"

"It's all just a myth, but if you look closely you can see Scylla fish-like with a tail, and because of what Circe did to Scylla I named this painting *Circe Invidiosa*, meaning she is 'jealous and hateful.'"

"Who is the model?"

"Her name is Allison . . . the model I told you about who's now in the theatre. When she comes back to sit for me I want to paint her as a water nymph."

"Then you will paint her nude?"

"Of course! Water nymphs don't wear clothes."

"Then she doesn't mind posing nude for you?"

"Not at all! It's her job as a figure model."

"I can't imagine a girl showing herself like that to *any* man not her husband . . . and maybe not then."

"Well you've got to know Allison. She's a 'nineties' kind of free-willed girl who doesn't mind taking off her clothes in front of a man and doing what she wants and saying what she wants. Not much of anything embarrasses her."

"Maybe I can meet her someday."

"You will soon enough if you sit for me. Allison comes by now and then . . . but be prepared for some off-colour talk. She's apt to say most anything."

"If I sit for you, what painting will you pose me for?"

"For *La Belle Dame sans Merci*. It's a story by John Keats about a faery-child . . . an immortal *femme fatale* who seduces a knight in armour to slumber on the moss with her. She must have been one of those free-willed girls of her own time doing what she wants when she wants," Nino chuckled.

"I want to paint her with long hair which is why I want you for the model. Keats's description of her goes, 'I met a lady in the meads full beautiful; a faery's child. Her hair was long and her eyes were wild.'"

"I don't have wild eyes, do I?" Muriel asked, surprised he may think so.

"Oh no!" Waterhouse laughed, "I'll paint yours to *seem* as wild . . . to look mesmeric . . . to look seductive. Your lovely blue eyes will do very well for that." Muriel blushed again at another compliment.

"And she won't be nude?" Muriel asked for reassurance.

"Oh no! I plan to paint the faery-child draped to her feet in a light and airy medieval dress. I think maybe purplish in colour and adorned with pearls."

Muriel played dress-up when as a child, and the appeal of being a model and an actress was to wear costumes and play-act. The description of the dress for La Belle Dame with pearls, and the dress for Juliet with sapphires piqued her interest.

"The purple dress sounds pretty. Will it fit me?"

"It's not made yet, but when finished I'm sure it will, and you will be pretty in it." Muriel smiled again at another compliment.

Waterhouse removed a volume of poetry by John Keats from his bookcase and opened it to *La Belle Dame sans Merci*.

"Take this home and read the poem. Decide if you want to pose as the faery-child. Talk it over with your mother, and remember you *will* be draped." Nino grinned.

Muriel lowered her eyes, now sheepish that she made such an issue of not wanting to pose nude, but she stood by her decision. It was nothing she could ever do.

"If you want to sit for my painting then come back a week from today, at ten, and we'll start with pencil sketches." Thinking the interview was over Muriel rose to leave.

"Thank you for the coffee, Mr Waterhouse. It was delicious, but I should go now." Muriel said "good-bye" to Circe and stopped to look at the pigeons again still on the patio.

"Would you like to feed them?"

"Oh yes!" Muriel exclaimed.

"That's what they're waiting for. I feed them everyday about this time." Waterhouse handed Muriel a tin of cracked maize and opened the patio doors. A cool breeze with the fragrance of garden roses wafted in.

"Your roses smell so nice," Muriel commented, then tossed a handful of maize onto the patio and at once the barbs pecked hungrily. With "chirps" and "cheeps" a pair of house sparrows flew down and joined in, and within a minute the maize was gone.

"How much fun!" Muriel exclaimed. "May I feed them again next week?"

"Of course! Anytime you're here. I'll dub you 'Royal Pigeon Feeder' as part of your job." Muriel laughed.

"I like feeding pigeons in the Waterloo station. Sometimes when I'm seated they get in my lap and eat from my hands. I feed them crumbs from my sandwiches . . . but they aren't always polite if they stay too long, if you know what I mean."

Waterhouse smiled again, amused by Muriel's humour, and led her down the hallway reluctant to see her leave. She retrieved her shawl from the hall tree; checked herself in the mirror; pushed some hair back in place; and exited through the front door held open for her.

Mrs Waterhouse sat in the quadrangle garden with the family Welsh corgi enjoying the warming rays of the late-morning sun. Muriel turned her attention to the corgi wagging its tail at her approach.

"And who are you, you pretty thing?" Muriel cooed as she bent down to pat the corgi.

"Her name is 'Pandora,'" Mrs Waterhouse replied, "We named her that because she brings trouble on herself getting into things. She sleeps in a box for a bed. We call it 'Pandora's box.'"

Muriel laughed as she arose to leave and said "bye-bye" to Pandora. "Now you stay out of things . . . okay?" Pandora lay with her head on her paws looking up at Muriel with big bright eyes still wagging her tail, knowing she was talked about.

"How are you getting home?" Waterhouse asked.

"By an omnibus sir . . . the same way I came. I can ride from the zoo down to Piccadilly and walk the rest of the way home across the bridge. It's a sunny day."

"But that's too far for you to walk."

"It's only a mile, sir, from the bridge to my home. I've walked it many times."

"That may be so, Miss Foster," Waterhouse argued as a concerned father might take charge of a situation, "but I can't allow it . . . not today anyway. You made a long trip here and you have another one back."

The thought worried him. How could Muriel sit for him on a regular basis having to travel so far south of the river. Omnibuses on any route are almost always too crowded to find a seat, and in inclement weather she wouldn't come at all.

Nino removed a florin from a waistcoat pocket and offered it. "Take this and ride all the way home. Use the rest to return next week. A florin will take you home and back, won't it?"

"Yes sir, but I can't accept it. It's too much, and I came today on my own."

"I won't hear of it. I offered to pay your transportation for sitting, and by coming today for an interview you missed a day of work. So here," he said as he handed Muriel an extra three shillings. "I want to pay your missed earnings, and if you sit for me it will well be worth it."

"But sir . . . I can't accept your money . . . and besides I haven't agreed to sit for you. My mother may not allow it."

"Nevertheless, take the money. It's the least I can do to help with your time and expenses for coming today."

Muriel took the coins reluctantly but they were worth a days earning as a flower girl. "Thank you sir . . . it's very kind of you," she said, embarrassed that Waterhouse gave her money.

Muriel said good-bye then turned and left. Waterhouse couldn't help but watch her walk to the gate and fall to that universal temptation of men the world over to observe the gentle sway of a woman's hips. By her grace, Muriel didn't disappoint him which added to her appeal as a seductive and alluring young woman.

During her visit now deemed much too brief, the lovely Miss Foster made a powerful impact on Waterhouse as both artist and man smitten with her youthful beauty, impish wit, and charming personality. And when during her interview she took down her hair and stood before him with eyes closed, Waterhouse fell in love with her. But now as quickly she was through the gate and gone. Would she ever sit for him? Would he ever see her again? His heart grew heavy thinking that he might not.

CHAPTER TWO

THE LETTER

The week passed all too slowly for Waterhouse anxious as he was to see Muriel again and to start sketches. His work to finish *Circe Invidiosa* kept him busy in the interim, also with a visit to the Royal Academy to visit Fred Pickersgill after Pickersgill's return from an exhibit of Pre-Raphaelite works.

"Did you see anything out of the ordinary other than red-haired beauties?" Waterhouse asked facetiously.

"As a matter of fact I saw a watercolour by Rossetti painted over a photograph . . . unusual for his style. I knew he worked from photographs but I hadn't seen one painted over."

"It's a growing practice of artists to use photographs in lieu of sketches and studies."

"I know, but you're right about Rossetti. His watercolour was of Lizzie Siddal, red-haired of course."

"Rossetti knew how to pick exotic models," Waterhouse commented. "Zambaco and Spartali were Greek and Italian stunners who sat for him."

"Of course!" Pickersgill replied. "Rossetti was half-Italian with a roving eye for beautiful women, and with a fiery temper I might add. Did you know the child model of his who couldn't sit still once sent Rossetti into such a rage he threw things around his studio, stamped about, and the poor girl was so frightened she screamed in terror and went into hysterics?"

"I hadn't heard that story," Waterhouse laughed, "but there is nothing more exasperating to an artist than a model who can't sit still. I do know that Rossetti found the young girl working the streets and took her on as a sitter. She couldn't have been more than thirteen. She *was* but a child. No wonder she couldn't sit still."

"Rossetti was always fascinated with prostitutes," Pickersgill chuckled, "making drawings of them on the streets even when he was a young man."

"I once met his model and mistress, Fanny Cornforth, an exceptionally good looking woman with ankle-length hair. She was . . . well . . . to put it politely . . . a 'companion of gentlemen' before she started modeling. And what was that famous line of Rossetti's about a prostitute . . . the one about the guinea?"

"Let's see," Pickersgill mused. "It was so long ago now, but I think it was something like 'Laughing lazy languid Jenny fond of a kiss and fond of a guinea.'"

"That was it! It's still funny."

"Hmmm," Pickersgill mused, looking askance at Waterhouse. "Maybe Rossetti's active . . . well, let's call it social . . . life was because of his Italian heritage."

Waterhouse fidgeted. He knew what Pickersgill implied. Though he was English, Waterhouse was Italian born and he returned on occasion because of his love for the country and the beautiful people using pretty Italian girls for models. But he didn't consider himself a hot-blooded romantic like Rossetti who in no way was the first or last artist to fall in love with red-haired sitters.

"Do you remember," Pickersgill asked, "John Ruskin's infatuation with his ten-year-old student?" Again, Waterhouse fidgeted. He once became so enamoured with a ten-year-old himself that he sought permission to paint her. "Yes, but I never knew much about it."

"There was a thirty year age difference between Ruskin and the young girl . . . 'Rose' I seem to remember her name . . . but an intense friendship developed between them. She grew enamoured with Ruskin as her art instructor and he proposed to her when she turned eighteen. The girl accepted, but her parents were so unhappy with the engagement they convinced her to break it off."

"I have to admit I'm enamoured with a young girl myself, actually a young woman, though not to propose marriage to of course," Waterhouse chuckled. "She must be twenty years or more my junior, but she's a very attractive."

"Well don't let young age worry you if she's that pretty redhead I saw selling flowers in the Waterloo station."

"She's the one! The one you sent to see me. With her beauty and long hair she came off to me during her interview as the *La Belle Dame* I want to paint."

"I thought as much after you and I talked about it that time. When I saw the pretty thing in the Waterloo station I bought a boutonniere just to make her acquaintance. She must have thought I was carrying on with her," Pickersgill chuckled, "when I asked if she wanted to be a model."

"That's a common come-on with pretty girls by artists."

"I know . . . but when I convinced her I was serious she said 'yes.' I gave her your name and address and suggested she interview with you but I apologize I didn't let you know before I left the city."

"Well it's important she came to see me, and I have you to thank. She's pretty enough that I'm thinking already beyond *La Belle Dame* to use her for the nymphs and mermaids I want to paint. Say! Did she have her hair up or down when you saw her?"

"It was up under her bonnet."

"Then you have never seen such long and lovely hair. It hangs all the way to her knees, and I think of lines from poets that 'nothing to a man is deadlier than lips or hair.' And 'this is my sorrow . . . she has bound my neck with a noose of hair.' Two other lines I remember off-hand are 'to mesh my soul within a woman's hair;' and 'about my neck her hair enwound.' I get ideas like those from poetry, and that's my idea for *La Belle Dame* with a noose of hair around the knight's neck in a scene of seduction. She's pulling him down to her for an invited kiss."

"That's a good idea. No one I know has used it."

"I have to admit that during her interview when she stood close to me with her eyes closed, I had the same thought about that long hair of hers wrapped around *my* neck," Waterhouse chuckled.

"Well, red hair *has* done in many a man. Look at Rossetti and his lovers. Think about Sandys, Burne-Jones, Millais, Hunt, Leighton, and Morris who have been smitten with red-heads . . . even Draper and Alma-Tadema . . . and I have myself," Pickersgill chuckled. "I'm not so old that a young crumpet like that red-haired flower girl of yours doesn't still turn my head. Why do you think I bought a boutonniere from her, and asked her to pin it to my lapel for me?"

"Because you like boutonnieres?" Nino grinned.

"No numskull! It was because of the flower girl! Buying the boutonniere was only an excuse to stand close when she pinned it, and oh my, her perfume. Even at my age perfume still works on my libido. I asked her name. 'Muriel' I believe she said."

"Yes . . . Muriel Foster."

"Well don't let her get away."

"I hope not to. With her lips, face, and hair, and that tall and slender body of hers, I could paint her as such an enchantress she could seduce the armoured pants off any knight."

"Then watch your own. That armoured wall of propriety you've built around yourself since your marriage could crumble like Jericho's wall with *that* pretty girl.

"But to be serious about it, let me advise you to proceed with your version of *La Belle Dame* soon. Anna Lea Merritt, the American, has already painted one . . . and Frank Dicksee is making sketches. I've heard that Frankie Cowper, the young lad who paints in such vivid colours, has expressed an interest. And who knows what Burne-Jones may do. He's made drawings. Rossetti once considered a painting . . . and Lizzie Siddal painted a watercolour although I understand it's been lost. The competition and interest is out there, so get on with it."

"I hope to start next week, *if* I can get Muriel for a sitter. She may not however. She's of an age to do as she wishes but she still lives under the thumb of her mother who may not let her. Besides, the young woman has her own senses of modesty and propriety. She insists she will sit only draped, and only then if she can convince her mother to allow it."

"Then by all means pay a visit to the girl's home and meet the mother. Convince them both of your good faith . . . that you are a man of good character and your relationship with the girl will be formal. Assure them that she runs no moral risks by being a sitter. But keep trying and the sooner the better. By the way, do you happen to know how Dicksee plans to portray his *La Belle?*"

"He wants her on horseback as Keats wrote: 'I met a lady in the meads and set her on my pacing steed.' Keats also wrote that the knight and faery-child 'kissed and slumbered on the moss.' The eroticism as I imagine the scene is the young seductress already off the horse and down on the moss pulling the knight down to her with a noose of hair. There, both are only a step away from everyone's fantasy of what they will be doing next when Dicksee still has the lady up in a saddle."

"Excellent idea. That's as close as you can get to showing people embraced without criticism."

"I'm going with it . . . the girl . . . the knight . . . the noose of hair. I'll darken the canvas to portray the seclusion of a wooded scene, and suspend the viewer at the most striking moment when the knight kneels to slumber with the faery-child. That's more sensuous than what Dicksee wants to paint. Women will fantasize they are seductresses of virile knights, and men will imagine they are knights anxious to shed their armour."

Pickersgill smiled at the scenario. "I wonder how quickly a knight can get out of a suit of armour if haste is important . . . but good thinking. If you portray the eroticism of the moment and titillate viewers to imagine the scene through to consummation you'll have a winner . . . but likely not without criticism by the moral press."

"I know," Nino remarked. "Remember the controversy last year over Greiffenhagen's *Idyll*. Critics called it immoral. Greiffenhagen and I laughed about that."

"Fortunately, an art-loving cleric came to his defense, as you may remember, saying there was nothing morally wrong with a man kissing a scantily-dressed woman. Bravo for the cleric."

. . .

After his visit with Pickersgill, Waterhouse felt compelled to take a cab to the Waterloo station to see Muriel again and learn for certainty that she would be in the Studio the next day. Aside from that, he wanted to buy a boutonniere from her but to his sorrow Muriel wasn't there. Disappointed, Waterhouse returned to Regent's Park by cab and strolled along the Broad Walk through to Primrose Hill; happy at least he would see her the next morning at ten.

But disappointment continued. Ten o'clock of the next day came and went and Muriel didn't show. Waterhouse waited out in the garden half-reading and half-watching the gate but by eleven and still no Muriel his heart grew heavy.

At twelve, Waterhouse was as disappointed as he had ever been about anything. He and Esther ate sandwiches in the garden to keep watch on the gate but Waterhouse wasn't hungry. Pandora gladly ate half of his. For a week he had hoped to be sketching Muriel by ten but now at one he knew she wasn't coming. Her mother must have told her "no."

Pandora pricked her ears to the sound of the postman delivering mail including an envelope to Mr JW Waterhouse, Esquire, Primrose Hill Studios No. 6, written in ornate script suggestive of female penmanship. There was no name or return address but Waterhouse knew the letter came from Muriel. He hesitated to open it. It could only mean bad news.

Waterhouse studied Muriel's handwriting for a long moment, to then turn his attention to the green and violet Queen Victoria stamp studying as always colour combinations. Esther, known for chronic, testy impatience, fussed.

"For goodness sakes, Nino, just open the blooming letter! You can be so exasperatingly slow sometimes." With intent to keep Esther fussed, a habit long acquired, Nino slowly removed a penknife from a waistcoat pocket; slowly opened the blade; slowly opened the envelope; slowly unfolded the paper; and slowly read the letter. The penmanship was exquisite.

6 April 1893

Dear Mr Waterhouse:

Let me say first how much I enjoyed my visit in your home talking about modeling and feeding your pigeons.

I am unhappy, however, that my mother won't allow me to sit for you.

She has opinions on the reputations of models and actresses and she doesn't want me to be either. I regret her refusal will disappoint you as I know how much you want me for your painting, but mama is my mother and I live under her roof. I must abide by her decisions and she said "no" to modeling.

When I interviewed with you last week I went without my mama's knowledge. She thought I was at work, but had she known otherwise she wouldn't have let me go, and certainly not without a chaperone.

I need to return your book of poetry. I'll carry it to the Waterloo station each day and if you could find me there some day soon I can give it back and tell you more about my mama's decision not to let me be a model.

Most regretfully
Muriel Foster

P.S. Please feed the barbs for me and say hello to Mrs Waterhouse and Pandora.

Waterhouse read the disheartening news with a great deal of sorrow to have lost his model, then read the letter another three or four times more adding to Esther's growing impatience. "I'll go see her tomorrow," he said as he handed her the letter.

Waterhouse awoke early the next morning with Muriel on his mind and left looking for a cab. By a stroke of good luck he found a hansom idle in front of the nearby Primrose Hill Bookshop. At Waterloo, girls with baskets stood about purchasing flowers from carts, but Muriel wasn't there. Perhaps he was too early. He remembered she told of following tracks into the station. He took a seat watching.

A London and South Western locomotive belching steam and coal smoke departed with a train of carriages for Bristol. Soon thereafter, a girl carrying a basket and a brolly stepped onto the now empty track and followed the rails into the station. Nino watched her step quickly from tie to tie but sometimes two at a time to hurry herself along. But was she Muriel?

"Aha!" he exclaimed when she drew close enough to recognize.

Muriel stepped from between the rails and up a flight of steps onto the loading platform and was walking towards the flower carts when she saw Waterhouse watching. She returned his wave and smile, and slowed as she approached his bench. Waterhouse stood to greet her. Muriel curtsied and offered an outstretched hand. "You must have gotten my letter."

"Yes, it came yesterday," Nino replied, pleased to hold her soft hand in a handshake, and there in front of him under a floral hat stood the prettiest girl in England.

"Thank you for your letter," Waterhouse said over the noise of the station. "I was sorry to learn you can't model for me, but I feel compelled to speak more on the matter with you and your mother. I won't give up on you."

Muriel looked flustered, detecting by the tone of his voice and by the expression on his face that Waterhouse was indeed disappointed in the contents of her letter.

"Sir," she spoke up to be heard over the noise of an arriving locomotive, "I had too much to say in my letter which is why I suggested you meet me here. I can explain more about my mother's decision not to let me sit for you, and return your book of poems which, incidentally, I read most of them."

"I'm impressed you read even some of them in a week since much of Keats's poetry is difficult to understand . . . but may we sit awhile and talk?"

"Yes sir, but not for long. I need to purchase flowers before the carts depart in half an hour. Let's go inside the terminal where it's quieter."

The noises of locomotives chugging in and out of the busy station with hisses of steam from boilers, valves, compressors and pistons, and shrills of whistles and clangs of bells created quite a din. Passengers rushed to board trains as conductors called out routes. Vendors sold foods and wares from carts and baskets, and newsboys hawked papers. "'Ere's your Mornin' Times!" one called out. "Get it for a penny!" The Waterloo station was large, crowded, and noisy.

"Don't buy flowers today," Waterhouse asked to Muriel's surprise. "Let me give you what you would sell them for, and with no flowers to sell we can go someplace quieter and talk about *La Belle Dame*. I know a pretty place."

Muriel blushed. An offer of money and somewhere quiet sounded a bit like propositions she sometimes hear. Her eyes lowered momentarily thinking on what to say.

"I can't accept money from you, and go somewhere alone."

"You went alone for your interview last week didn't you? And that was hours by yourself all the way across London."

"Yes sir. But my mother wouldn't have let me go had she known. So I went alone, but the point is I wasn't with a man."

"I see. But you walked to work this morning, and your mother knew ahead of time that you were coming *here* without a chaperone."

"Yes sir, but that's only because my mother can't walk with me on days we both work."

"I can understand that. You need to get to work on your own, but my point is that you sometimes go somewhere alone."

"Yes sir."

"Now when here at work and you sell flowers, you accept money from men don't you?"

"Yes sir."

"And you accept gratuities from men don't you?"

"Yes sir."

"Then you accept money from men."

"Yes sir, but . . . but . . . that's all part of the job," Muriel stammered. "Why are you asking me all these questions?"

"Well first, let's go to the flower carts. I have an idea for something to do . . . and I'm of a mind that you can do about anything you want, if you just will. You are certainly old enough."

"Yes sir."

"Then you *are* of an age to do anything you want."

"Yes sir, but I___" Muriel started to argue but was interrupted.

"As an example, you *can* be alone with me here in the station can't you?" Waterhouse asked facetiously, smiling at her. "That is, if you take a fancy to it."

"Yes sir Mr Waterhouse, but we're not alone in here. There must be a hundred people about . . . maybe two hundred."

"My point is that if you walk with me to the carts then you'll be going somewhere with a man without a chaperone."

"Sir! You've got a kooky way to twist things around. But I *can* walk with you to the carts," Muriel giggled.

"Okay then! Now when we get there I'll tell you what I want you to do, and you decide if it's proper or not, and if you have a mind to."

"What are you going to do?" Muriel asked anxiously.

"You'll find out soon enough."

Waterhouse walked with Muriel down the loading platform into the station proper weaving in and out of crowds of travelers. People stood queued for tickets. Some held dogs on leashes and some pushed prams. Some hurried for departing trains while others sat on benches awaiting arrivals. Children darted here and there, and pigeons scurried to keep out of the way. High overhead, a huge station clock hanging from the ceiling read eight forty-five.

"Flower carts leave at nine," Muriel remarked, as she checked her wrist watch. Nino took out his pocket watch to check its time too. The country, trains, flower girls and men run on railroad time.

At the carts Nino asked: "From which of these do you buy flowers?"

"No certain one sir. I buy from whichever cart has the freshest and prettiest. The prices are all the same."

"Then may I pick a cart for you?"

"Yes sir," Muriel replied, but puzzled that he asked.

Waterhouse scanned the three carts quickly and pointed to one. "There," he said, "the violets in the middle cart. How many do you buy?"

"Ten dozen, sir, but I tie a half-dozen each to a bouquet . . . so I get twenty bouquets which I___"

"Never mind all of that," Nino interrupted. "How much do you pay?"

"Two shillings six."

Waterhouse fished coins from a waistcoat pocket and counted out money to pay the vendor himself, but Muriel pulled back his hand.

"Sir," she whispered, "I can't allow you to buy flowers for me. I already have the money. And besides, if *you* buy them the vendor will charge you retail at five shillings. I don't imagine he will think you're a flower girl with a beard and a bowler," Muriel laughed, "so I have to buy them. But sir, what are you doing?"

"You don't want me to give you money for not selling flowers do you?"

"No sir. It wouldn't be proper."

"Then buy your flowers wholesale like you always do and I will buy them from you at your retail price. That way you'll earn your profit in two minutes and not take all day."

"But sir!" Muriel protested.

"No need for any 'buts.' It's a deal that sounds good to me, and with no more flowers to sell you'll be free to spend the rest of the day with me." Waterhouse smiled at Muriel's flustered expression.

"But sir! I . . . I . . ."she stammered, not knowing what to say.

"May I call you Muriel?"

"Yes sir."

"Then Muriel, I see this as a legitimate transaction between seller and buyer. Big business deals like this happen every day in the corporate world among Captains of Industry." Waterhouse smiled. "Now no arguments please."

Waterhouse winked, and in return Muriel grinned at the mention of 'big business deals among Captains of Industry' over a few shillings plus and some violets.

"Then take your two shillings six and pay the man."

"Yes sir."

Muriel carried her basket of violets to a nearby bench and sat with it across her lap. Waterhouse sat beside her.

"I tie these in bouquets of six each," Muriel explained as she removed a spool of purple thread and a pair of scissors from her basket.

"You can help me tie them if you want."

"I don't need flowers tied to buy them do I?"

"No sir. I can sell them however you want."

"Then I want them untied," Waterhouse said as he paid Muriel five shillings at her retail price plus another one as a gratuity for being such a charming business woman. If for nothing more, the gratuity was worth seeing Muriel smile.

"Thank you sir," Muriel said smugly as she put the payment in her purse, "but what in the world are you going to do with ten dozen violets?"

"I'll sell them myself."

Muriel grinned at the humour of his answer, imagining him selling flowers. There sat Waterhouse with a lap full of violets; a distinguished, moustached, bearded, and handsome man wearing a tweed suit with a waistcoat, tie, and bowler. Muriel had to laugh, humoured by the whole idea of a gentleman of his stature selling flowers.

"What's so funny?" Waterhouse asked, now laughing himself at Muriel's contagious display of amusement.

"If you will pardon me sir," she giggled, "you are so funny . . . a famous painter sitting with a lap full of violets. And I have never sold so many flowers so fast in all my life." Then both broke out laughing again. "My God! She is such a delight," Waterhouse mused to himself.

"How, sir, are you going to sell all those violets by yourself?" Muriel asked, curiously. "It takes me half a day or more." Another flower girl walked up to buy flowers.

"Do you know her?" Waterhouse asked.

"Yes sir. Her name is Jennifer Beasley."

"Would you ask Miss Beasley to come here, please?"

Muriel arose, puzzled by the request, but waved to Jennifer and walked to her. The two girls entered into an animated conversation during which Jennifer looked over at Waterhouse with a curious look as he sat with ten dozen violets in his lap. The girls returned. Waterhouse set the flowers on the bench, stood and introduced himself.

"My name is Mr Waterhouse Miss Beasley. I'm a friend of Miss Foster and I have a business offer I doubt you can refuse."

"What sir?" she asked. The young ragamuffin with a dirty face in a tattered dress couldn't be more than thirteen.

"What if I offer you these violets . . . all ten dozen of them . . . for one shilling. Would that be a good offer?"

"Yes sir!" Jennifer exclaimed with a look to Muriel for approval. Muriel nodded 'yes.'

Jennifer gave Waterhouse a shilling and a hug; then stepped back embarrassed by the show of gratitude. Her face flushed.

"Think nothing of it Miss Beasley. It's a pleasure to be hugged by such a charming young lady . . . and for that here's a gratuity." Waterhouse returned her shilling.

"Thank you, sir," she said smiling, to then sit to tie bouquets.

"That was generous of you sir. Like I do, Jennifer lives with a widowed mother who is poor."

"Then I'm glad I could help. And now with no more flowers to sell will you spend the rest of your day with me?"

Muriel lowered her eyes again, briefly, trying to decide how to answer, then looked up.

"I'm sorry sir, but I can't."

CHAPTER THREE

THE TEAROOM AND THE GARDENS

"But you can if you will, and you *know* you can, so let me take you to my favourite tearoom for pastries and coffee. The tarts are most delicious ... the best ever baked ... and the tearoom is next to the beautiful Kew Gardens where I make sketches. Both places are well worth the trip, and it's a pretty ride through the parks and over and back across the river."

"But I brought something to eat. You may have half my sandwich if you're hungry."

"That's kind of you to offer, and it must be delicious if you made it. But join me instead for pastries and coffee. We can discuss modeling, La Belle Dame, and a plan to convince your mother to let you sit for me." And while there I want to make a sketch of you."

"But sir! My mother would object."

"No need for concern. The tearoom and Gardens are quite public and quite safe I can assure you, but a much prettier and quieter place to sit and talk than here in this madhouse of a station."

Muriel knew her mother would object to a sketch, no doubt severely, and being alone with a man without her permission and without a chaperone. Well she didn't even want to think about it. But Muriel and her mother both knew she was of an age to make her own decisions.

"So why not?" Muriel asked herself. Her defenses began to weaken in the decade of the nineties when young women with new attitudes and new behaviour began making decisions of their own independent from their mothers.

The day was warm and sunny, so why *not* spend a day with Mr Waterhouse if she wanted, and so long as she was home on time. Her flowers were already sold and paid for, and maybe she owed the man a sketch if she couldn't sit for a painting. Muriel thought for a moment to decide on an answer. Then a smile lit up her face.

"Okay, I'll do it. But sir I *must* be home by four."

"I promise."

A jubilant Waterhouse hailed a hansom with two blasts on his carriage whistle [one blast hails a four-wheeler] and with instructions to the cabby for a ride to the "Maids of Honour" tearoom in Kew, the two departed for a ride across the Thames. By the time they crossed over Westminster Bridge, Big Ben struck the ten o'clock hour. Continuing east they passed St. James and Green Parks, Buckingham Palace, then Hyde Park where they passed The Serpentine; a man-made lake popular with boaters, fishermen, picnickers, and bathers.

"The Serpentine," Waterhouse pointed out, "is another of my favourite places. Trees through the park and around the lake are pretty . . . especially the weeping willows with canopies that drape the ground. I'll take you there sometime." Muriel smiled at the offer but said nothing.

The hansom rumbled on through residential areas of stately brick homes then back across the Thames over Kew Bridge and down Kew Road to the "Maids of Honour" tearoom. Waterhouse led Muriel inside to a cozy table in a back corner looking out onto a gated area with an ivied fence of age-old bricks, and gardens of flowers. Muriel knew them all. Looking up through the window Muriel's attention was attracted to the peculiar antics of a flock of pigeons.

"Look sir! Look at them tumble!" Muriel watched amazed at the way the pigeons flipped backwards in mid-flight and tumbled down to near treetop level, then spiral high to tumble down again.

"I've never seen such a thing. Do you know what kind they are?"

"They are Birmingham rollers raised for their tumbling behaviour."

"Then they must be the pigeons Mr Keats mentioned in his poem *Sleep and Poetry*. I wondered about them when he wrote of things he loved in nature, like a wind in summer and a pretty hummer . . . leafy dales and nightingales . . . and then he mentioned a pigeon tumbling in summer air."

"You're right. Keats wrote about a Birmingham roller . . . but the 'hummer' was a hummingbird hawk moth in case you wondered. They feed in daylight, and are fun to watch when they hover over flowers. I must say, however, I'm impressed by your memory. Do you memorize things easily?"

"Well no, except for things that strike my fancy. 'Summer and hummer and dales and gales and the tumbling pigeon' caught my fancy . . . but I do like novels and poems. I love to read."

Muriel looked up again at the pigeons. "They are fun to watch aren't they sir . . . but how do you know so much about pigeons like barbs and Birminghams Mr Waterhouse?"

"I raised pigeons when I was a boy, and I paint them in my pictures . . . MISS FOSTER." Muriel smiled amused at the way Waterhouse stressed her name.

"Why did you say my name like that?"

"Because you called me 'Mr Waterhouse.'"

"But sir, I have to call you Mr Waterhouse . . . that's being respectful. My mother would scold me if she heard me not say 'Mr Waterhouse.'"

"Then be *dis*-respectful, and be rest assured that I'm not going to fuss about it, and I'm certainly not going to tell your mother if you call me 'Nino.' I can handle any measure of disrespect to be on a first name basis with you."

"That's easy for you to ask . . . but I'll feel awkward calling you 'Nino.'"

"There! You just did it."

"Did what sir?"

"You said 'Nino.' You *can* say my name . . . so please call me 'Nino.' I insist."

Muriel flustered not knowing a reply to Nino's request. After all, she called every other man 'Mr,' and then there was Nino's habit of polite but firm insistence about things; not that she objected. She rather enjoyed his manner of taking charge of things.

The day of her interview he insisted she accept help with carriage fares. An hour ago he insisted he buy her flowers. Then he insisted she leave the station with him and without a chaperone, and now he insisted she call him by his nickname. Muriel relented.

"Okay . . . NI-NO," she stressed the syllables and smiled, "but only in private. At other times in front of people I must call you 'Mr Waterhouse.'"

"Then it's agreed?"

"Yes sir," she replied.

"And there's another thing! You don't need to curtsy when we greet."

"But sir, it's a show of respect to someone of honour. Girls even curtsy to school teachers, and certainly to people of importance such as you."

"That may be, thank you, but personally, curtsies make me uncomfortable. I am embarrassed by them. Curtsies should be reserved only for the nobility of which I am not so honoured and wouldn't want to be. Otherwise, I feel persons who expect curtsies are pompous and accursedly pretentious about rank and class which I detest. A simple handshake on greeting is sufficient respect."

"Yes sir."

"Now that's another thing."

"What sir?"

"Just that! That 'sir' thing with you. A simple 'yes' or 'no' is sufficient. You don't need to tack on a 'sir.' I hope you and I can converse without formalities other than a 'please' or 'thank you,' or a 'may I' and an 'excuse me.' Those are conventions enough I think to be polite with one another. Otherwise, you call me 'Nino,' and I'll call you 'Muriel.'"

"Yes sir . . . er sorry sir . . . I mean 'yes,' Nino."

"By Jove!" Nino exclaimed with exuberance, "I believe you've got it. It's 'Nino' without the 'sir!'" Muriel smiled at Nino's exclamation of triumph. He returned her smile but then his demeanour turned reflective.

"I was impressed by your letter. You expressed yourself very well."

"Well thank you . . . but that may be because I do so much reading."

"You said you read the book of poems."

"Well, much of it."

"How did you like Keats?"

"I found much of his poetry sorrowful and not easy to read and understand, and the knight in *La Belle Dame* was sad . . . the 'wretched wight so haggard and woe-begone,' as Mr Keats described him.

"But in one poem his, *Give me Women, Wine, and Snuff* struck my fancy. I pictured Mr Keats in a bawdy pub down in Wapping somewhere banging his fist on a tabletop demanding of some poor barmaid, 'Give me women, wine, and snuff until I cry out hold, enough!' Muriel emoted with expression and a laugh. I had to wonder which of the three vices Mr Keats got enough of first."

"Wager on snuff first, then wine," Nino laughed. Muriel blushed by implication of which vice came last and most wanted, then continued.

"Lamia was scary . . . both a woman . . . 'a maid more beautiful,' as Mr Keats described her . . . and a serpent . . . and he wrote of other creatures like nymphs, satyrs and fauns. He wrote of fears of dying . . . and who was Fanny? He wrote of her several times."

"You seem to understand the nature of Keats, but maybe the sadness in his poems is explained by knowing that most of his best poetry was written after knowing he was dying from consumption. He coughed up blood one day and knew its curse.

When Keats was twenty-three, his brother died. Then Keats died two years later when he was only twenty-five."

"How terrible to die so young... but who was Fanny?"

"Fanny Brawne was his hopeless and tragic love. He met Fanny when she was a teenager... maybe about your age... when he became ill, and his failing health made it impossible for their relationship to run a natural course. They wanted to get married but never did.

"The 'tragedy' of it was that while Keats fell more in love with Fanny he grew more ill. She and her widowed mother lived next door to him in Hampstead near the heath, and Fanny must have been much like you... a girl of vivacity, maturity, and wit with an articulate vocabulary."

"That's complimentary of you to say those things, but you speak of me in ways I never think of myself."

"But it's true of you... and Fanny was a lady Keats wanted to marry. But he learned his illness was terminal. Knowing he was dying of consumption was why they never married, and having not long to live resulted in much of his best, though some of his saddest poetry."

"And that's when he wrote *La Belle Dame*? Was he writing about Fanny?"

"Maybe! He knew he was dying when the poem was written and the poem may have been inspired in part by knowing he would never have Fanny. Keats was in a life-death struggle with his disease and himself, and wanting to live for Fanny. The faery-maiden in *La Belle Dame* was life, and Keats suggests the knight was dying by saying, 'And on thy cheek a fading rose.' Keats may have written about himself. The true meaning of *La Belle Dame*, however, is complicated by scholarly differences in interpretation. Some say the story has nothing to do with Keats's dying or his love for Fanny, and that it's best to read the poem only as a fable and nothing more.

"But there are those who believe the story of the knight and the faery-maiden is an allegory of Keats experiencing the relations of joy and sorrow. The knight's joy of finding the maiden and then his sorrow of losing her . . . the joy of Keats's being in love with Fanny but the sorrow of not having loved her . . . if you understand my meaning."

"I'm not sure."

"Was there intimacy between Keats and Fanny? Had he loved her in that regard? Some of his poetry suggests it, though it may have been only in fantasy. Keats most likely wanted to avoid intimacy in his closeness with Fanny because of his highly contagious disease, and only dreamed of unrequited desires. He wrote in *La Belle Dame* that the knight dreamed 'ah woe betide.'

"At the time, Keats also had a chronic sore throat that lasted for months, and for both reasons Keats may have never kissed her. In a letter he said her lips grow sweet to his fancies, suggesting kisses with her were just that . . . fancies. Keats died not long after the poem was written."

"How sad it must have been that Mr Keats may have died without intimacy with his beloved Fanny. What happened between them?" Muriel asked, anxious to know the ending to Keats's bittersweet story.

"Keats moved to Italy the last year of his life to live in a warmer, drier climate for his health, but before leaving he and Fanny exchanged locks of hair and rings as parting gifts."

"Did she ever see or hear from him again?"

"She never saw him again but she heard from him. He wrote to her until he died, and the poignancy and beauty of his letters became literature in themselves."

"The poor man," a misty-eyed Muriel said sadly with a look of deep compassion. "Such a love Mr Keats had for his lady . . . such as every woman should be so fortunate to have . . . and to have poetry written about her."

Muriel's tender expressions of sympathy and compassion were impressionable on Nino. He saw in her a caring young woman with a sensitive soul not yet hardened to unashamed displays of emotion. Muriel turned to meditate for a moment as she gazed through the window refreshing in the beauty of the flowers.

With her head aside Nino studied Muriel's profile as he did

the week before. Her beauty was such it was hard not to look at her; to study her perfect face; to imagine the ways in which he could paint her, but all too quickly Muriel turned back and caught his gaze.

"Were you looking at me?" she asked demurely.

"Yes," Nino admitted. "I was studying your profile for La Belle Dame."

"What did you see?"

"What Keats must have had in mind when he wrote in *Endymion* that 'a thing of beauty is a joy forever.' You will be a joy forever." Muriel blushed.

"It's flattering of you to say that, but I think Mr Keats wrote about objects . . . not people . . . or why did he say a 'thing' of beauty? Am I a 'thing?'" She giggled.

"Oh no!" Nino exclaimed, and laughed at her humour, "but a painting is a 'thing,' and I looked at your profile perfect for *La Belle Dame*. Paintings preserve the beauty of images which in their natural manifestation age and die, but as long as a painting . . . one of you . . . hangs for the world to admire, your beauty will never pass into nothingness. Those red lips and hair of yours and the blush on your face will last forever for people to enjoy." Muriel lowered her eyes from the intimacy of his expressions.

Muriel sensed Nino's love for poetry and art. She sensed his fascination with her, and now she felt more sorrowful about her letter that she couldn't sit for him. She reached across the table and touched her hand gently to his, the first time ever to touch a man in such manner, then quickly withdrew it.

"I *must* paint you," Waterhouse lamented. "Your letter was disheartening . . . that your mother won't allow you to be a model. Do you still want to be one?"

"Yes, but with the reservation I mentioned during my interview . . . that I model draped only."

"What do you hope to get from being a model?"

"I've thought a lot about that. Financially, you offered me more money than I could ever make as a flower girl. Maybe I could save enough for school someday . . . maybe to be a nurse or a teacher . . . but if I can't sit for you I may always sell flowers?"

"You won't *always* sell flowers."

"I'm afraid I will, but to what end in my future? An hour ago I looked at Jennifer Beasley tying flowers to work all day for a pittance. It was like looking at me her age sitting on that same bench tying flowers. Now here I am still selling flowers . . . still earning a pittance.

"And look at my clothes . . . clean for now because I didn't work today in that grimy railroad station. Each night, however, I scrub out the soot so I can wear these same clothes the next day . . . but I can't wash away the patches. And look at the other young ladies in here of obvious means, prim and proper and well-dressed, and how they glance at me. They must think me a ragamuffin."

"You are being unfairly harsh on yourself. There are things more important than the clothes one wears."

"But these people in here don't know me, and clothes are what they see. Even our waitress is better dressed than I am. There has to be something more in life for me than what has been."

Muriel paused again, gazing out the window, regretting she just bared her soul to a man who was really still a stranger. But Nino's was a friendship she enjoyed and wanted. He was a gentleman. He was amusing and made her laugh. The feeling was mutual. Nino wanted to know more.

"Please go on. Tell me what you want in life."

"I expressed some of that during my interview when I said I wanted to be a model, and maybe an actress. I want to improve on my station in life and my financial situation so my mother and I can live in a pretty neighbourhood like yours in Primrose Hill on a tree-lined, lamp-lit street with a lawn and gardens. I don't want to live forever on a dirt alley, muddy so much of the time from so much rain, and awakened nights by passing trains."

Muriel paused again to gaze out the window.

"Please go on."

"These are changing times for girls and I want to be more than a flower girl. I want to climb the social ladder a rung or two to have a better job and educated friends . . . like you . . . and you may be the only person I will ever know who is scholarly and famous.

"You said your model Allison is in the theatre. Perhaps if I sit for you she and I can become friends and she could help me start as an actress . . . and you mentioned Mrs Waterhouse is a theatre critic. Being with you as a sitter would introduce me to a new world of friends and opportunities, a whole new life for me.

"Maybe my name would appear someday on playbills and in marquee lights . . . and my face on theatre posters. Maybe I would become famous."

"Then why does your mother object to all of that if you want to model and act?"

"So far as modeling goes, she thinks that . . ." Muriel paused looking out the window again, hesitant to say.

"Go on," Nino urged.

"If I tell you what my mother thinks, her views may offend you as an artist and a gentleman and dishonour your profession . . . but let me assure you she is speaking with no specific knowledge of things she says. She speaks only from what she has heard, true or not."

"What has she heard?"

"Excuse my language in repeating it, but if you really want to know, mama says that artist models are thought by just about everyone as studio pets and . . . well . . . as strumpets, to put her terminology as politely as possible. I don't want to say the 'w' word my mother uses."

"What else did she say?"

"That sitting as a model is not a respectable occupation because models are alone with men who want to see them nude and seduce them, and for excuses pay them to be sitters. She says that no matter what her age, any woman who takes off her things before a man and accepts money for the use of her body as a model is a strumpet . . . that she might as well sell her body on street corners. She says that even if a model is a virgin she's 'damaged goods' to have been looked upon before marriage."

"That was a lot to say."

"That wasn't the half of it. Mama said that models are the naughtiest of the naughty. She says they are morally suspect, and they throw away hope for an untainted reputation. She said gentlemen won't marry a girl if they know she is or was a model. She says gentlemen want only to marry ladies, and that ladies would never be models. Mama said that if I model I can never be received in respectable circles." Muriel paused again to gaze out the window.

"That was a lot to say. Did she have anything else?"

"Oh yes, plenty!" Muriel said, turning back. "Mama then started in on actresses." Nino threw up his hands.

"Enough already! I get the picture, and after all of that you still want to be a sitter?"

"Yes . . . but with the same reservation. I don't want to show any part of me unladylike."

"Well, your mother may be correct in some things she's heard about."

"Such as what?"

"That painters have love affairs with sitters. Art history is full of them but whether sitters are seduced or not, I don't really know. I rather think, however, attractions between artists and models are more often mutual than not, and models grow fond of men who paint them, draped or undraped.

"As for you not wanting to model undraped, I must tell you I have ideas to paint nymphs, mermaids, and the like . . . ladies of myth who wore no clothes . . . and I have in mind a mermaid picture for membership as an Academician in the Royal Academy."

"That's quite an honour, isn't it?"

"It is, but it's the only one I want. I'm not a man chasing after honours, but I need a Diploma Picture for membership in the Academy."

"What kind?"

"Anything I want, though professionalism has to be approved by a committee. I'm thinking of a mermaid sitting on a shoreline with waves breaking at her feet . . . well her tail," Nino chuckled, "and she's combing her hair and singing, which mermaids have propensities to do. I got the idea from Tennyson's poem, *The Mermaid*. He wrote of 'a mermaid fair singing alone and combing her hair.' 'I would be a mermaid fair' she sang, and 'with a comb of pearl I would comb my hair.'

"Tennyson's poems and those of Keats inspire me with ideas and that's how I think I'll paint the mermaid . . . sitting alone and singing while combing her hair. I'll add something to the scene symbolic of mirrors mermaids are said to have . . . maybe a shiny abalone shell."

"It sounds pretty, but why do mermaids comb their hair and sing?"

"It's thought that combs and mirrors satisfy mermaid vanity, and a maiden of any kind combing her hair is sensual to men. Mermaid singing and hair combing allures sailors on passing ships, and when sailors get distracted they turn from their course and steer in the direction of the singing where they wreck on rocks. According to stories, sailors drown from the lure of mermaids."

"How terrible!"

"But stories also say sailors save themselves by plugging their ears with wax so not to hear mermaid singing."

"What other pictures like that do you want to paint?"

"I painted one already called *Ulysses and the Sirens*, in which sirens took bird forms as harpies with bodies and wings of vultures but heads of women. And since I couldn't paint wax in sailor's ears I wrapped their heads to deafen them. According to Homer, Ulysses was also bound to the mast of his boat to help keep him from being lured overboard to his doom, and I got the idea of sirens in bird form from an ancient vase in the British Museum."

"You do like mythology, don't you?"

"Like I told you during your interview, I have enjoyed mythology since I was a young boy. The ancients, anxious to know and explain everything, created theories and made up stories handed down from generation to generation."

"What other stories do you want to paint?"

"I have sketchbooks full of ideas. I like to tell stories on canvas with brushes and paints. One is a siren playing a lute, and I want you as the model . . . and for the mermaid. That long hair of yours is perfect for my needs."

"It's flattering of you to say that, but you will paint them nude, won't you?"

"Have you ever seen pictures of mermaids wearing clothes?"

"No sir," Muriel said, to then put her hand to her mouth about the 'sir' word. "Oops," she said. Nino smiled.

"And remember," Nino continued, "that in ancient times bare breasts were stylish, and period artists like me paint accurate to the times. Moreover, in some parts of the world today women wear nothing above their waists. Gauguin paints Polynesian women that way in the South Pacific. Naturalists photograph bare-breasted women in primitive parts of the world such as in the Amazon and dark Africa and the outback of Australia. And in stylish Europe, artists paint necklines showing ample cleavage." Muriel lowered her eyes, embarrassed by thoughts of women with "bare breasts" and "ample cleavage."

"I understand what you are saying. I've seen ladies in fashion journals wearing low-cut necklines, but I would never wear one. And remember, I saw your *St. Eulalia* of Roman times. Unfortunately, so did my mother, but I still don't want to pose . . . well . . . pose like what you just said about women back in ancient times, and how you painted St. Eulalia. There's a limit on how much of me I'm willing to show. I would rather die than have men look at me wearing little or nothing in a painting."

"I understand, but paintings and sculptures are art if for nothing more than the sake of art, and nudity *can* acquire respectability even when images elicit titillating fantasies. Think about Pygmalion, the story of a sculptor who made a statue of a young virgin so smooth to the touch and beautiful to look at that he fell in love with his own creation. He gave his statue a name,

'Galatea,' and dressed it . . . her . . . in fine clothes and jewelry. He kissed and caressed her as if she were alive, and took her to bed with him, though the story gives none of the details," Nino chuckled. Muriel lowered her eyes.

"That sounds quirky to me!"

"Well, sexual attraction to statues, or images in paintings, is not uncommon and is known as 'Pygmalionism.' The story of Pygmalion however is only a myth, but women in art *au naturel* are acceptable and admired. As puritanical as Queen Victoria may seem, she enjoys nude art, and commissions such works for gifts to Prince Albert, and he for her.

"And as interesting as it may seem, some of the most erotic of modern paintings are those of voluptuous little faeries so dainty and small they could sit on toadstools and wear bluebells and foxgloves for hats. Sensual young faeries are painted draped with their own hair, or clothed in moon mist or spider silk so translucent to add little to nothing to propriety. And consider statues like *Venus de Milo*. And what about statues of men like *Apollo* and *David* with ripples of ribs and muscles, and their manhood without fig leaves? You've seen etchings in books I'm sure."

"Yes, and I saw statues like them in the British Museum where my school class toured one day. But the statues embarrassed me. I didn't want to look for fear someone would catch me looking."

"I suspect you did, however, and need I ask where you looked?" Nino chuckled.

"A woman can't help where she looks," Muriel answered demurely to avoid a direct answer, but she gave away the truth with a blush and eyes lowered.

"Your answer makes the point that if statues and paintings are ever forbidden because of how people look at nudity then the world must be prepared to abandon art. But a Nude is not naked. Consider it clothed in art and the queen would say as she does, 'Shame on you who think ill of it.'"

"Well don't just talk about women. What about men? You know what parts of nymphs and mermaids, and your *St. Eulalia* and *Venus de Milo*, men dwell on . . . and men no doubt ogle naked faeries. I embarrass myself thinking that men would gawk at me in a painting and think what men think."

"You do know that *La Belle Dame* will be draped to her feet. I've told you that. There's nothing to be nude about her."

"I know . . . and I know you plan to paint her beautiful, so its a lovely compliment you want me for your model. But even if *La Belle Dame* IS draped to her feet I will still have a problem with my mother." Muriel paused again looking out the window. Nino felt a need to change the subject.

"Would you like another tart?" Muriel looked back.

"No thank you. They are delicious, but another would be one too many and I wouldn't be slender anymore like you say you want me." The two exchanged smiles.

"Would you come here again with me sometime?" Nino asked, hopefully. He found himself very attracted to the alluring young woman opposite him and he enjoyed her company.

"I would like that. This is a lovely tearoom with all the flowers."

"Then we'll come back . . . and soon I hope, but for now let's walk out into the Gardens and find a bench by the lily ponds. I want to make a sketch of you. I need to know if you can sit still," he grinned.

Nino's remark was facetious, but Muriel took it seriously. During her interview he said she couldn't be a sitter if she couldn't sit still. Now she was apprehensive.

Nino walked with Muriel along the Broad Walk through the Kew Gardens to the lily ponds. Along the way he pointed out rhododendrons and azaleas, and beach, hazel, chestnut, oak, maple, and willow trees; the kinds that fill his sketchbooks.

In under trees, carpets of bluebells grew in with anemones, ferns, and primroses. Scents of violets, the sweetest of smells, blended with those of roses and honeysuckles. Red squirrels with elevated tails scampered about chattering as squirrels do, and not far in the distance woodpigeons "cooed" soulfully to mates. "Coo-coo-coo, coo-coo."

In the ponds and along edges, water-lilies, crowfoots, daffodils, irises, and wild roses added splashes of white, yellow, and pink to the greens of the pond. Twittering fork-tailed swallows skimmed the surface drinking on the wing, and fast flying swifts hawked insects high overhead. Blue, and red damselflies flew about while peacock, tortoiseshell, painted lady, orange-tip, and red admiral butterflies—the latter on migration up from the Mediterranean—fluttered among the flowers. Nino and Muriel took a park bench seat to take in all the scenes and scents.

"How pretty!" Muriel exclaimed.

"Yes you are!" Nino remarked, catching Muriel off-guard with opportunistic flattery.

"No, silly!" Muriel laughed, "I was talking about all the flowers, and the butterflies."

"OH! The butterflies." Nino chuckled. "Do you see the yellow one fluttering about the primroses? It's a 'brimstone,' named from the colour of sulfur . . . also butter . . . and the story goes that early-day people called it a 'butter-coloured fly,' thought to be origin of the name 'butterfly.' See how it flutters and glides, flutters and glides. Well butterflies were once called 'flutterbys' because they flutter-by-the-tip-of-your-nose just like this," Nino remarked, fluttering his hand in front of Muriel's face and brushing the tip of her nose. Muriel laughed, amused by his humour, and wiped away the tickle.

"How funny," she said, fluttering her hand back at Nino.

"Since butterflies flutter and so many aren't yellow, I think 'flutterby' is a better name.

"See the one flying around the willow trees . . . the maroon one with white borders on is wings? That one is a summer migrant up from Africa and out of north Europe, first discovered here in England over in Camberwell just south of the river."

"I've *been* to Camberwell. It isn't far from where I live, and not far from the Waterloo station. How interesting!"

"Well, because of where it was discovered it's called a 'Camberwell beauty.' But because of the hem-like border on its wings it's also known as a 'white petticoat' or 'mourning cloak.'

Camberwell beauties usually fly around willows, but often around blackberry bushes to suck juice from over-ripe berries."

"Once I had a butterfly . . . er flutterby . . . land on my flower basket. It must have wanted nectar from a violet but it flew when I tried to pet it."

"They're known to do that," Nino laughed amused she should try to pet a butterfly. "Have you ever been to Steven's Auction Rooms in Covent Garden near St. Paul's church?"

"No."

"Then I'll take you sometime. You would enjoy seeing the flutterby specimens sold there from all over the world . . . and we can visit St. Paul's, known also as the 'actor's church' where the theatre crowd attends services. The Theatre Royal on Drury Lane in Covent Garden is where you might act someday. Covent Garden and adjacent Soho are popular places for theatre crowds, street musicians, and performers like jugglers, contortionists and mimes . . . and where ladies of the night perform."

"My mother says they aren't 'ladies.'"

"Not the kind you would want to be."

"That was one of my mother's concerns . . . that actors hang around in parts of the city where the oldest profession occurs, except she says acting is really the oldest profession since the Devil played the part of the serpent in the Garden of Eden."

"That's something I hadn't thought about . . . that Satan played a role as a serpent. I can see it now in marquee lights; Theatre Royal's presentation of *Eden and Evil*, starring Satan as the serpent. Maybe Satan was also an artist painting on fig leaves," Nino laughed, slapping his knee.

"Well laugh all you like, but my mama thinks temptation, sin, acting, modeling and nakedness are all wrapped up together as one big bundle of ungodliness . . . and when scholars learn the Devil was also a painter of nudes, just to ogle Eve, artists and actors will close out the chapter on the four oldest of the world's nefarious professions."

"Four oldest? What's the fourth?"

"The legal profession! Mama says it started when the Devil tricked Adam and Eve."

"Well enough with all that nonsense your mother fills your pretty head. I'm going to sketch it. Do you see the lily pads off to your left?"

"The ones with the white blossoms or yellow blossoms?"

"The white ones. Now look in that direction, but sit up straight . . . that's the way. Get comfortable against the backrest. Now lift your chin a bit but look down a little and gaze out across the pond. Turn your head and shoulders a little to your left . . . a little more . . . a little more. There! That's perfect. Now hold that position for the next ten minutes or so, and for God's sake don't move."

"For ten minutes?" Muriel fussed.

"That's what I said. The important thing is sit still and don't squirm, and don't get the giggles. You may breathe, however."

"Ha! . . . Ha! . . . Ha!"

"No frowns either. Now look pretty like the good Lord made you." Muriel made a sourpuss face like licking a lemon.

"I thought I said no frowns!" With a great show of the effort Muriel wiped the frown from off her face leaving an exaggerated smile like some clown face. "How's that?" She asked, holding the smile.

"Fine," Nino laughed, "but a bit too much smile. Look like Mona Lisa with only a hint of one. It's okay to talk, but keep your head still."

"YES SIR!" Muriel responded with an exaggerated military style salute.

"One more thing," Nino said. "Would you kindly remove your hat?"

"But___"

"I need to sketch your head without your hat. But you don't need to let your hair down," Nino hastened to add. Somewhat reluctant with memories of her bare-headed interview, Muriel pulled the pins and removed her hat.

Nino removed a sketchbook and pencils from a deep coat

pocket, always carried for opportunities such as this. Nino had sketched for only a minute when Muriel whispered his name.

"Yes?"

"I need to scratch my nose. It itches something fierce."

"Why in the devil didn't you scratch a minute ago?"

"Because it didn't itch then."

"Oh all right! But don't move your head, or as sure as the sun arises each morning the clouds above will rain down all over you."

For the next several minutes Muriel sat with time to think, daring not to move, not wanting to get rained on. But malevolent thoughts with good reason wandered through her mind, wondering if Nino didn't have a sadistic side to him deriving sadomasochistic pleasure from making her sit so still.

Muriel's back began to ache. Her derriere grew numb on the hard bench. She wanted to squirm but she knew Nino's opinions of squirmers. Pure torture it was. Yes! That was it! Nino was the Marquis de Sade behind his beard and beneath his bowler.

Muriel heard the faintest of pencil scratches on drawing paper, and once she heard the Marquis mutter "drat" when he used an eraser. She hoped for God's sake and maybe her future as a model she hadn't moved. She prayed not to think of something funny. Even a giggle would surely end the briefest modeling career in art history.

"Okay, it's done!" Nino finally said. "You may move if you want." The words were about the kindest thing ever said to her. Muriel gladly took Nino's permission to move, and she squirmed to improve her sitting position from numb to less numb and scratch her nose again.

"May I see it?" she asked anxiously.

Muriel gasped with jaw dropped. "What in heaven's name is that!" she exclaimed as she looked at a full-face, cross-eyed, snaggletoothed caricature of herself with thumbs in her ears. But she couldn't help but laugh.

"Oh no!" Nino exclaimed with a feigned look of shock. "I gave you the wrong sketch," and with a hearty laugh handed her the real one.

Muriel gazed surprised at the drawing [title page] almost as if looking at a photograph. It was her face—no question about that—but she blushed seeing her image with hair down and with bare shoulders as if she wore nothing. But she was otherwise drawn as posed with chin lifted, and looking out over the pond with the suggestion of dreamy eyes; highly seductive in that alone. Her hair parted down the center of her head hung tousled over the sides of her face and down her back. The result added sensuality to it all.

Muriel's eyes and eyebrows, slightly up-turned nose, mouth, curvatures of chin and jaw lines, and face shaded light to dark by the hardness and softness and flat surfaces of pencil leads gave a three-dimensional effect to her features.

"I love it! But do I really look like this?" Muriel asked, admiring the drawing. "But what happened to my hair? You drew it down!"

"I drew it the way I wanted it to look. That's known as 'artistic license.' I wanted your hair the way I remembered seeing it during your interview. I can draw and paint from memory."

"Well I love the sketch!" Muriel remarked "but I've never dressed to show bare shoulders, and be out in public with my hair down and without a hat. I would never be so daring. My mother would murder me dead. That's why I didn't tell her I took off my hat and let down my hair in your studio."

"Well the face and hair is you all right, and that's just in pencil on paper. In oils on canvas you will be even more beautiful with your auburn hair and blue-grey eyes, and as much more of your fair skin showing as you will allow me to paint."

"And all of London will see me like this?"

"And half the world. Thousands will queue up at exhibits just to see your face and ask, 'Who IS she?' Men will fall in love with you like Pygmalion, and bags of letters will beg for your hand in marriage."

"Will you just hush with that kind of silly talk? You know that isn't going to happen."

"And why not? Just wait until the world sees you painted."

"Is this the way La Belle Dame will look?"

"Oh no! You're the perfect model for the faery maiden . . . no question about that . . . but this is an idea I have of you as a water nymph." Muriel lowered her eyes, knowing he would want to paint her nude as a nymph, and his sketch of her with bare shoulders suggested it.

"You would be in a group of nymphs with dainty arms and long hair, half hidden by water-lilies in a pool shadowed by trees . . . just like over there." Nino pointed across the pond. "Imagine that the nymphs are young, beautiful, and graceful, and they are looking around for men," Nino chuckled. Muriel blushed.

"That's not really true, is it? I mean looking for men."

"Not really, but the ancient Greeks imagined nymphs were man-hungry. Did you know the Greek name for water-lily is *Nymphaia*? Botanists named the family 'Nymphaeaceae,' and Greek for a water nymph is *Nymphe*. Moreover, the generic name for the water-lilies with white flowers is *Nymphaea*. And the Camberwell beauty . . . the flutterby we saw flying around the willows . . . is named *Nymphalis antiope* in the family 'Nymphalidae.'"

"How can you remember all of that biology stuff?"

"Because I study water-lilies and flutterbys, and use them in my paintings. But there's more. A place like over there where nymphs might live is a *Nymphaeum*. Ancient Greeks saw water-lilies bloom in the morning, then disappear below the surface in the evening. They fancied them as heads of water nymphs coming up to look around during the day, then going down for the night."

"But don't they drown?"

"Not in myths. The Greeks lived in a world of fantasy. They imagined that water nymphs were born from water-lilies and could, if they wanted, emerge naked in human form and walk about, or frolic. Sometimes they danced in circles as if frantic, as if man-crazed with insatiable urges . . . if you will pardon me for saying so," said to Muriel's blush. "That's where 'nymphomania' came from applying to women. And men who dream lustfully about nymphs suffer from 'nympholepsy,' a fantasy about nymphs, especially about precocious young girls thought of as 'nymphets.'"

"Well don't think of me as one!"

"I'm sure you aren't," Nino replied to assure her with a laugh, "but do you want to know something else? The two colours of water-lily blossoms you see out there are different species. The white ones, sometimes called 'Ladies of the Lake,' or 'Swans of the Lake,' are the largest flowers in England. The yellow ones are sometimes called 'brandy bottles' because of their seed pod shapes. Yellow lilies have larger pads but the white ones have larger flowers.

"My idea is to have two models represent the two species. I want Allison for one and you for the other, as pretty a 'lady of the lake' as I could hope to paint."

"Why, thank you," Muriel said with lowered eyes. But she sighed knowing that Nino would want to paint her nude. Not wishing to even ask, Muriel paused to pin her hat back on, and to change the subject asked: "How did I do sitting?"

"Fine, except for scratching your nose."

"Well, I defy you not to scratch *your* nose if it itched," Muriel fussed, "and do I really have to sit so long without moving? That's nothing but torture."

"Then I'll give you a rest every several minutes if it will keep you from fussing about it. Just remember your position before a rest break so you can retake it, and I'll paint you no more than four hours a days including as many rests as needed."

Muriel beamed at such a concession. "But," she said, "I'm afraid there won't be *any* modeling for me if mama won't allow it."

"What if I speak to her on your behalf?"

"That might help. Could you come Sunday afternoon for tea . . . say at three . . . and bring Mrs Waterhouse with you? Maybe the three of us could convince my mother to let me sit for you."

"Consider it done! We'll be there at three!"

Nino tore a page from his sketchbook for Muriel to draw a map and watched amused as she plotted criss-crossed lines going every which direction representing streets, alleyways, and railroad tracks centered by an 'X.' "My flat" she said smugly; proud to have drawn such a fine map. Nino rolled his eyes and smiled.

The two strolled back to Kew Road where they hailed a passing hansom letting Muriel, who asked, blow two toots on the carriage whistle. Muriel beamed when the taxi stopped.

"Mind your step!" Nino warned as he helped her in then gave orders to the cabby for a ride to Regent's Park at the Marylebone entrance.

"I'll disembark here and walk to Primrose Hill. It's not far. You can see it over there," he said pointing.

Nino instructed the cabby to take Muriel home and paid in advance with a handsome gratuity to get her there by four.

Muriel extended her hand from inside the cab; said "good-bye;" and thanked Nino for the day, the tarts, and the drawing. "I love my drawing," she said smiling as she held it beside her face for comparison. "See! It's better than a photograph, but you will understand why I can't show it to my mother," Muriel laughed.

"You mean 'murder you dead?'" Nino said in humour to repeat her earlier remark, and laughed.

"That or worse! And thank you for agreeing to meet with my mother on Sunday at three. Her name is Henrietta."

"I won't forget," Nino replied, and as the hansom pulled away Nino waved good-bye and asked, joking. "And what was your name again, *mademoiselle?*" He asked in jest as if he had forgotten.

Muriel laughed at the *mademoiselle*; leaned out the cab holding to her hat and looking back. Above the noise of the street she replied in pretense French using most of the only words she knew. *"Je m'appelle Muriélle, monsieur. Je suis la mademoiselle Muriélle La Belle Dame,"* she said in fun, rhyming all the "elles" but with an emphasis on her own.

Nino laughed at her humour and called back, *"Au revoir, mademoiselle Muriélle,"* said with the emphasized "elle." As her cab disappeared in the traffic Nino waved a last farewell, sad to see her gone so quickly and missing her already. "Oh my!" he said to himself. "She tugs on my heart strings so."

Nino walked the Broad Walk through Regent's Park back to Primrose Hill worrying along the way about a meeting with Muriel's mother, and rehearsing already things to say. Would she allow Muriel to model? She must! But what if she doesn't? Nino feared a confrontation.

CHAPTER FOUR

THE TURNING POINT

Big Ben struck the three-quarter hour as Nino and Esther crossed the Waterloo Bridge over the Thames en route to an 'X' on Muriel's map, to be there by three. The cabby spotted the turn from Waterloo Road then drove to an alley along the railroad tracks.

"I believe the house must be the one over there," he said, pointing. "Do you want me to turn in?"

"Park here . . . but wait. We shouldn't be more than an hour."

"Aye-Aye sir!" the former boatswain in the Royal Navy replied. "An extra shilling will buy you an hour and a nap for me and my horse."

Nino and Esther hadn't long to wonder about the right location. Muriel waved from the front door when she saw the carriage arrive. Nino waved back.

"How are you ma'am?" Muriel asked as she approached and extended her hand to Mrs Waterhouse . . . "and you . . . sir?" Waterhouse understood her need for the 'sir' word. "Thank you for coming, but be forewarned my mother remains adamant not wanting me to be a model."

Muriel led the Waterhouses back from whence she came to an upstairs parlour door at the top of a stairwell. "Mr and Mrs Waterhouse are here," she announced through an open door. From back in the kitchen came a clatter of dishes, then footsteps.

The comely lady who answered the door seemed no more than in her late thirties who could be none other than Muriel's mother. Were she half her age she and Muriel would be thought sisters with the same height, blue-grey eyes and auburn hair. Muriel's mother was not who—or what—Nino expected. He had imagined she would answer the door on a broomstick.

"Please come in," she asked cordially. "I am Muriel's mother. Call me Henrietta." She ushered the Waterhouses to a sofa in front of an open window. "Its cooler here," she said. And just as soon said a breeze blew in fluttering the curtains.

Muriel pulled up a chair for her mother. "You visit with the Waterhouses while I tend to the tea," then said to their guests: "If you will excuse me, I'll be back in a moment."

"I'm impressed with your daughter's manners," Esther remarked as Muriel exited into the kitchen.

"Mr Foster and I taught Muriel and her brother proper behaviour from the time they were toddlers. But aside from manners," Henrietta continued, "I taught obedience. I expected the children to behave . . . to do as told and not to argue. I taught them to respect God foremost, then me, and their father at the time, others in the family and elders whoever they are. Since Muriel and Thomas could talk they addressed adults by 'sir' and 'ma'am' and said 'please' and 'thank-you.'" Esther glanced at Nino.

On return, Muriel smiled at Nino having heard the tail-end mention of "sir" and "ma'am." Nino smiled back. "The tea is steeping. It will be ready in a minute," Muriel said as she took a seat.

Henrietta then continued to Muriel's chagrin and the Waterhouse's disinterested benefit. "We raised our son and daughter to fear the Lord and know His wrath if they sin." Muriel fidgeted and glanced at Nino and Nino glanced back at Esther.

Nino and Esther sat taken aback by the fervor of a God-fearing Henrietta. Nino thought there was little chance she would ever allow Muriel to sit as a model.

The purpose of the visit now seemed useless. But Muriel glanced at Nino, anxious to talk about sitting, and as Nino started to broach the subject Henrietta offered tea. "I believe it's ready," she said as she stood. The inviting aroma wafted about the flat. Nino and Esther nodded agreement, and Henrietta excused herself into the kitchen.

Nino leaned close to confide with Muriel. "I'm afraid your mother will never allow you to sit for me . . . not after hearing what she just said, and knowing of her objections from what you told me in the tearoom. Do you still want to be a model?"

"Yes sir."

"Then understand that while I'm not playing the Devil's advocate here, your decision to model will be contrary to your mother's telling you 'no,' and we know how she feels about obedience. If you want to be a sitter, remember you *are* of an age to make that decision on your own, but be aware a decision to model will cause you to have trouble living here."

"I know . . . and mama would disapprove severely if I choose to model. She's very strict with rules and discipline but you have offered me more than I can earn selling flowers."

"Then you may have to live elsewhere."

"I've thought about that, but I have no other place to live. I could never afford a flat on my own, and I don't want to have to marry just to live elsewhere. Besides, there's no man in my life anyway. Mama wants me free of sin and temptation and to her, being a sitter is sinful and men are temptation." Muriel gazed forlornly out the window. "I don't know what is to become of me."

"Do you still want me to discuss modeling with your mother?" Muriel turned back to face him.

"Yes sir. Today is as good as any, and we need to get this matter settled." Nino now feared a confrontation.

"Does your mother know you came to my studio for an interview? Does she know you went with me to the tearoom?"

"I told her about the interview, and that you offered me a job as a sitter which is why she said so much to me . . . the things I told you in the tearoom. But mama doesn't know about the tearoom, and I didn't dare show her your lovely sketch of me for the reasons you know."

"I trust you got back on time?"

"Yes sir. The cabby got me home by four, so that wasn't a problem, and I came home with the money you paid me for my flowers. Mama thought I worked all day or I would have had to tell her the truth had she asked. I can't lie to mama, so I got off the cab a few blocks away. I usually walk from the station anyway."

"Muriel honey," Henrietta called from the kitchen. "Will you help me please?"

"Yes mama," and on arising Muriel spoke quietly. "Please excuse me for a minute . . . but after tea will you discuss wanting me for *La Belle Dame*? Be sure to mention that I will be draped all the way down to my feet."

"That's fine," Nino replied, and after Muriel left to help with tea, Nino and Esther discussed quietly the sitting problem.

"Esther, if Muriel needs a place to live she can stay with us. We have that extra room."

"We would have to care for her, and what, forbid, if she gets sick? We couldn't just send her back here. And have you noticed her shoes and dress. She's in need of a whole new wardrobe. I'm sure she's wearing her best for us."

"There was never a problem when Allison stayed with us."

"But Allison was older, and had a sister to stay with much of the time. Muriel doesn't. She would essentially live with us full time."

"Well I have numerous paintings in mind for her long after *La Belle Dame* is finished, and if she eventually wants lodging of her own I'll be more than willing to help . . . providing of course she lives near and continues sitting for me. It's not uncommon as you know for artists to provide favourite models with allowances to keep them close and available, and with bad weather and commuting from here so far, there could be days she wouldn't show at all. And omnibuses are almost always so crowded to not even have a seat."

"It *is* a long way. It took longer than I imagined here."

"Something else to consider is that with Muriel's upbringing she should be no problem living with us. She could be of help around the house."

"Extra help would be nice," Esther admitted. "My interests outside the home with theatre reviews and visits to family and all keep me busy."

"Muriel can help me in the studio. I can teach her how to size and prime canvases, grind pigments, mix and thin paints, and clean brushes. If she wants to help with a painting she can do the varnishing. Allison helped that way, and she got good with studio chores."

"Well, model work is your business, but I think it best not to make Muriel an offer to live with us in front of Henrietta . . . not today anyway. We don't want to force a conflict and turning point this afternoon."

Henrietta returned with a tea tray followed by Muriel with a platter of glazed biscuits. "I baked these by myself," Muriel said proudly.

"Do you like to cook?" Esther asked, surreptitiously.

"Yes ma'am. When mama isn't home I prepare meals."

"How nice of you to help like that," Esther replied, smiling to herself with a glance at Nino.

"Muriel *is* a good cook," Henrietta confided, "and she's good about the house. She knows what needs doing and does it without being asked." Nino smiled to himself and glanced at Esther.

"Otherwise," Henrietta continued, "Muriel keeps to herself reading. She seems always to have her nose in a book. Muriel was a good student in school."

"Then she doesn't go anymore?" Esther asked.

"Not since she finished required schooling after her father died. Muriel had to work to help with expenses, but that didn't stop her from learning. Would you believe she taught herself some French of all things? And just last week she read a book of poems." Muriel exchanged smiles with Nino at the mention of the poetry book.

After another several minutes of small talk mostly about Muriel, to her continued chagrin, Henrietta asked: "Would anyone like another cup of tea, or a biscuit?"

"Not for us," Nino replied. Esther nodded agreement. "The

tea and biscuits were delicious but we need to be on our way soon. We have a carriage waiting."

But Muriel glanced at Nino, and then at her mother as a signal to discuss the subject of modeling.

"Henrietta . . . ." Nino started hesitantly, "you know I interviewed Muriel last week for a sitter for the *La Belle Dame* I want to paint."

"Yes . . . I know that!" Henrietta replied, agitated that the subject was raised. "Muriel told me, but I told her she can't be a sitter, and that's final!" Muriel lowered her eyes, dejected.

"Why shouldn't Muriel sit for me," Nino argued, "if that is what she wants to do? And let me add that I will pay her well."

"Muriel told me. Your offer was generous. It's more than she earns selling flowers . . . but any amount would be akin to selling her body and that is immoral in the eyes of the Lord. Her father would turn in his grave if he knew his daughter posed for an artist. He and I raised Muriel to abide by the teachings of the Lord, and the fifth of God's Commandments is 'Obey thy father and mother.' So that settles the matter. Muriel will live here with me and obey what she's told."

"I believe in the Commandments myself, and I respect your convictions Henrietta," Nino rebutted, "but I___"

"I'm sorry Mr Waterhouse," Henrietta frowned and interrupted, "but my decision stands. I will not allow my daughter to be a sitter."

"My sisters Jessie and Mary sat for me, and so has Esther," Waterhouse argued. "Mary sat for *The Lady of Shalott* in the Tate where millions view it. Other artists use members of family for sitters but I don't believe any believe they are selling themselves . . . certainly not my sisters and Esther."

"I didn't know your family modeled for you . . . and I must say Muriel and I saw *The Lady of Shalott* which is how we know of your talent and fame as a painter. It's a large and beautiful painting. However, we also saw your *St. Eulalia* in the Tate which makes my point. Do you have daughters?"

"No."

"Do you see how pretty my daughter is?"

"She is very pretty!" Muriel blushed at the compliment.

"Would you want her to pose for a painting half-naked like your *St. Eulalia* for men to ogle and have covetous thoughts. I can't believe any parent would want that for a daughter. Muriel's body is not to be seen."

"The *La Belle Dame* I want to paint of Muriel will be fully draped all the way down to her feet."

"Muriel told me. But it makes no difference. I won't let her be a model."

"I have to commend you on raising Muriel to be the proper young lady she is, but I sincerely believe you can protect a child only so long and so much. There comes that time in life when they are old enough to take off on their own."

"Muriel isn't old enough!" Henrietta snapped, "or does she know what she wants."

"Oh mama!" Muriel objected. "I *am* old enough to know what I want!"

"I agree!" Nino spoke up in support. "During her interview Muriel expressed to me very well what she wants."

"Mr Waterhouse! I agree that a child eventually takes off on his or her own. Thomas did . . . but girls don't leave home until they are married, and I will keep Muriel here until she does."

"Oh mama," Muriel interrupted. "How long will that be? When am I ever going to marry? You won't allow anyone to call on me. Am I to live here the rest of my life?"

"Please don't interrupt!" Henrietta scolded, and continued her reproach. "So long as Muriel lives under *my* roof she will abide by *my* rules and I will not allow her to be a model."

Nino responded in a voice bordering on exasperation. "As Muriel's mother, you are exercising parental will in what you have decided is best for your daughter, regardless of what Muriel wants. I mean no disrespect but I think you should consider what Muriel wants. It's *her* life." Henrietta's eyes flashed and Muriel and Nino exchanged nervous glances.

Esther detected Nino's exasperation. The confrontation he

feared even before they came was heating up and going nowhere. Esther wanted to end it. It was obvious a totally uncompromising Henrietta felt backed into a corner and that no matter what Nino added to his arguments she had no intention of changing her mind.

"What my husband asks is not something that needs an answer today. He won't begin painting his *La Belle Dame* until he has a sitter, but we ask that you give the matter additional thought. In the meantime we need to be on our way."

"Yes," Nino concurred, looking at his watch. Nino and Esther arose to say 'good-bye.'

"I'm sorry to disappoint you Mr Waterhouse," Henrietta said as she walked them to the door, "but I *had* wanted to meet you anyway when Muriel said you were coming. As I said, I know your name as a painter, and it's one to which Muriel and I can relate."

"How do you mean?"

"I don't know if Muriel told you, but she and I are 'Waterhouses' ourselves." Nino looked surprised by the disclosure with a quick glance at Muriel and a long look at Henrietta.

"*You* are Waterhouses? How is that?"

"My father . . . Muriel's grandfather . . . was a Henry Waterhouse, hence my maiden name. I was named Henrietta after him, but like me, Muriel has no middle name. Had her father and I given her one we considered 'Muriel Waterhouse Foster' since by marriage I was 'Henrietta Waterhouse Foster.' That way, Muriel would have been named for both her father and me."

"I see! That stands to reason, but I can hardly believe you are Waterhouses," Nino said, looking fondly at Muriel. "I don't know of a 'Henry' on my own family tree, however."

"I don't know much about mine beyond my grandfather," Henrietta remarked, "but the Bible tells us we all came from Adam and Eve."

"So!" Nino remarked to Muriel with a chuckle, "then somewhere back . . . maybe about the time of Moses . . . you and I became cousins." Muriel smiled at the remark but Henrietta didn't. She wanted no thought that she and Muriel were related to an artist.

"Heaven forbid," Esther thought to her self that her husband and Henrietta might be related from somewhere back. "No two people could be more different, or at odds."

"Thank you for tea," Esther interrupted to move an awkward situation along, "but we need to be on our way."

While Esther was saying 'good-bye' to Henrietta, Nino leaned close to Muriel and whispered: "Walk with us to the carriage. There is something more I want to say." He then bid farewell to Henrietta who seemed more cordial now that her controversial guests were leaving.

The three walked slowly towards the carriage rehashing the conversation with an unyielding Henrietta. "I have the feeling," Nino said, "that no amount of argument is going to change your mother's mind. She has no intention to let you be a model."

"I knew that even before you came but I hoped she might change her mind if she knew you personally."

"Well, she didn't change her mind, and I'm afraid I only made your mother harden her stance."

"You did your best. You made a good argument when you said members of your own family sit for you, and she admitted your painting of *The Lady of Shalott* was beautiful. But, unfortunately, she remembers your half-draped *St. Eulalia*.

"I told mama you wouldn't paint me like that . . . I wouldn't allow it myself . . . but for all the reasons I told you in the tearoom she won't let me be a model, and she made that very clear today. So, I'm sorry Mr Waterhouse. I can't sit for you."

"There *is* an option if you are serious enough."

"What sir?"

"That you live elsewhere on your own . . . just as your brother Thomas."

"I know . . . and Thomas is better off for it . . . but sir I have no other place to live and I can't live with my brother. My aunt, who lives up in Sheffield would dearly love to have me live with her but that doesn't help me here."

"Then live with Mrs Waterhouse and me. We have an extra room . . . the one Allison lives in when I paint *her*." Muriel looked startled by the offer.

"I don't know what to say, that you would take me in."

"It would be convenient for you to live in Primrose Hill and not worry about bad weather and the long commute everyday. Moreover, I feel now we are family anyway . . . *cousin!*" Nino said grinning. "Why didn't you say something about being a Waterhouse during your interview, or in the tearoom?"

"I didn't want you to employ me as a 'Waterhouse' if that would have swayed your decision otherwise, but when you offered me a position on merit it didn't seem important, and besides we could only be distant relatives at best. Lots of people who aren't related share surnames. I mean how many 'Smith's' and 'Jones's' are there?"

"You're right about that, though there aren't as many Waterhouses. Nevertheless, we want you to live with us if you can't model staying here."

"Your offer is kind, but I can't up and leave my mother. If it's at all possible to change her mind it would be best I stay here. She needs me."

"Well keep in mind you can live with us if you can't work out a solution here."

"I'll talk more with mama tonight, but how will I let you know if I decide I can't live here?"

"Well, let's see. We don't have a telephone for you to ring us . . . not yet anyway . . . so just come. Bring your things. Knock on our door day or night, and if the carriage gate is locked walk around the corner on Kingston to the side fence. Ring the bell on the caretaker's gate. He will let you in."

Nino fished a crown from his waistcoat pocket. "If you decide to move your things to Primrose Hill use this for a four-wheeler."

"But sir, I can't accept your money. You know that!"

"Then consider it a loan. You can pay it back by sitting."

"Yes sir, and thank you," Muriel said as she took the coin, "but I don't have much to move . . . mostly books and clothes."

"Bring what you have. A four-wheeler should move it."

"Sir . . . ma'am," Muriel said as she extended her hand to say good-bye. "I need to get back. I suspect mother is wondering about me . . . likely watching from the parlour window."

Muriel turned to walk away. Nino watched for a moment sad to see her go then helped Esther into the cab and spoke with the driver. When he looked back Muriel was gone, once again. His heart grew heavy. Would he ever see her again?

. . .

Day after day Nino hoped to see Muriel at the gate with her carriage, but saw nothing. He thought to look in the Waterloo station but Esther convinced him Muriel should be left to sort things out on her own.

Nino believed Muriel must have talked with her mother—that same day no doubt—but that was nearly two weeks ago. What was the decision? Her mother must have told her 'no.' But why hadn't Muriel come for a visit, or written? She wrote once before.

After meeting Henrietta, Nino knew she could be, and was, self-righteous in her puritanical views, and intolerant of Muriel's desires contrary to her own. There was no 'middle ground' with Henrietta which left Muriel with two options. She could rebel against her mother and leave home, or submit, stay home, and abandon her dreams.

Nino spent his days finishing *Circe Invidiosa*, painting a darkened background of trees and rocks along a shoreline of sea water turned green by Circe's magic potion. Circe, herself, was long completed but he finished then repainted Scylla the sea monster; not satisfied with it the first time. A painting had to be perfect before Nino would sign it.

Waterhouse was glad to be finishing Circe. He had worked on it for weeks, but now that Muriel might be coming to sit for him he was anxious to clear his easel for *La Belle Dame sans Merci*. But would he have a sitter? As each day passed it seemed more and more likely he would need to find another. His heart grew heavier day by day thinking about that. He wanted Muriel, not only as a model but—he had to admit to himself—her sharing his home with him.

Twelve long days passed since Nino had visited Muriel and her mother. He would give her two more days, and if nothing was heard he would look for her at the Waterloo station. He *had* to see her again and know why she hadn't kept in touch.

Esther was away for the day on her usual doings outside the home. Nino typed a letter to the Art Gallery of South Australia in Adelaide making further plans to crate and ship the Circe painting on the SS Orient. Letters by sea from the other side of the world took weeks.

Nino made tea while listening for the postman, hoping each day for a letter saying Muriel was coming to live with him. With teacup in hand and Pandora trailing close behind Nino walked out onto the patio to sit and await the postman. Impatience, however, soon drove him to pace the quadrangle.

Then he saw a four-wheeler parked outside the carriage gate. His heart raced. "Can it be Muriel?" he wondered, anxiously, but he saw no passenger; only the driver sitting atop his perch as if waiting to pick up someone. His heart sagged.

But Nino was curious. He walked to the gate and asked "Are you wanting to come in?"

"Yes sir, but the gate is locked and my passenger went around the corner on Kingston to get a key from the caretaker. She talked as though she lived here so I supposed she must have forgotten her key."

Nino's heart raced again being almost afraid to ask. "Is your passenger a young lady with red hair?"

"Yes sir, she's a right pretty young thing." Nino knew she was Muriel.

"Damn it!" Nino exclaimed to the driver. "The caretaker isn't here today and there won't be anyone to answer his gate bell. I'll open this one for you, and please drive to studio six . . . the one in the left corner of the quadrangle. Park there! Did she bring any baggage?"

"Yes sir . . . a trunk and boxes of things."

Nino knew Muriel had come to stay. His heart raced faster as he unlocked the gate to let the carriage enter then walked rapidly for the corner on Kingston and down the fence to intercept her.

"My God!" he exclaimed to himself. "Muriel is here! She's got her things. She has come to sit for me." His pace quickened.

As Nino neared the caretaker gate he heard the bell ringing dingle-ding, dingle-ding. Then he saw her. "Muriel" he called out. "It's me! Nino!"

Muriel turned in the direction of the shout, waved back, then walked to meet him. "Your caretaker must be a sound napper this afternoon. I've been ringing and ringing."

"He isn't here today . . . it's his day off . . . but you look exhausted."

"I am! I've had almost no sleep for two days, and little before that. My life has been in turmoil the past two weeks . . . but how did you know I was here?"

"I saw your carriage. The driver said you came here for a key. Does that mean you plan to stay?" Nino asked hopefully.

"Yes," Muriel replied, apprehensive of his response, "if you still want me."

"Of course I do! I've been half-sick not hearing from you. What happened?"

Muriel smiled though weary, relieved by his answer. "All that's happened these past two weeks is too long a story for now, but let it suffice for the moment to say I no longer live with my mother. The day after your visit, mama packed me off by train to Sheffield to live with my aunt Sophie, 'to keep me free of sin' she claimed in her note to my aunt.

"I didn't want to go, but mama made me, and when I got to Sheffield my aunt was sympathetic to my troubles. She had been through them herself with mama, and my aunt sympathized with me knowing I was of age anyway to do what I want. Despite mama's note to keep me in Sheffield my aunt gave me fare and money for a trip back to London to live with you, and with new clothes and everything."

"That's wonderful news, but there is plenty of time to tell me all of it later. Right now you need rest."

"I do. I'm dead on my feet, but before we go please understand that all of this is such a turning point in my life I've been sick from worry over what is to become of me. Reassure me you want me here and that everything will be all right."

"Everything will be fine."

"I have nowhere else to go, and except for my brother and my aunt you are all I have who care about me." Muriel's eyes grew misty from malaise, weariness, and from relief knowing Nino still wanted her.

Nino unlocked the caretaker's gate and closed it behind them, then gave Muriel a heart-warming hug lifting her onto her tiptoes. "Welcome to Primrose Hill," he said.

Muriel broke down from the show of affection and the welcome. She was emotionally drained. With a long, tiring trip from Sheffield with little sleep, fearing all the while despite what was said two weeks earlier that Nino really didn't want her, and with worries of what would happen to her if he didn't, Muriel's stamina finally failed. She grew faint and her knees buckled.

Nino caught her, then lifted her into his arms with her head upon his shoulder and carried her in through the blue front door of Studio 6. Muriel Foster's long journey was over. She was in a new home with a room of her own, but ahead were conflicts from the requirements of a figure model coming of age as a spirited and venturesome young woman. But for the moment she slept the rest of the day and all through the night.

CHAPTER FIVE

THE METAMORPHOSIS

Within the day of Muriel's arrival rumours spread among residents of Primrose Hill Studios. Those who peered through curtains to watch her carriage unload of baggage whispered that a close member of the Waterhouse family had come for a lengthy visit. Why, she was so close Nino carried the young woman across his threshold which caused murmured discussion. "Hmmm," they said.

Those who saw Muriel the next morning wearing a blue frock and poke bonnet, and sweeping the front door walkway said "no," she must be a live-in servant. But then why would Nino carry a maidservant across the threshold? "Hmmm," they said.

But those who saw her later that day walking Pandora while wearing a fashionable day dress and twirling a parasol said: "She couldn't be a servant . . . not dressed like that." Maybe she was a noblewoman who had come as a guest for a portrait. After all, Nino did paint portraits of wealthy and beautiful female patrons. But the question persisted. Why did Nino carry her across the threshold? "Hmmm," they said.

By evening, before anyone knew for sure, some imagined she was a red-haired lass from one of the Irish clans, or of Scottish descent. In fact her name "Muriel" heard whispered around was an Anglicized variant of the Scottish Gaelic "Murieall" and the Irish Gaelic "Muirgheal." There was the romantic idea she might be a descendent of the historic William Wallace clan.

Not until one of the gentlemen rapped his head and exclaimed "Of course!" did Muriel's identity come to light. He remembered buying flowers from the young beauty in the Waterloo train station, and had been so enamoured with her he bought two bouquets and tipped her twice. But now more intriguing was the question: Why did Nino carry a flower girl across his threshold, and why was she living there? More 'hmmms' that day were hummed.

Within Muriel's first days, Studio families came to know her. She was out and about walking Pandora and making friends. They learned how it happened that Nino carried her faint through the door, and that she was living there to sit for a painting. Of course! That was it! That explained it all! Other models had come and go, or stayed for awhile in the big middle of a painting, but there was still another "hmmm" or two just to have something more to "hmmm" about.

Muriel crossed paths with Mrs Greiffenhagen who remembered letting her through the gate the day of her interview. The Waterhouse Welsh corgi and the Greiffenhagen Scottish Aberdeen were friends already. They wagged their tails and did doggy sorts of things whenever greeting despite the fact Scots and Welsh weren't all *that* friendly.

Others of the Primrose Hill Studios began to speak and wave. Two were reporters and sketch artists for the *Illustrated London News* with tours of duty in the Zulu wars and the Balkans. There was a designer, an illustrator, and a Prince; His Highness Prince Demidoff, an artist, naturalist, and big game hunter, and Sir Henry Wood, a Knight, an eminent musician and conductor.

A neighbour who became one of Muriel's favourites was Joseph Wolf, a painter of birds and other animals. Another who became a friend and confidante was Mrs Edyth Starkie Rackham, a painter herself, married to Arthur Rackham who painted storybook characters for fairy tales by the German brothers Jakob and Wilhelm Grimm.

All were as one family with common interests visiting one studio and then another with critiques of works. The men, 'sans wives,' confabulated out-of-doors in the quadrangle courtyard while drawing on imported briar pipes, American cigarettes, and Cuban cigars, and while sipping domestic ales, swapping tall tales, and discussing news of the times.

There was the new diesel engine and Ford's first auto cars with speculation that Ford would compete with Germans Daimler and Benz. Plans for British cars by Charles Rolls and Henry Royce were on the drawing boards, but no cars yet built could outrun a smartly trotting horse, and horses would long be needed to pull cars from mud on country roads. Moreover, horses never got flats, and how close can one find petrol for auto fuel when grass for horses grows along every roadside.

Progress was discussed on building the Westminster Cathedral off Thirleby Road built from a hundred different marbles imported from all over the world. It was estimated twelve million bricks would wall the structure by time of completion. The artists in the group, and Waterhouse in particular, called it an ugly red-brick Byzantine hulk banded by stripes of white Portland stone to be towered over by a campanile nearly three hundred feet high. "Such a monstrosity," Nino complained. "It will clash aesthetically with all of London," and had the city fathers asked him he would have gone with 'neo-Gothic.'

"Here-here," everybody chided-in as they took another puff on their smokes and a sip of their ales.

There were confabs on the New Scotland Yard in 1890 that Sherlock Holmes knows was built on the very site of a never solved murder; the first tube railway and the Forth Bridge; progress on the Tower Bridge; the new corridor carriages from London to Glasgow; fluctuating world coffee prices caused by problems in Brazil backed by the London House of Rothschild; and the strong comeback of the British market since the ruinous depression of the 1870s and social unrest of the 1880s. And what had been the success of the free tuition Education Act?

Queen Victoria was in her seventies. Prince of Wales Edward VII was in his fifties. Was he ready for the throne, and what would an Edwardian rule hold in store for Britain? Waterhouse foresaw an era of architecture to replace the gaudy Victorian. "Here-

here," everybody chided-in again as they took another sip of their ales.

Such were the erudite discussions by scholarly gentlemen enjoying their smokes and drinks while confabulating on the quadrangle in Primrose Hill Studios. Muriel wondered how any of them could talk and not cough amid such clouds of smoke. The aromatic sweet smells of garden flowers were smothered by the robust aromas of Cuban tobaccos and American burleys.

Muriel felt inadequate in her knowledge of national and worldly topics and contemporary issues, but she was a woman, and women were not expected, or encouraged, or even permitted, to join manly discussions of politics, business, the military, naval warfare, maritime law, bowling and cricket—or women. But women had motherhood, needlework, cooking, gardening, and afternoon teas with endless gossip.

Muriel did know about barb and Birmingham pigeons, and if anyone should ask she could quote a line from Shakespeare's *As You Like It*. Most everyone knew "Wherefore art thou Romeo?" or "To be or not to be, that is the question," and "Every dog has its day," but how many knew "I will be more jealous of thee than a Barbary cock-pigeon." Not many she imagined.

Muriel knew about brimstone and Camberell beauties, and that butterflies were once called "flutterbys;" knowledge not that common to the average person, much less women. She had some knowledge of water-lilies and water nymphs in Greek mythology. She knew the names of garden flowers and she was on top of the British market of wholesale cut flower prices.

From working at the Waterloo station Muriel knew a little about railroad operations and train schedules. She knew by sight just about every engine-driver and train conductor who pulled in daily at the Waterloo station on the Great Western; Greenwich; the Liverpool to London; London and North Western; and the London, Chatham and Dover Railways. Railroad men waved and said "hello" when she sold flowers on the platforms.

Muriel knew more than most other women about inside and outside designed two and three cylinder engines; and 2-2-2, 2-

4-2, 2-4-0, 2-6-0, 4-2-2, and the American made 4-4-0 wheeled locomotives. She understood the workings of coupled drive-wheels, and once saw a 2-6-2 ten-wheeler with triple drive-wheels eight feet high, higher than she could reach on tiptoes.

Once a flirtatious engineer let Muriel pull the cord on his steam whistle but she realized later that what he really wanted was to hold her hand helping her up into and down from the cab. The second time he asked Muriel if she wanted to pull his whistle cord she said "no thank you."

But that was about the extent of Muriel's worldly knowledge. She knew the three "R's," and most children left school by the time they were fourteen—Muriel did—and boys were better taught than girls. Girls, it was believed, had less need for schooling and if too educated had less chance for marriage. Men didn't like to marry women smarter than them.

Girls were considered educated if they knew little more than something about music, art, and needlework; knew how to cook and clean, wash and iron; and had a general knowledge of the British Monarchy. A girl really needed no more refinement for marriage and motherhood than be amiable, clean, inoffensive, quiet, and dutifully available when wanted by her husband.

But Muriel was a bookworm. She read widely and avidly to learn more. She read adventurously for entertainment to escape the drudgery and boredom of her home life—"always had her nose in a book" her mother told Nino. Her book collection contained *Magnall's Questions*, a catchall text of history and worldly facts, and such titles as *The Arabian Nights*, *Aesop's Fables*, *Grimm's Fairy Tales*, and those by Hans Christian Andersen from which she fantasized romances with handsome princes.

Muriel read a wide assortment of writings by Charles Dickens, Jane Austen, and the bittersweet romance novels of the Brontë sisters. She had a grammar, French and English dictionaries, and a book of poetry by Elizabeth Barrett Browning.

By age thirteen Muriel reached levels of maturity when she awakened from day dreams and sleep to restless desires she really didn't understood but was titillated by imaginative romantic fantasies of aggressive lovers and willing or unwilling heroines read about in her novels; the sources of her daydreams. But her fantasies conflicted with a strict, moral upbringing, and a puritanical mother who suppressed her awakening sexuality.

Muriel had favourite heroines imagined to be herself, as Charlotte Brontë's fourteen year-old orphan Lucy Snowe in *Villette*; the ten year-old orphan Jane Ayre; orphans Caroline Helstone and Shirley Keeldar in *Shirley*; nineteen year-old Agnes in Anne Brontë's *Agnes Grey*; fifteen year-old maidservant Pamela in Samuel Richardson's novel of the same name; all of who struggled through adversities striving for education, security, happiness, recognition and social status not unlike the wants of Muriel.

Muriel was bewildered by what seemed incomprehensible that fifteen year-old Caroline in Charlotte Brontë's *Caroline Vernon* lost her innocence to the man of the house. That she could lose hers to Nino was absolutely unthinkable. Although she and Nino never determined how far removed her Waterhouse ancestry was from his—they were as he once joked, "kissing cousins"—but that she and Nino would ever kiss for any reason was unimaginable.

Muriel's avid reading gave her a wide array of knowledge and ideas. It improved her reading and comprehension skills, and development of an articulate vocabulary in keeping with her precocious mental maturity. Muriel hoped Nino and her scholarly Primrose Hill neighbours would be mentors for a broader education.

Muriel settled into a routine around the house in which she helped with volunteered household chores; diligent especially in keeping studio windows clean of coal-fired smudge and gaslight fume. Nino appreciated the brightness of studio light. She helped cook, wash dishes and clean house, clean brushes, grind pigments, mix paints, prime canvas, and dust studio clutter on promises she would never move any of Nino's paints or papers. "Keep my papers and sketchbooks where I leave them," he once said. "Dust around and over everything but not through any of it."

Muriel took pride in her room. She enjoyed privacy respected by Nino and Esther. They didn't pry through her things. They included her in family affairs as if she was their own. Well, she lived with them, and was herself a Waterhouse. She became an equal in an adult world. She had come of age.

Muriel enjoyed the pigeons. She made friends with them, and in time they ate from her hands. As 'RPF,' the honorary title of 'Royal Pigeon Feeder' Nino bestowed on her, she fed them daily relieving Nino of the chore, but for Muriel it was fun to do. In fact, she thought nothing else was quite half so much fun as "fooling around" with her feathered friends.

One day Muriel asked if she could pin to a studio wall the sketch Nino made of her in Kew Gardens. After all, there was that other sketch of a girl. Muriel picked a place seen easily by anyone entering the studio, and visiting neighbours recognized her if they noticed. Prince Demidoff noticed as did Sir Henry Wood. So, Muriel was already famous.

Weeks earlier she was only a flower girl but now she was known and recognized by nobles; well at least two of them and they were neighbours, but Muriel beamed when she thought about it. Moreover, they called her "Miss Foster" and tipped their hats to her.

Sir Henry Wood spoke French for Muriel and tutored her to learn more. He gave her piano lessons. Joseph Wolf sometimes walked with Muriel and Pandora along footpaths on Primrose Hill and taught her all about plants and animals. Mr Wolf was considered one of the world's greatest wildlife painters and he seemed to know everything about nature. Muriel began knowing a better part of the world. She was happy, and stepping up that social ladder talked about that day in the tearoom.

Muriel was out of an alley flat and living in the comfort of a picture-window flower-garden kind of home she always wanted in a neighbourhood of tree-lined lamp-lit streets. No more living on a muddy alley in a cold and drafty flat, and no more awakenings in the night by rumbling trains. She now lived well provided for. Nino paid her enough as a sitter that she no longer needed to sell flowers. In dutiful exchange for her good fortune Muriel worked attentive to volunteer chores, and she promised herself daily, "I will, I will sit still." Sitting still for Muriel began in earnest for sketches of *La Belle Dame sans Merci* while Nino also finished *Circe Invidiosa*. Fellow Academicians came to see the colourful painting before it was crated for shipment to Liverpool for display, then on to Australia with the usual raves of Nino's artistry.

"Waterhouse is imaginative and creative in his interpretation of the Circe myth; artistic in the compelling pose of the draped figure, and ever faithful to the beauty of the model. He is admirably accomplished and masterful in his strong but sensitive, harmonious use of deep blues and striking greens, and colours on every canvas he puts his hand.

"Waterhouse's paintings steeped in romance, mythology, and classical literature are artistic bridges between his inner imaginative self and his visual creative genius. Waterhouse thinks in paints and paints what he thinks. Viewers are charmed by Waterhouse perspectives of the beautiful old stories. With Waterhouse, the haunting beauty of the model comes first and the story and the imagery are wrapped around her. One looks first at the sitter, then the imagery, and then the sitter again always painted sensual and beautiful; the lovely face and sensuous form of a model is always the focal point and centrepiece."

"Centre yourself on the sofa," Nino asked.

"How do you want me to sit?"

"Up straight. That's the way. Turn to your left and look up. I want to sketch your right profile. For now, put your left arm over the top of the sofa and your right arm in your lap, but keep your elbow down. Draw up your knees. That's the way. Now remove your shoes and stockings and let your feet hang off the edge of the cushion so that I can sketch you barefoot." Muriel stiffened.

La Belle Dame was to be fully draped—so Muriel thought. That's what Nino told her when she interviewed for the sitter position. When he said *La Belle Dame* would be draped to her feet, he somehow failed to mention "bare" feet. Yet, she had just been asked to bare her feet which in front of a man was most improper. A gentleman doesn't ask to see a lady's feet, and a lady doesn't show them until she's married and maybe not then. When during her interview Nino said there would be no nudity in the painting Muriel assumed 'no nudity' included feet.

A young lady showing bare feet to a man not her husband is inappropriate; not even in swimming attire at the beach. Women are required by the demands of decency to wear cumbersome swimming dresses from head to foot *including* swim shoes, and now Muriel had just been asked to bare her feet. And if asked to bare her feet then what else, pray tell, would he want to see her bared? She didn't want to think about it.

"What you are asking is sinful," Muriel protested. "MUST I show my feet?"

"Yes ma'am! *La Belle Dame* is a faery-child, and faery children don't go around wearing shoes . . . certainly not like those you wear."

"Oh Nino . . . no man has ever seen my feet."

"Then I will have the honour of being the first one, and get used to the idea because when this painting is on exhibit half the world's men will see your bare feet . . . tops, bottoms, heels, insteps, ankles, and toes . . . all ten of them . . . with some showing toenails. But I promise to paint them manicured."

"Don't talk like that!" Muriel fussed.

"Well men will love your feet," Nino said as he laughed and winked at Muriel but she sat shocked by what he seemed so rude to say. To her dismay Nino continued.

"A maiden's feet are sensual to men, and the story of La Belle Dame is both Sensual and Seductive spelled with capital letter 'S's.' And you, young lady, are the model for this Sensual Seductress so I need to paint your feet. Just be glad I'm painting *La Belle Dame* otherwise draped, or whatever else of you alluring to men could be bare and showing." Muriel glowered, and Nino barely managed to stifle a grin.

"Shame on you!" Muriel protested. "You are wicked and sinful talking like that."

"Wicked and sinful is all a matter of opinion . . . yours not mine. I'm the artist here and you're the model, and I need to paint La Belle Dame with bare feet. Now remove your shoes and stockings like I asked."

"Well then be a gentleman and turn your back . . . and don't you dare look!" Nino turned and Muriel glowered as she begrudgingly slipped off her shoes and stockings. She sat on her stockings to hide them, then covered her feet with the hem of her dress.

"You can turn back around!" Muriel fussed.

"Sometime later I *will* need to see your feet, 'Little Miss Modesty who needs her job.'" ("And heaven help me when I need to see you nude for nymphs and mermaids," Nino muttered to himself.)

"Can't you sketch my feet without looking? You already know what feet look like. You painted Allison's in *St. Eulalia.*"

"But I don't know what *yours* look like. All feet aren't pretty. Some are mis-shaped and downright ugly, and what if I imagine you have ugly feet. You wouldn't want me to paint them ugly now would you? I need to paint feet I can see. I need to see everything I paint . . . and I need to be sure you even have toes."

"Of course I have toes! How silly of you to say that."

"Well *I've* not seen them, and for all I know, you may not have toes . . . not yet anyway . . . just nubbins of some sort waiting to pop out as toes when you get older."

"Don't talk like that. You know nubbins never happen. Do I have to show you my ankles too?"

"Only your right one . . . but I'll tell you when I'm ready."

Muriel buried her face in her hands again slowly shaking her head. "Oh me!" she grieved. "God will strike me dead."

"Please don't grumble! The good Lord isn't going to strike you dead. Allison isn't dead and she posed for *St. Eulalia* showing a lot more of herself than feet.

"Now get your face up out of your hands and sit up straight. These first sketches will be of you in various poses until I find what I want. Remember how I sketched you in Kew gardens? Sit just as still."

Muriel groaned, but at least she sat on a soft cushion and not a hard bench. Nino continued.

"After sketches I will do an oil study before the finished painting, so we have days of work ahead. The sooner we get started the sooner we get sketches and the study done . . . and the sooner half the world can admire your feet in the finished painting on exhibit."

Nino stifled another grin watching Muriel squirm. What a difference he thought when Allison posed for *St. Eulalia* for hours on her back bare-breasted with arms outstretched. Allison was so unconcerned about a naked pose she went to sleep, and here's a flustered Muriel sitting fully dressed who doesn't want to bare a toe.

But Nino didn't ask Muriel that day to expose her feet. He let her keep them covered. Maybe on the morrow she would be less hesitant after a night thinking the matter over.

Over the next two hours Nino sketched one pose of Muriel after another giving short rests between them but had to turn his back when she slipped her shoes and stockings on and off. But he was pleased she sat as still as she did. The story of Gabriel Rossetti's model who couldn't stop squirming kept coming to mind.

"Okay precious . . . that's all for today." Nino paused, discomposed by what he just said in innocence with a slip of his tongue but without thinking. "You don't mind if I call you that, do you?"

"I guess not . . . so long as it's said in private. I know you meant it endearing and that's sweet of you but not in front of anybody who might misconstrue its meaning."

"I promise. Now would you make lunch? Esther won't be back until this afternoon late and you make delicious sandwiches." The making of meals, the cooking of puddings, and the baking of pies and breads was almost as much fun to Muriel as eating everything.

Following a lunch of corned beef sandwiches and a tasty plum pudding Muriel had baked the day before, she spent time in her bedroom reading more of Jerome K. Jerome's witty new book *Three Men in a Boat (To Say Nothing of the Dog)*. It was the odyssey of three zany friends rowing a boat up the Thames to Oxford with a feisty fox-terrier on board named Montmorency. The dog had an atrocious attitude problem, and reputation as a cat, rat, and chicken killer as well as dog fighter *par excellence*.

Fox-terriers, said in the book, are born with four times more sin in them than other dogs, and it seemed in the story that Montmorency's other ambitions aside from fighting were to get in the way of everything and everybody. There was something about being cursed that Montmorency felt existence as a terrier was justified.

The stories of a "fight" between Montmorency and a whistling tea kettle, which irritated him no end, and his face-off confrontation with a tomcat meaner than he was were stories so funny Muriel dog-eared the pages to reread time and again.

Pandora lay beside Muriel as she laughed, unknowing she was amused by the antics of a dog, or Pandora might try to outperform Montmorency for more of Muriel's attention. Muriel became Pandora's favourite care-companion. She took her on daily walks; fed and bathed her; brushed her hair; and kept her perfumed with sprinkles of rose-water.

Pandora decided Muriel had read enough for the afternoon and began her daily routine tugging on the hem of Muriel's dress for a walk to the top of Primrose Hill. There, Pandora savoured the sounds and scents of animals wafting up from the zoo below, and walks were Pandora's favourite things to do except eat, sleep, and listen for the postman.

Muriel enjoyed walks herself to look out over Regent's Park and much of London. She picked wildflowers along the way and, like Pandora, listened to sounds of animals. She thought calls of peafowl must wake the dead, and only mournful howls of wolves or blasts of elephant trumpets might be louder. Muriel timed her walks to return home for afternoon mail delivery.

Muriel never got mail but she enjoyed looking through deliveries for foreign stamps. But on this particular day, much to her surprise, she received an envelope addressed to her in care of Mr JW Waterhouse, Esquire, Primrose Hill Studios London. Inside was a letter from her aunt in Sheffield.

6 May 1893

My dear Muriel

 I received your lovely thank-you note after your arrival back in London. Please, there is no need to repay the money I gave you for train fare and new clothes.

 I received a long letter from your mother who now regrets sending you here. I wrote her the day you left, so she knows you are back in London with Mr and Mrs Waterhouse.

 Your mother feels I betrayed her wishes not to keep you here in Sheffield but I think she knew you would have left home anyway, just as Thomas did a year ago.

 Henrietta worries of course about your salvation. She suspects by now you are already modeling and sinning in the eyes of the Lord. Be assured that I don't see it that way myself. I never became the zealot your mother did.

 She will disagree with me on this but these are the nineties and changing times for women. You are no longer a child at home. You are a young woman now with freedoms these days not available to girls when your mother and I were your age. You have rights to a life and a career of your choosing.

 Make the best of your new opportunity as a model and be the best sitter you can be. Mr Waterhouse is a way for you to be on your own and live like you want.

 Please keep up with your reading, and come see me again when you can.

Love,
Your Aunt Sophie

Muriel read the letter, wiped her misty eyes, and took the rest of the mail inside to Nino. There was an envelope from South Australia with a rose-coloured five shilling Queen Victoria stamp. She knew he would be anxious to read the letter. Muriel went to her room followed by Pandora, closed the door, and laid down on her bed. Pandora jumped up with her and Muriel reread her Aunt Sophie's letter.

Muriel seemed subdued that evening during dinner but Nino and Esther let her be. She turned in early to go to bed. Nino commented it was the earliest since living with them. "She did her first sittings today," Nino remarked. "She's just tired."

By ten o'clock the next morning Nino was ready to sketch again and Muriel was in better spirits. She wanted first to feed the barbs and held out a handful of maize hoping they would feed from her hand.

Muriel named the tamest and most daring of the hens 'Belle' who came cautiously, cocked her head and looked first at Muriel and then at the feed in Muriel's open hand. Slowly, Belle reached out with the full length of her neck, pecked a single piece of cracked maize and pulled back. She cocked her head again and looked. Belle must have thought her situation safe enough that she hopped up on Muriel's hand and pecked vigorously at the feed.

Muriel laughed quietly at the tickles, and before the food ran out other barbs now brave gathered on and around her hand pecking feed. Muriel couldn't contain herself any longer and squealed in delight which frightened the pigeons. But in forced silence and with another handful of maize the barbs returned.

"Nino . . . did you see?"

"I saw! But I think anything would like to eat from your hands."

"Will you just hush with that kind of silly talk? You are embarrassing me."

"Well, if you are embarrassed already then you might as well take your position on the sofa again . . . same as yesterday . . . but this morning I need to sketch your feet."

Muriel blushed again at the idea of baring her feet but she took her position on the sofa influenced by her Aunt Sophie's letter. "Make the best of your new opportunity and be the best sitter you can be."

Muriel sat abashed by what she was about to do but she didn't ask Nino to turn his back. Sheepishly, she removed her shoes and stockings being careful to show nothing more than feet and ankles, though once again she sat on her stockings.

"How do you want me to pose my feet?" she asked softly with eyes lowered.

"Hallelujah!" Nino exclaimed to himself. "A good night's sleep must have done it." God must have smiled upon him.

Muriel remarked the day before that no man had ever seen her feet. Nino was now the fortunate first. Her feet were slender, lovely, and delicate with translucent skin as though neither had ever seen the sun. They were exactly what he had in mind for his *La Belle Dame sans Merci*.

In expectation the night before that Nino would sketch her feet on the morrow morning, Muriel painted her nails a delicate pink, adding to her beauty, and when she removed her shoes and stockings it was as though she had metamorphosed and emerged into a "painted lady;" a Nymphalid "flutterby" of God-given beauty.

What else of Muriel would be lovely to see for the painting of undraped nymphs and mermaids? Would he be so fortunate again to have God smile down upon him?

CHAPTER SIX

THE ARMOUR AND THE KNIGHT

Over the next week Nino sketched Muriel many times unable to decide how best to portray the faery-child. One day for the fun of it he sketched her wearing a lily pad for a hat. "Hmmm," he mused. It gave him an idea for the naiad he wanted next to paint.

Muriel grew accustomed to baring her feet for sketches, but the trouble of putting her shoes and stockings back on for all the rest breaks became too much a bother. For convenience she left them off about the studio, but one day she was barefoot half-way out the door when the postman blew his whistle. "Oops!" she said.

The sketch Nino selected depicted Muriel sitting before a roughed-in image of a kneeling knight with a noose of hair around his neck. Nino needed next to sketch the armour in detail, and put a face inside the helmet to kiss the faery-child.

"Who will model for the knight?" a dreamy Muriel asked. "Will he model here so I can meet him?"

Muriel fantasized being the faery-child herself, but real kisses for her were just that—fantasies. She had never been kissed, and certainly never slumbered with a man. And a knight in armour? "Why my Lord," Muriel mused. How does a girl unbutton plates of steel, or otherwise get a suit of armour off? Ideas of a can opener or a hacksaw amused her, and what—if anything—do knights wear beneath their armour?" The same nothing perhaps Scotsmen are thought to wear beneath their kilts. "I don't plan to use a sitter for the knight. I have an artist friend named Seymour Lucas who lives not far from here in West Hampstead. Seymour's home is a museum of armour suits. I can use one of his for the knight and make up a face. Seymour is also a fine costume designer. In fact, he made your dress."

"Well I love it. It's what every faery-child should wear. Does Mr Lucas have other dresses?"

"Lots of them! Seymour has a changing room full of dresses . . . racks of them . . . but most are old attire like Shakespearian and Elizabethan clothing. Recently, he designed costumes for a new theatre production of Henry VIII . . . back in Tudor times."

"When was that?"

"Oh some years ago . . . back before you were born . . . back when I was just a lad," Nino replied joking. "Back in the good old days when a bloke could earn a tuppence a day and buy four tankards of ale at a ha'penny each in any pub, or two tankards and a roast chicken. Yeah, the good old days. I remember them well."

"You don't drink ale do you," Muriel joked back, "that bitter old stuff my mother's minister once said was tapped from horses . . . whatever that means . . . but I don't think he meant it to mean anything nice."

"Probably not."

"The news outright shocked my mother. She gasped and fanned her face to hear of such a thing."

Good-humoured bantering between Nino and Muriel became everyday amusement. Nino delighted in it to carry on with Muriel, and she him, but feeling a need to change the subject of ale from horses Nino said: "Now when we go to Seymour's house I'm sure he will let you see and try on dresses."

"When can we go?"

"Now if you want. Esther is gone for the day and you can use her bicycle. How are you riding one?"

"Not too good," Muriel joked. "It seems every time I ride a bicycle and run into something, the front wheel stops but the back wheel keeps right on going."

"Don't worry," Nino laughed at the scene. "Esther and I have bicycles with the new safety brakes and Dunlop tyres, and if you don't bowl along too fast you'll do fine." ("I hope," Nino muttered to himself.)

"When you meet Mr Lucas you will notice he walks with a limp from a train wreck last year in Spain. His traveling companions were killed but Seymour survived with a badly fractured leg that will cause him to walk with a limp the rest of his life."

"How unfortunate . . . but what an interesting man, and what an interesting name. I've never known a 'Seymour.'"

"It's his mother's maiden name, Elizabeth Seymour. I'll gather my pads and pencils while you get out of the faery dress and into something else."

"Can't I wear it? It's such a pretty dress, and mauve is fashionable these days. Haven't you noticed girls wearing purples?"

"Oh all right! And yes, I've noticed. Seymour would like to see you in his dress anyway."

"Can you wait for me to put up my hair and put on a hat?"

"Oh all right! But be sure to put your shoes back on and wear long stockings in case your dress blows. Hanging around the studio barefoot is one thing, but outside is something else."

"Of course I'll wear shoes and long stockings! Why did you say that?"

"Because at first I couldn't get you out of your shoes and stockings but now I can't keep you in them."

"Ha! ha! ha!"

. . .

"Now that we're here, I hope Seymour's home, and you went much too fast around that last turn when you sideswiped me."

"I swerved to steer away from where a horse had been. You wouldn't have wanted that mess all over Esther's new tyres, would you? And besides, you are such a 'slowpoke' on a bicycle. Why ride at all if you can't ride fast? What's the fun in that? I could have walked faster than you were going."

"Well, maybe," Nino fussed to sound disgruntled by her reproach, but smiled. "It's a wonder you didn't tear your dress and rip my trouser leg."

Nino rapped again. The latch clicked, and the door squeaked open. There stood Seymour. "Hey Waterhouse, you old rascal. Where have you been since that last night at the V & A?" [Victoria and Albert Museum.]

"That's right! I enjoyed seeing the armour you donated, but before you give it all away I need to sketch a suit."

"No problem! I have several left. Come on in and take your pick . . . and who's your pretty friend? I recognize the dress."

"Seymour . . . meet Muriel Foster. She's sitting for my La Belle Dame painting. You know . . . Keats's poem about the faery-child and the knight . . . the reason I needed this dress."

"Of course I remember. You said Miss Foster was tall and slender . . . five foot eight and about eight stone or so . . . and that's the size I made it. I must say it fits her nicely."

"So THAT'S why Nino wanted to know my height and weight during my interview? I thought he asked just to carry on with me."

"That I would suspect, Miss Foster, knowing Nino as well as I do, back from the sixties when we made the pubs together and chased the girls about. He always carried on with pretty barmaids when he sized them up for models. I remember one especially from the Old Cheshire Cheese down on Fleet Street." Muriel smiled at Seymour's humour but Nino frowned.

"So you're ready for a suit of armour. Take your pick."

Nino had visited Seymour's studio many times, but Muriel stood in awe her first visit looking not only at the size of the huge room with its vaulted ceiling and massive sixteenth and seventeenth century oak furnishings, but propped upright around the room against oak-paneled walls stood suits of medieval armour with lances, swords, and shields.

"Where did you get all of these things, Mr Lucas?"

"From around Europe and here in Britain. I'm an antiquary."

"Oh come on now Mr Lucas," impish Muriel said in jest. "You're not old are you? You couldn't be a day over forty." Nino and Seymour who were the same age at forty-three laughed.

"No-no Miss Foster! An antiquary is someone who studies and collects antiques. I collect arms and armour and I design old costumes like the dress you're wearing. I'm not an antique myself. Nino, maybe," Seymour laughed.

"I see!" Muriel exclaimed, "Well I couldn't believe you were suggesting you're old.

"I do love my dress Mr Lucas. What kind is it?"

"It's a thirteenth century cotte, close to the body but loose and flowing, like a shift or a chemise. It's quite unlike the fourteenth and fifteenth century dresses that became so grotesque in appearance . . . the farthingale for example. A cotte could be worn by itself like you are wearing it, or under a sleeveless tunic."

"Whatever it is Mr Lucas it's pretty, and feminine."

"Why don't you go down to that room at the end of the studio where I keep costumes. Look around. If you see anything you like maybe I can trade you to get my cotte back," he said with a chuckle. "That's how much I like it . . . and you in it Miss Foster."

Muriel blushed at the compliment bordering on flirtation, but she was delighted with the offer to see the costumes. Both men watched her walk to the dressing room and close the door behind her.

"She's certainly a beautiful girl, and I like that walk of hers. What a find! Does she have a twin?"

"No, unfortunately. Are you looking for a model?"

"I need another about Muriel's age . . . but I hate looking for sitters. It's hard to find one, then learn she can't sit without squirming, or she quits before a painting is finished. It's a chore to find and keep good models."

"I agree, which is why I pay sitters well to keep them, and I want to keep Muriel. I have paintings in mind for her as nymphs and mermaids."

"Nude, no doubt."

"Of course! *if* she consents, but she may not. Muriel is outgoing and friendly, and fun to carry on with, but she's modest and virtuous. I had a problem getting her to let me sketch her feet."

"I think sometimes I got on the wrong side of painting women. You paint yours wearing little or nothing and I paint mine wearing so much drapery all one sees are hands and faces. You paint parts of women I only dream about, including feet," Seymour laughed.

"I tried to tell you back when you were a student at St. Martin's, and when we painted figures in life classes at the Academy. But you, Charlie Green, Ed Abbey, Ernie Crofts and others of your ilk insisted on being costume artists. You paint women clothed to their necks, and with ruffs you don't see necks. I tried telling you nude was the only way to paint women but you wouldn't listen."

"Seeing Muriel makes me wish I had," Seymour chuckled. "She seems to fill whatever space she occupies with beauty. But what do you see in armour that you like? Are you interested in a full suit, three-quarter suit, or a half-suit?"

"A full suit. The best dressed knights wore armour from head to foot and I want my knight for *La Belle Dame* to look his best."

"Well, let's see. I've got a fifteenth century suit of German field armour made by Anton Peffenhauser in Augsburg. It's the one over there," Seymour pointed, "and the one next to it is a Peffenhauser in heavier metal with a volant piece for jousting. Then the one over there is an Italian suit made by Lucio Piccinino in Milano. You know Milano, Nino. You've been there."

"Several times . . . in Milan, Rome, Naples, Venice, Turin, and other places. Italy is a beautiful place."

"And filled with beautiful women," Seymour laughed.

"Of course! Lots of them."

"In the Piccinino armour note the T-shaped opening in the helmet, but with the helmet on you can't see a face."

"I want to show a face. What about that suit over there?" Nino pointed. "It looks more like what I have in mind."

"That's a nice one. It's French Burgundian with a globular helmet as you can see. The movable visor pivoted at the temple dates it to late fourteenth century, and with the visor up you *can* see a face."

"That one will do. Is there any chance we can get it down into a kneeling position?"

"No problem. The pieces are buckled together. How do you want the armour posed?"

"Kneeling down and humped over leaning forward. I want the knight with visor up looking down into the face of the faery-maiden, driven by desire to kiss and slumber on the moss with her. Well, you know Keats's story, and let's call him . . . well lets see now . . . we'll call him 'Sir Wants-her-alot.'" Both men laughed.

"Or better yet," Seymour chuckled, "paint the scene after the fact with his armour off and call him 'Sir Gal-he-had.'" Both men laughed again.

"And how about this?" Seymour said, still laughing. "Paint yourself as the knight who slumbers on the moss with her . . . with Muriel that is."

"That's an idea, but the only way I'll ever get close to Muriel is in a painting. But I don't allow myself to dwell on such thoughts anymore . . . not since I got married ten years ago."

"Oh come now! I don't believe that for a moment. We all know you have a persona supposedly as impenetrable as that German field armour over there, but you're talking now with an old school buddy who knew you otherwise. We go back to some rousing good times with the girls."

"We had them, didn't we? But we were younger then and mostly dreamers and talkers, like the time we tried talking that one barmaid into modeling for us. Was she ever pretty, but we had a few too many ales which is probably why she wouldn't sit for us. She probably thought we couldn't see straight to paint her.

"Now that I'm married, I think you know me about models. I admit I still have immoral thoughts, but who of us haven't with sitters as pretty as Muriel. Allison lay nude in front of me for hours when I painted her for *St. Eulalia*. I had thoughts but that's all they were. I stayed on my side of the easel.

"But say . . . speaking of temptations . . . Hacker must have desires for the model for his *Syrinx*. What a beauty she is!"

"I haven't seen her."

"Well, you must. I met her not long ago in Hacker's studio. She covered up when I entered but I saw his painting. That exquisite girl could drive any man delirious. Hacker must have a lot of willpower."

"Or maybe he doesn't," Seymour chuckled.

"I don't know about Hacker, but *my* willpower gets tested with Muriel. I think of her in ways . . . well you know what I mean."

"I've been there myself with models, and I can think of artists at the Academy who've more than fantasized. Now that I've seen Miss Foster I understand your dilemma."

"Well, she's fun to carry on with but that's as far as it goes. Otherwise, she's straight-laced and overly modest which is why she didn't want to bare her feet for *La Belle Dame*."

"I see a big problem on your hands when time comes to paint those nymphs and mermaids you talk about."

"It worries me. I want to paint her next as a water nymph."

"Nude I imagine."

"Of course! Have you ever seen a water nymph wearing clothes?"

"Well . . . no. But to be truthful about it I've never seen a nymph."

"Then do what I do. Stroll through the woods until you come upon a pond of water-lilies. Imagine the blossoms are heads of nympho nymphs lusting for men, and they see you coming. Without the constraints of God, morality, decency, or marriage, visualize the blossoms emerging in human form with youthful bodies and the daintiest of limbs to avail themselves of your manhood. But you have to use imagination to see them."

"Nino, it's plain to see you are stricken with nympholepsy. You've got nymphs on the brain, and an imagination like no other person I know. Unfortunately, my mind doesn't work like yours. The women I see and paint don't poke their heads up out of lily ponds, or look like Muriel. But the next time you stroll through the woods would you mind if I tag along?"

The two old friends enjoying good-humored raillery since classroom days and barroom nights paused to reflect on things just said; starring off for a long moment in pensive thought.

"Well anyway, Seymour," Nino finally said to break the silence, "can we get this armour down and on it's knees?"

. . .

Nino's sketches were masterfully done. Every forged and hammered part from helmet down to sabatons was drawn in detail. Back in Primrose Hill Muriel watched Nino sketch the armour on the study and position the kneeling knight in close to the faery-child "face to face," except he had no face and she looked longing into a hollow helmet.

Nino sketched a woodland background, then in time painted over his penciled lines with greens and browns for grass and trees; a sliver of blue for a mountain stream; a purple for the dress in flowing folds; gun-metal greys for the armour; and splashes of white dabbed with pink for flowers. Flesh-coloured tones of the maiden's face, hands, and feet captured the scene as if luminous in the shadowed setting.

"I thought the painting would be larger. It's not big like *Circe Invidiosa*," Muriel said, disappointed.

"That's because this is only a study," Nino reassured her. "But the finished painting will be larger. On studies I make sketches first to establish the outlines of the composition. Then I colour details for ideas in the final work . . . the one the public sees. You'll see when it's done."

"But aren't you going to paint a face for the knight? You painted mine already."

"A face comes next, and our knight errant needs hands."

"What exactly is a knight errant?"

"A man looking for adventure. He wants excitement in his life so he goes in search of it."

"It seems to me that what the knight has in mind excites his lady too. Does that make her a lady errant?"

"A lady? Not exactly, but 'errant' yes. This faery-child is an enchantress known as a *femme fatale*. She's the one doing the seducing to then abandon this hapless knight after a night on the moss . . . a roll in the hay if you will pardon me. When he awoke the next morning and found himself abandoned, his miserable soul was essentially destroyed, to become the sorrowful creature that he is . . . a 'wretched wight so woebegone,' as Keats said of him."

"You make her seem pitiless."

"That's exactly what she was. She was a seductress *sans merci*, without pity, who lured men down from off their lofty heights . . . the saddles of pacing steeds . . . only to destroy the wretched souls when loved and abandoned. This unfortunate knight was not the first of her men to unsaddle and unman.

"Keats wrote she had others too . . . kings and princes and warriors . . . all of whom she held 'in thrall,' which means they were enslaved by her hypnotic eyes to do her bidding."

"Can a woman really do that?"

"Seduce a man with her eyes? Oh yes! Right along with everything else she has to offer, and once a *femme fatale* mesmerizes her victim she can do with him as she pleases. Our faery-child here is who Freud calls a 'nymphomaniac;' a woman with excessive desire for lovemaking. She gratifies herself by seducing victims, and when they awake from her spell they find her gone . . . perhaps unaware of what really happened. Our knight here loiters about 'haggard and woebegone.' For the knight there are no more pleasures . . . no 'birds sing.'"

"So *that* is what Mr Keats meant when he said 'her eyes were wild.'"

"Exactly! She had hypnotic eyes. Keats created a woman

who was attractive and mesmerizing but wicked and pitiless. Men fell in love with her beauty . . . her face, her tempting lips, her hair, those pleading, seductive come-hither-make-love-to-me eyes . . . but unknowing of her Circelike powers until snared with her noose of hair like a bug in a web.

"Then it's too late. And after her pleasures are satisfied she leaves her victims abandoned and alone. 'What happened? How could she do this to me?' they ask themselves once awake and out of her spell."

"But don't men do that sort of thing to women? I mean love them and leave them. I've heard of such."

"Don't confuse the issue. We're talking about women here . . . not men."

"But still . . . don't men do the same thing to women?"

"The subject is *femmes fatales*. Have you ever heard of *hommes fatales*? I think not. Now you may hear of *hommes d'affaires*, or business men . . . or *hommes du monde*, men of the world. There are *hommes en vue*, or men about town, but nowhere in the French language I know are there *hommes fatales*. I suppose there could be but I'm not French. I *will* grant you there are *hommes a femmes*, or 'lady's men,' but that doesn't have the meaning of *femme fatale*. What does *La Belle Dame sans merci*, and *femme fatale* mean? You know some French."

"The words suggest a pretty woman who is deadly without mercy . . . but I think that 'heartless' or 'pitiless' is better meant than 'deadly,' don't you? *La Belle Dame* isn't really 'deadly' is she, like a spider with a bug?"

"A *femme fatale can* be. Salome and Turandot had men beheaded, but this faery-child was a heartless woman who captivated a knight, loved him, then left him. Now that's 'pitiless.'"

Muriel blushed, thinking of herself as *La Belle Dame*, not just the sitter. Could she be cold and heartless in a love affair? "Never!" she thought. To be a *femme fatale* she would need to lead men astray—down "primrose paths" so to speak—to then abandon them *sans merci*. No way could she do that, she assured herself.

But then Muriel smiled, thinking she did in fact walk down paths on Primrose Hill with Pandora, but never with a man; well, except for nature walks with Mr Wolf, but that was different.

"Nino . . . ?" Muriel paused after starting to ask a question.

"Yes?"

"Well . . ." Muriel paused again, thinking. "That's my face in the sketch isn't it?"

"You are the model."

"Then *La Belle Dame* is me. It's just that I've come to think of me as the faery-child, and I don't want *me* to be a *femme fatale*. Look at the way you drew my hair around the knight's neck. If I ever do that to a man I will love and want him . . . not devastate him."

"That's very commendable . . . but virtue is not in keeping with Keats's story, and *La Belle Dame* is not virtuous. She *is* a *femme fatale* and I want to paint her seductive according to the story."

"But you don't always paint true to the story. I mean I read about St. Eulalia, and the book said she was tortured, mutilated, and burned . . . but the gentle side of you didn't paint her disfigured. Even though she's dead in your painting she is whole and beautiful."

"That's keenly observant . . . and true. I don't horrify viewers with my paintings. I painted St. Eulalia beautiful even though she was, as you said, burned and mutilated. I painted her with compassion though dead as a martyr to her Christian beliefs and not with the horror of what the Romans did to her.

"But what has that got to do with the faery-child? There is nothing horrific to be painted. In the poem, Keats described her as 'full beautiful' which is how I intend to paint her, er you, and *you* are beautiful." Muriel lowered her eyes.

"I chose you for *La Belle Dame* for that long, lovely, auburn hair of yours, hair that most any man . . . any knight errant . . . would sell his soul to tangle in." ("Including me," he thought to himself).

"Why would a man want to tangle himself in my hair?"

"It will occur to you someday when it happens," Nino smiled, "but I knew your hair was perfect for the knight's seduction the day I saw it drop to your knees. I choose sitters for my needs . . . not as they want or don't want to be painted. Keep that in mind for the future." Nino turned and winked at her.

"I will! I will!" Muriel fussed. "But who will look at me in your painting and know that I'm supposed to be wicked?"

"Because of the *sans merci* which implies the faery-child behaves less than nice."

"Why not shorten the name just to *La Belle Dame*? Leave off the *sans merci*. Then no one would know the faery-child is merciless. Since it's me you're painting I want to be *La Mademoiselle Muriélle La Belle Dame* 'avec compassion,' not *sans merci*."

"You are being argumentative. The name of the painting stands. Now if you want to think of yourself as *La Mademoiselle Muriélle La Belle Dame*, or whatever, that's fine since you *are* pretty and the name is befitting. I'm painting your body, your face, and your pleading, hypnotic eyes as the seductive young enchantress she is . . . sensual and beautiful, yes . . . fawnlike and graceful, yes. I have no argument there but the story remains as Keats wrote it. *La Belle Dame sans Merci* is a *femme fatale* and a promiscuous predator."

"How terrible of her!"

"Well remember, the story is only a myth but she was certainly not the only of her kind. Delilah, Salome, Judith, Turandot and others like Circe and Lamia were all perverse women who turned holy water into love potions to seduce men.

"Keats may have been inspired from folk mythology, the Bible, classical literature, Renaissance poetry, or medieval ballads. The sources for *La Belle Dame* tales are many, and the great old stories were his inspiration . . . as they are mine."

"Yes . . . but___"

"There are no 'buts' about it. You have transferred your virtuous 'good-girl' persona to the image and are trying to change the meaning of the painting. As a model you have to disassociate yourself from the painting. She is not you, and you wouldn't want to be her anyway."

In a pretense of grumpiness Nino fussed. "Muriel... lesson number one for a sitter is to sit still and don't argue. Lesson number two is sit in the position asked and don't argue. And lesson number three is don't argue... not about anything... or," Nino said with a chuckle, "you will find yourself arguing to keep your job."

"*Yes sir*! but don't think of me as a *femme fatale*. If I ever kiss and slumber with a man it will because I love him."

"I will keep that thought in mind. But for the purposes of getting this painting finished just think of yourself... not that you are mind you... just think of yourself as a seductress." ("And you, you lovely thing, could seduce the pants right off any fortunate man.")

Nino added hands to the kneeling knight, painting first the left one holding to a tree for support. Nino painted the right hand gripped firmly around his 'rigid lance' symbolic of the knight's desire for the faery-maiden.

"What's he holding?" Muriel asked curiously.

"For the moment his lance but I may decide to make it his staff... the banner staff of his heraldry, that is, which in the finished painting would add a splash of colour to the purple of your dress. I might make the banner red. The manner in which he grips his staff symbolizes desire. Suggestive imagery even if subliminal adds eroticism to a painting."

"But how so with the way he grips his staff? I don't understand."

"Well its nothing you would know about now... when you're older perhaps... but this is a story of lust, and what one imagines is a matter of personal knowledge, experience, perception, and interpretation. It's a question of what you think you see or want to see. Viewer interpretations vary as to what one imagines in a romantic painting but the imagery must tell a story and excite imagination. It must titillate, and the more a painting arouses imagination the more it will be studied and enjoyed, and everyone has a right to interpret works of art as he or she likes."

"You certainly put a lot of feeling and high expectations of viewer enjoyment into a painting, don't you?"

"Of course! I wouldn't consider myself a good painter if I didn't strike a viewer's fancy. I want acclaim for my work, and what artist doesn't? I crave rave . . . to be poetic about it . . . and viewers will admire my work if it's good. To achieve that level of success I pour my feelings into what I create on canvas."

"Well you seem to be pouring a lot of feelings into this particular painting, the way you speak of it."

Intuitively, Muriel struck home. Nino wanted the knight symbolic of himself. He wanted to be the one to "slumber on the moss" with her. He had just argued the faery-maiden is wicked—a *femme fatale*—but he doesn't think that of his sitter. It was quite to the contrary.

Sitting before him she is in truth the graceful fawnlike girl with auburn hair and hypnotic eyes he is painting. The desire he strives to depict of the knight for the maiden is his own for the sitter but he suppresses his yearnings within a suit of armour symbolic of impenetrable propriety. His identity inside the helmet without his beard is hidden by a visor.

"I want this painting to shout of desire," he replied to her comment. "Are the knight and the faery-child to become as one on a bed of moss? That is the titillating question. On first view the painting is a scene of seduction. The end of the story rests in viewer imagination."

"Well *my* imagination is titillated. I want to know who the knight will be. Who will I kiss to sleep? I have never kissed a man, and when I do I want him to be handsome, whoever he is. Can you draw in a face?"

"So you want to know who the lucky man will be. Or," Nino added with a grin, "who the unlucky man will be." Muriel slapped him playfully on his arm.

"Well . . . if it will satisfy you more than idle curiosity I'll sketch a profile."

Nino pondered aloud. "Now let me see. Who would Muriel want to kiss . . . Quasimodo, Blue Beard, or Jack the Ripper?

Probably not! How about the Sandman, Jack Frost, Jack who climbed the beanstalk, or Jack who jumped over the candlestick? How about the Pied Piper, Scrooge, Rumpelstiltskin, or Johnny Appleseed? No, none of them. The man in the moon? Now there's a possibility." Nino smiled watching Muriel frown at his suggestions. "Oh, I've got it! Jolly old St. Nick." Nino laughed and Muriel looked daggers.

"Why do you always tease me like you do? You should be *Le Homme sans Merci*."

"I wouldn't tease you if I didn't love you," Nino said carelessly without thinking. The unintended remark escaped Muriel, however, and she acknowledged it with an indifferent smile and a casual "I love you, too" said in return with no more meaning than a bouncy comeback.

Not knowing for certain, however, Nino leaned into his easel trying to concentrate on his work while dwelling on Muriel's unexpected reply. Was her remark innocent or meaningful? It could only have been innocent, he concluded.

The deeper meaning of his careless remark however disquieted Nino, for not only had he said he loved her but it was his wish to kiss the lovely Miss. And dare he admit—now that he was baring his soul—that it was his yearning to slumber on the moss with her.

Muriel watched intently. She was curious. Who would be the knight she would kiss? Nino painted a vaguely discernible profile shadowed in the helmet by a visor. Surely his beardless face would go unrecognizable. Muriel stood close resting her hands lightly upon his shoulder watching every stroke of his brush.

Muriel watched fascinated by the masterful way Nino mixed colours on his rosewood palette with thumbhole fitted to his left hand; amazed at the speed he mixed and thinned pasty paints with drops of linseed oil. Daubs of colours spread across his palette from light to dark from left to right; from white and yellows through the warmth of reds and browns and neutral greens to the cools of lighter blues and the darker depths of Prussian blue and black.

Muriel's closeness with the touch of her hands upon his shoulder was sensual. The softness of her almost imperceptible inhalations of which warm, sweet, exhalations wafted in front of him mingled with the heady fragrance of her rose-scented perfume acting like an aphrodisiac. Nino inhaled deeply the scent of her so as to become one with her. Unwary to Muriel, Nino took breath by breath something from her she was oblivious in giving.

"Does it bother you for me to watch you paint?" If only she knew.

"Not at all" Nino replied nonchalantly trying to sound indifferent about her concern. "Watch as close as you want."

Nino knew there would be weeks and months ahead of her closeness, even if just in the same house, and he always painted in the privacy of his studio where they would be alone with the door closed.

"I'm anxious to see if the knight will be handsome."

"This study won't show too much now but when the painting is finished in coming weeks you can decide then. There won't be much of a face to show anyway. It will be hidden under the visor but I hope the knight will be someone you will think handsome and want to kiss."

CHAPTER SEVEN

MURIEL'S MODEL FRIENDS

To Nino's chagrin, Muriel's pleasurable closeness was interrupted by a knock on the door. She answered, and there in the afternoon sun holding to her bicycle stood a very pretty dark-eyed, dark-haired young woman tall and slender who seemed familiar. Muriel looked intently into her face shadowed by the brim of her hat.

"Why I know you," she said in surprise. "You are Circe."

"Yes," the young woman replied with a big smile to be recognized by a painting, "I'm Circe. My name is Allison."

"I'm Muriel."

"I assumed as much, seeing all that hair of yours. Esther told me some weeks ago that you were living here for a painting. I've wanted to meet you, and see Nino and my painting."

"Is it still here?"

"No, unfortunately. Circe is up in Liverpool for an exhibition, and then it's going to an art gallery in Australia . . . in Adelaide I believe Nino said."

"Wow! Australia, the far other side of the world. I'll never see it now. I should have come sooner . . . but how are you and Nino getting along?"

"Fine, I think."

"Does he carry on with you?"

"All the time," Muriel laughed. "There seems to be no end to it."

"Then he likes you. It's Nino's way of flirting, but he's always a gentleman. He was with me when I lived here. Is he home by the way . . . and Esther?" Allison asked as she peered down the hallway towards the studio.

"Nino's here, but Esther is away for a few days visiting with her sister somewhere over on the Devon coast. But you don't need an invitation to come in. You've been here more than I have."

"I stayed weeks at a time in the big middle of a painting, in what must be your room."

"The very one! Share it with me anytime."

"I would like that. I know Nino wants me back for another painting." Allison hung her shawl on the hall tree and checked her appearance in the mirror. She brushed back some hair blown by her bicycle ride.

"Is Nino back in the studio?"

"As usual. He seems to live in there. I sometimes find him asleep on the sofa with a book across his chest. It seems he would rather read and sleep in his studio than up in his bedroom."

Allison leaned close and whispered. "I think Nino disengaged himself from anything affectionate in his marriage long ago . . . if you know what I mean. Esther can be such a fusspot. It's no wonder they have no children."

Nino interrupted the whispered conversation when he walked into the hallway to see who knocked. Upon seeing Allison after many weeks, the biggest grin Muriel had seen on Nino spread across his face as he hugged her in a warm embrace.

"Are you here to sit for me, or are you still doing your theatre thing?"

"My theatre thing for at least a year. I have that part you know about that I don't want to give up right now . . . but let's sit in the studio and I'll tell you all about it."

"You two go ahead," Muriel suggested. "I'll make tea."

Nino and Allison walked the length of the hallway into the studio with Nino's arm around her shoulders. Muriel watched, not having known the two were that close as friends, and it was obvious they were elated to see one another. Nino had known Allison for years and no doubt well.

"Before we sit, take a look at the study for my next painting." Propped on an easel, Allison studied it for a long moment.

"What do you think?"

"It's great. The colours are excellent, and Muriel is so beautiful."

"The story is by John Keats about a knight and a___"

"I know the story. So Muriel is your heartless faery-child? She certainly looks a seductress the way you looped her hair around the knight."

"In the painting she's heartless, but otherwise 'no.' Muriel is innocence personified. She's a sweetheart of a person."

"So, what you are saying is that Muriel isn't like me," Allison laughed.

"Not . . . at . . . all like you, so far as sitting goes. You're a sweetheart too, and always have been, but the two of you are as different as black and white."

"And I'm the 'black' one. Is that what you're saying?"

"Not exactly, but when it comes to baring any part of herself Muriel is the lily-white one. It was a bother just to get her out of her shoes and stockings when you never had qualms to take off everything," Nino laughed.

"To tell you the truth, I did at first, but you were a gentleman from my first sitting on and you promised never to sketch or paint me in suggestive positions and with anyone watching. It never bothered me to pose nude for you after the first time or two."

"I hope that will be the case with Muriel. I want to paint her next as a naiad, and later as a hamadryad."

"Nude of course."

"How else? They are nymphs! And later I want both of you nude in a pond full of nymphs that I have in mind."

"That will be fine with me, but keep hoping about Muriel for your naiad. Maybe it will happen. But let Miranda and me work on her. If anyone can get Muriel out of her clothes and stripped of her prudery we can do it. And Miranda is well experienced taking off clothes in front of men," Allison laughed.

"Ah yes . . . Miranda! The mention of her name is like a ray of sunshine," Nino commented with a big smile.

"Who is Miranda?" Muriel asked as she entered with a tea tray, amused in the way Nino seemed delighted to hear mention of her name.

"You tell her Allison. She's your flatmate, but I did see the canvas Hacker is painting of Miranda as *Syrinx*, the virgin nymph. Have you seen it? Miranda is exquisite."

"I've not seen the canvas, but Miranda has a sketch on our bedroom wall . . . a full frontal view sparing nothing to see . . . and you're right, Miranda is exquisite. I see her nude about the flat, and she's not at all bashful in front of me, or Mr Hacker, which is what makes her such a good model," Allison said for Muriel's benefit. Allison looked at Nino and winked, hoping Muriel got the message.

"So who is Miranda?" Muriel asked again, blushing at what was just said of her.

"She goes by her stage name, Miranda Marie . . . like I do. Allison Paige is my stage name . . . and as Nino mentioned, we share a flat in Covent Garden to be near the theatre. We are in the Drury Lane Troupe."

"How old is Miranda?"

"She's my age . . . twenty-four . . . and a stunner of a brunette with curly brown hair and big brown eyes. She's got a body men would die for, and she doesn't mind Hacker painting her nude." Allison laughed with another wink at Nino.

"From seeing Hacker's study of *Syrinx*, I have to agree about the 'men would die for' part," Nino replied and grinned.

"Well I wouldn't know," Muriel remarked dryly, but the knowledge that Miranda, like Allison, was a model and an actress piqued Muriel's interest. Both were doing what Muriel wanted to do and she had just met Allison.

"I hope I can meet her someday."

"Well you've got to. Miranda's a real kick in the arse," scampish Allison said and laughed, but Muriel blushed at use of the "A" word.

"Sorry for my language," Allison apologized, but it comes from hanging around the theatre crowd and the roles we play. If one is playing St. Joan or St. Agnes then a whole lot of saintly 'thees' and 'thous' and 'Hail Marys' are said, mixed with smatterings of 'Holy Mother of God' as one's strongest language.

"But if one's role is a trollop in a bawdy port-side tavern with a boat load of drunken sailors breaking up the place then there's a lot of profanity uttered much worse than 'arse,' if you get what I mean. That's unless 'arse' is spoken in terms of endearment knowing what it is a trollop has to offer . . . and then its not profanity but an expression of affection for the lady." Muriel turned as red as red-heads can.

Muriel had been warned by Nino days before that Allison's language was "saucy" but Muriel blushed mostly on hearing such earthy things said in front of Nino. "Oh me oh my," she muttered.

Nino leaned close to Allison and whispered: "See what I mean about virtuous?"

"I see what you mean," Allison whispered back. "But again, let Miranda and me work on her. We'll get her out of her clothes and prudery and turned around to think like us."

"How is your acting going, by the way?" Nino spoke up to change the subject.

"Very well. As you know I play the role of Mary in the Payne and Irving comedy, *Charles the Second*. I want you to come see it tonight. The play starts at eight in the Drury Lane Theatre." Muriel listened with interest.

"I know about the play," Nino commented. "Esther wrote a review of opening night for the *London News*. She said the theatre was packed, and the play was well received with curtain calls. But I apologize I haven't seen the play myself."

"Then you must tonight. All of us in the cast read Esther's review. She only panned opening jitters concerning missed cues and slow scene shifts but predicted the play would be long running to packed audiences when we ironed out the wrinkles. Well she was right. We have a full house every night."

"Can we go?" Muriel asked excitedly. "I would love to see the play. I can pay for the tickets."

"No need for tickets," Allison said, "and you couldn't get them on short notice anyway. Seats are sold out days in advance but I have passes for two, for tonight only, in the Prince of Wales box if you want them."

"The Prince of Wales box!" Nino exclaimed. "How in the world did you manage that?"

"Any night Prince Edward is not scheduled to attend, the theatre and troupe assign his seats to guests of the cast and dignitaries. Tonight's my turn to have two guests, which is another reason I came by. Since Esther isn't here and has seen the play already I would like to invite you and Muriel."

"I would be delighted to take her."

"I know this is on short notice," Allison said to Muriel, "and it's only a suggestion, but come home with me if Nino will let you use Esther's bicycle. Nino can meet you at the theatre before play time and you can stay the night with Miranda and me."

"May I go?" Muriel asked Nino anxiously.

"Of course! But there's no need to ask. You're of an age to make your own decisions about things you want to do."

"Then it's all agreed," Allison said.

"Where should I meet Muriel?"

"At the door of the lady's dressing room at seven-thirty."

"Excellent idea," Nino grinned. "I've never been to the lady's dressing room," he chuckled.

"That doesn't mean come in," Allison laughed, wagging her finger. "Just knock and wait outside. The play starts at eight. Your reservations are for the two Prince of Wales seats overlooking the stage. You'll have an excellent view."

"Sounds good to me," Nino said as he looked and smiled at his two models; both pleased to be making plans for the evening.

"But I need to get ready," Muriel said.

"Don't worry about that here. You can have a bath at my place and wear one of my dresses. Just pack a toothbrush and a change of drawers."

"ALLISON!" Muriel fussed. "Don't talk about things like that in front of Nino. That's embarrassing!"

"That's nonsense! I suspect Nino knows what you wear. Most women wear drawers, and Nino knows what drawers look like."

"But you don't have to mention them."

"That's why people call them 'unmentionables,'" Nino interjected and chuckled.

"Nino's seen every pair I ever owned," Allison remarked, "in and out of them when I modeled for him, and mostly out of them." Allison and Nino laughed but Muriel blushed at more of Allison's saucy talk.

"I don't mind posing nude for Nino's paintings," Allison added for Muriel's sake, "but I can't hold a candle to Miranda's body. Wait until you see her and mine for yourself."

"*ALLISON!*" Muriel fussed.

"Someday," Allison continued, "when Nino makes sketches of you, like the charcoal one of me there on the wall," she pointed, "he'll need to make yours in sanguine . . . assuming you're a true red-head that is." Naughty Allison grinned and winked again at Nino.

"Don't talk about things like that!"

"I guess that's because I've known Nino longer than you have. Now get your things together so we can be on our way, and don't worry about anything to wear. I've got clothes you can borrow. Miranda and I will dress you up and do your hair to be such a stunner Nino will need a stick to beat the men away."

"I'll carry a cane just in case," Nino joked.

"You two are teasing me again!"

"Not this time," Allison replied. "By the time Miranda and I get you dressed for the theatre you'll look like Cinderella. Now begone my friend and hurry," Allison emoted with a backward flip of her hand as Shakespeare might have written such a scene.

"Just pack your . . . oh you know what I mean . . . your unmentionables," Allison grinned. "We need to get to my place in time to get you ready. All that hair of yours will take awhile."

"How do I find the lady's dressing room?" Nino asked.

"It's backstage and up three flights of stairs. Tickets for the Prince of Wales box are good for stage passes."

"How will you get to the theatre and back?" Muriel asked Nino.

"I'll hail a cab for there and another home."

"Okay, but you will have to get home by yourself. I will stay the night with Allison."

"In case you hadn't noticed, young lady," Nino retorted, stroking his bearded chin, "I'm a grown man. I'm forty-three and quite capable of finding my way home myself, thank you."

"Do you have enough room for me?" Muriel asked Allison.

"All you need. You can sleep on a lumpy sofa in the parlour, or on a floor pallet in with Miranda and me . . . or," she said facetiously, "on the fire escape outside our bedroom window. It's cooler out there anyway. Tonight is going to be warm, and there will be a full moon to see."

"Never mind! There's no way I'm going to sleep outside with Jack the Ripper on the loose and for the world to see. I'll sleep on the floor in with Miranda and you, and if you have creepy-crawlies I'll crawl into bed with you," she laughed.

"Then share my bed with me. Before we got a second one Miranda and I slept together, so I'm used to it. I learned to knee and elbow to keep Miranda on her side. She hogs the bed and takes covers."

"You know," Nino remarked, "Charles Darwin based his theory of 'survival of the fittest' on two people in a bed."

. . .

The one-mile bicycle ride to Allison's flat six blocks from the Drury Lane Theatre was uneventful—well almost. Muriel didn't bowl along too fast—but almost. She raced down Broad Walk through Regent's Park dodging other cyclists, people strolling, mothers with prams, and dogs on leashes. She didn't sideswipe anyone—but almost. She didn't cause anyone a wreck getting out of her way—but almost. But something Muriel did—and a lot of—was turn heads as she sped along with ribbons on her hat flying and Allison in hot pursuit.

The two young models soon to become "bosom buddies" and "partners in crime" as they would soon consider themselves, arrived at Allison's flat in time to meet Miranda pedaling in from her modeling job. Three flirtatious young men who live in the row house next door, and who work as scene-shifters in the theatre, heard the sounds of the girl's screeching bicycle brakes and girlish voices. They opened an upstairs window and looked down upon the scene waving and whistling for attention.

Not always did they catch Allison and Miranda together, but today there were three of the beauties. "What luck!" exclaimed one. "It's just too, too, too much" exclaimed another counting out the girls. "Hey Miranda," the third called down, "it's tonight or never."

"Then it's 'never,'" Miranda called back.

"Hey Red, will you go out with me then? I'm available if you are."

"My name's not 'Red,' thank you," Muriel remarked sarcastically. "I only go out with older men."

"I'm twenty-three and older than you I imagine. That makes me an 'older man' doesn't it?"

"Not old enough. Add twenty years and make it forty-three then I might reconsider," Muriel replied, knowing Nino was forty-three. Allison and Miranda giggled at Muriel's now sassy talk.

"What's a forty-three year-old man got that I don't have and can't do better?" the young man protested.

"He's got maturity, a reputation, and good manners for starters. He's a gentleman. And what he can do is sweep a lady right off her feet which you're not doing at all."

"Ouch!" exclaimed the young man put in his place.

Allison interrupted the banter to give Muriel and Miranda a delayed introduction.

"I'm happy to meet you," Miranda said, ignoring the three young men. "Just pay them no mind," she said aside to Muriel. "They hardly leave us alone, but it comes with being models and actresses. Men throw themselves at your feet, but step aside and keep right on going. That's what Allison and I do. But don't ever step over one or they will look right up your dress and hope you had forgotten your drawers." Miranda and Allison laughed. The three young men above scratched their heads wondering what was so funny.

Despite her previous straight-laced demeanour and modesty Muriel laughed the loudest, now sassy herself influenced by her new older and more worldly friends. They had minds of their own. They did what they wanted, when they wanted, and said what they wanted.

Miranda's language was coarse, but Muriel liked her immediately. Allison's language was saucy too, but the two pert and sassy girls were experienced models and actresses. Muriel liked her new friends already, wanting to be just like them as "one of the girls."

"Hey Red," the one young man called down again. "If you change your mind you can find me backstage after the play."

"Well don't hold your breath or you won't be around that long," a spirited new Muriel retorted.

The three girls laughed again and entered their flat to prepare for a night at the theatre; a night to become the most memorable of Muriel's young life; a night which in the hours to come would change it forever.

CHAPTER EIGHT

THE PLAY AND THE QUEEN

One wall in Allison's and Miranda's bedroom was a gallery of pinned chalk and pencil sketches in black and sanguine. Some showed Muriel's new friends in nude depiction, and she wondered how either had nerve enough despite their claims that nudity in art was no big thing and the job of figure models.

"This is you as 'Circe!'" Muriel exclaimed to Allison as she studied the sketch. "In the painting you're draped but here you aren't. Why is that?"

"That's Nino's technique. He prefers to sketch models nude to start so that arms, legs, feet, and such, are properly articulated and in good posture, sort of like making a frame to hang clothes on. Then he drapes the sketch like dressing a mannequin, but Nino avoids too much clothing so that a model's femininity shows through.

"Well there's certainly no question about that in your Circes and Eulalia."

"That's Nino for you. He likes things bare or showing through. When he draped me for Circe with a cup, I had parts of me showing through garb so sheer I might as well have had nothing on. My nipples showed," Allison laughed. Muriel blushed. "In *St. Eulalia* Nino left me bare-breasted for men the world over to see."

"That's what shocked my mama and me when we saw the painting in the Tate. But in the *La Belle Dame* Nino is painting of me, I'm draped from head to foot and from the start. He didn't ask for nude sketches, and there's nothing bare of me showing but feet."

"I suspect he wanted to sketch you nude, though, to establish the posture of the faery-child before adding the drapery, but he knew of your objections."

"It's a good thing he didn't ask or he wouldn't have had me for a sitter."

"He knew that, but you can be sure he'll reveal outlines of your limbs."

"My hair is why Nino said he wanted me for *La Belle Dame*. He never said anything about limbs but we had an argument about feet. I finally had to give in and show them."

"You can't win an argument with Nino about poses. He knows what he wants in a work, so I never argue but I can tell you that any hair that's long and red is a fixation with Nino and he'll do with it as he pleases. That's why he's painted my hair red in Circe with the cup even though it's as plain as day that mine is black, but Nino changes hair colours in paintings if whimsy moves him.

"And if you want to know of something else funny, Nino made a tangled mess of mine getting it arranged for Eulalia like he wanted. I just lay there while he fooled around with it, but it seemed to take him forever. The truth is, I think, Nino was just playing around." Allison laughed.

"Well he fussed with mine, too, making that crazy noose he wanted, and while I held it posed like he sat me he combed the rest of my hair down my back, all the way down to my . . . well to where you saw in the study. And now that you mention it, Nino was just playing around."

"That's him for you. He likes to get his hands in hair," Allison said with a grin.

"Posing the noose was funny because I held it looped over the back of a Chippendale chair instead of a knight. There was nothing romantic about that. I never did get to meet a knight. Nino just made one up."

"You want to hear something else funny," Allison said for a bit more humour. "When Nino finished sketching mine I made him brush out the tangles. After all, he made them, I argued, but he didn't fuss about it. He must have taken a hundred strokes beyond anything necessary but I didn't fuss either, or ask him to stop. It felt good."

"Well the truth of *that* matter is," Miranda piped in with some tittle-tattle, "Allison was trying to seduce Nino with all the brushing."

"Ha! ha! . . . fat chance of ever seducing Nino!" Allison retorted. "That'll never happen."

To change the subject to something Miranda didn't mind hearing, Allison pointed to Miranda's full length frontal view of the nymph *Syrinx* with an arm raised and a breast lifted. "See! I told you she's fantastic." Miranda smiled at the flattery, and with a rare hint of blushing lowered her eyes.

"Well yes," Muriel replied, taking a long look, "but I could never pose like that."

"Haven't you ever undressed for a boyfriend?" Miranda asked.

"For heaven's sake! No man is going to see *me* until I'm married, and maybe not then."

"Oh piffle!" Allison fussed. "These are the nineties you know. Good times for girls are in. Let a boy touch you somewhere private if he wants. What do you think God made fingers for?"

"That may be for you but not for me. A boy once tried to slide his hand down my dress but I slapped him silly."

"Well sooner or later you *will* want a man to slide his hand down your dress . . . or up under," Miranda said and grinned.

"Haven't you ever had a doctor examination?"

"Only once, but the doctor looked down my throat . . . not up where you are thinking. I would have died."

"But someday you *may* need a doctor to examine up where you think I'm thinking."

"I'm not going to get sick down there."

"What about a woman? Don't you undress in front of other girls . . . or your mother?" Miranda continued with questions probing for chinks in Muriel's prudish armour.

"Mama said my body was not for viewing or touching until married, and that when my husband lifts my nightgown I'm to turn my head and grit my teeth. She says allowing oneself to feel pleasure by what men do is sinful. She says marital congress is God's command for procreation . . . not recreation."

"Blimey!" Miranda thought to herself, seeing problems from a puritanical mother.

"If you lived with a girlfriend like Allison and I do, and she saw you nude, would that bother you?"

"I don't know, but maybe not if she turned her back and didn't stare at me."

"Allison and I undress in front of one another every day and we certainly don't stare. We have only the one bedroom and bath anyway, and if time is of importance we bathe together to hurry things along."

"Yeah!" Allison interjected. "It's no big deal for us, and you'll see us bathe and dress right soon now to get ready for the theatre. Just pay us no mind, but get used to seeing *me* nude because Nino wants to paint us together as nymphs in a lily pond."

"I know! Nino told me a few months ago when he showed me a lily pond and drew a sketch of me. He said he wanted you for the other nymph."

"*Aha*! So you've been out with Nino already, and he sketched you naked in a lily pond did he?" Allison remarked in jest and laughed. "How much of you showed from neck down?"

"Don't be funny! Nino didn't sketch me nude and it wasn't in a pond. I sat on a park bench with people all about."

"Oh!"

"Would you believe," Miranda piped in, "that Allison and I skinny-dip in the very pond where Mr Hacker sketched me for *Syrinx*. It's a private place out in the country that Mr Hacker knew about. It's well hidden by trees and reeds and a fun place to sneak to at night with boyfriends to skinny-dip."

"That's true," Allison added. "It's a fun carriage ride down a long country lane to an old barn, and from there a short walk to the pond. There's also a fun hay loft up in it."

"Don't forget we have to climb over a fence to the pond and up a ladder to the loft," Miranda added with a giggle. "Maybe you can get Nino to take you sometime. Have you ever climbed a ladder?"

"Not up to where you are talking about, and not on your life!" Muriel frowned.

"We can tell you how to get there," Miranda laughed, "and don't forget to take towels and a blanket."

"Just hush you two with that kind of dumb talk! Nino knows I wouldn't do anything like that, just as he knows I won't model nude for him. He understands my concern, so he said."

"Well he *does* understand, and he said as much . . . but after *La Belle Dame* I know he wants to paint you nude for a naiad and a hamadryad."

"When did he tell you that?"

"It was this afternoon in his studio when you were making tea in the kitchen. Aren't you pleased he wants you for other paintings?"

"Not if he wants me in my birthday suit."

"Not now anyway . . . but do you want to know something else? Now understand Nino didn't actually tell me this but I think he's in love with you."

"No way!" Muriel exclaimed, unbelieving.

"I would say he is, certainly in the ways he speaks so fondly of you, even if he never confesses his love . . . and he won't. He'll just love you in silence from a distance."

"Well, he's *not* in love with me, and besides he's married and a gentleman. He has never so much as laid a finger on me, or even tried."

"And he won't. He never tried anything with me either, not even when he played around with my hair for *Eulalia*. And I lay nude on the floor right in front of him for hours. If *you* ever pose nude for something like that, the first time or two may make you nervous being flat on your back in front of a man, but you'll get used to it. Just think about other things to pass the time . . . or go to sleep. Models all do who've been up late the night before."

"I don't mind posing nude for Arthur," Miranda piped in to add, "and he's already making sketches of me for another nude when *Syrinx* is finished."

"Which one is that?" Allison asked surprised.

"Circe."

"Circe!" Allison exclaimed. "Nino's done two Circes of me already. How can Mr Hacker paint a Circe better than Nino?"

"It should be obvious!" Miranda snapped back.

"What is that supposed to mean?"

"That Arthur has *me* for the model, and *my* Circe is nude to show off *my* superior body, in case you've never noticed. Why do you think Nino draped your two Circes . . . huh? It was to cover over what you don't have to show."

"Don't have to show! Well he showed my breasts and nipples in *Eulalia*, and let me tell *you* something, mine are better to show than what you've got, or ever will have."

"Well let me tell *you* something. I've got___"

"Hush you two!" Muriel blurted out to break up the bickering. "If Nino wants *me* undraped then how can either of you claim a body better looking than anyone else's without seeing mine?"

Muriel paled. "Oh God no!" she groaned to herself. She couldn't believe she made such an impetuous and foolish comment without thinking. But in spite of it Muriel broke out laughing on seeing the shocked expressions of her two surprised friends. Allison and Miranda joined-in, taunting, and Allison pointed at Muriel's bosom.

"You . . . you have something there better looking than ours? Well a big 'ha' to that!"

"We're breaking some ice here," Allison whispered aside to Miranda. "Keep her going. I told Nino that if anyone can get Muriel out of her clothes and out of her prudery we can." Muriel overheard the comment and began to fidget.

Miranda goaded her on. "Well 'Miss Bosom,' if you think *yours* is better looking than ours then prove it."

"Yeah!" Allison piped in to keep her going.

Muriel turned crimson by the language and caught up in the dare of a bare bosom contest. She had just thrown down a gauntlet unthinking of the consequences. A foolhardy challenge had been made to prove who of them was a better contestant. Muriel couldn't back out now, and the dilemma was of her doing.

"Don't we need to get ready for the theatre?" Muriel asked, to make excuse for what she anticipated happening.

"Oh my gosh!" Allison exclaimed, looking at the clock on the wall. "We need to get our baths started."

"Is your tub big enough for three?" Muriel asked.

"Are you suggesting we take a bath together?" Allison replied, surprised with jaw dropped by Muriel's question.

"We don't want to be late for the play, do we?" a now adventurous and much bolder Muriel asked. Influenced by the peer pressure of risqué new friends, Muriel began unlacing her bodice to be "one of the girls" who undress in front of one another and bathe together.

"The last one in the tub is a rotten egg," she challenged. The unbelievable of minutes earlier happened. Pandemonium broke out as all three girls, giggling, began stripping to be first in the tub.

Squeals filled the room as each piece came off, and the three young men next door put their ears to the wall. Then Allison threw her petticoat at Muriel in the opening volley of a "war."

Muriel picked up the petticoat and her own and threw one back at Allison and the other at Miranda, and Miranda threw hers and a pillow at Muriel. Muriel returned the pillow and another resulting in a barrage of heavy artillery back and forth across all fronts.

Wall hits knocked pictures and the clock askew. More clothes came off in the melee, and Miranda stood bare in all her glory. But Muriel remained in corset and drawers reluctant now to remove anything more. Miranda scrambled to be first in the bath, but

Allison pulled her back to take the lead, though Allison still wore drawers.

With a devilish laugh and a downward pull Miranda popped Allison's buttons in yanking them off. That left a blushing Muriel the only one still wearing anything and wishing she hadn't instigated the affair. "Why didn't I just keep my darned mouth shut?" she reprimanded herself.

Allison saw Muriel's hesitance. "Gotta get her out of her clothes like I promised Nino," she remarked to Miranda, and the naked flatmates converged on Muriel retreating from their onslaught.

"Not so fast," Allison said as they grabbed Muriel by her arms. "You started this whole thing and we're gonna finish it."

"Yeah!" Miranda piped in. "It's bath time 'Miss Bosom!'"

Muriel squealed, slipped free, and made a dash for the bathroom to lock the door behind, but not in time. Amid more squeals, Allison and Miranda held Muriel prone across a bed to unhook the backside of her corset. Muriel kicked and thrashed. "Don't!" she implored. "I beg of you! I'm sorry I started this!"

"'Sorry' won't save you now," she said to Muriel. "Help me hold her down!" Allison commanded Miranda. "I'll sit on her and you hold her arms still!" Then amid begs for mercy Muriel's corset was unhooked and stripped off. With a struggle, the two girls flipped Muriel over starting in on her buttoned drawers trimmed with frilly lace and satin bows.

"Please don't pop my buttons!" Muriel begged, still struggling to get back on her feet. Allison spared the buttons, but despite pleas for mercy the girls held Muriel down and stripped her bare of the last of what she wore.

"Whew!" Miranda exclaimed, breathless from the struggle as Muriel, red faced, sat back up. "She's a real scrapper she is."

"And a real red-head," Allison added.

A blushing Muriel—red all over—scrambled to her feet amid more squeals as the three girls struggled to be first through the bathroom door.

Common sense prevailed when Miranda raised her arms like *Syrinx* directing traffic. "Hold it!" she called out. "So far as who of us has the better looking body, I vote for Muriel. Just look at her Allison! She's got curves men would die for." Muriel blushed furiously trying vainly to cover herself with arms and hands.

"I agree," Allison said, but Muriel was the diplomat.

"I give you both a tie," she said, then nudged Allison to vote for Miranda who won by a decision. It was Miranda's raising her arms like *Syrinx* with breasts lifted that convinced Muriel that buxom Miranda had the better looking body. Then all three girls stepped into the tub with more squeals from a cold water bath.

The young men next door felt the wall-shaking thuds of pillows. Even without their ears to the wall they heard muffled laughs, shrill squeals, and cries for mercy. Then through the wall came the sound of running water. The three men imagined a bevy of frolicking water nymphs.

"Mirthful merrymaking," said one. "Boisterous whoopee," said another. "Insatiable perversions," ventured the third. "They're just too, too, too much," said the one again counting out the girls.

. . .

Nino presented his theatre ticket for a pass then wandered backstage over and around curtain ropes and electric cables looking for the stairs leading up to the lady's dressing room. Hopefully, Muriel would be ready. There was a bustle of activity as stage-hands set up scenery for Act One, Scene One. Stage lights with colour filters tested on then off; curtains opened then closed; and others raised then lowered to make certain everything worked.

A buzz of activity hummed through the auditorium as ticket holders entered and took seats amid rumours Queen Victoria and two of the royal princesses with an entourage would attend. The royal party would occupy the queen's box opposite the Prince of Wales box where in the absence of Prince Edward and his princess, Nino and Muriel would sit as theatre guests courtesy of Allison and her Drury Lane Troupe.

Nino hoped the queen wouldn't look his direction, recognize him, and remember to her consternation and his embarrassment that he once arrived a day late for her garden party. The queen received him nevertheless for afternoon tea and she showed him the Royal art collection including to Nino's surprise a number of nudes.

Nino walked about backstage feeling out-of-place in black evening dress with a tailcoat and matching trousers, an embroidered waistcoat, a velvet-lined black cape, a black bow tie, black velvet top hat, and carrying a silver-tipped cane. Others on stage wore work clothes or fifteenth century costumes for the play including a group of sailors for a rowdy barroom scene.

Up three flights of squeaky stairs Nino knocked on the door of the lady's dressing room with the knob of his cane then stood back waiting amid aromas of perfumes and powders. From inside came sounds of voices and laughter amid which he heard Muriel's. He knew her happy laugh, and much to his pleasant surprise Miranda answered the door dressed as her character, Lady Clara. Nino's heart skipped a beat to see Hacker's beautiful model again. The last and only time he saw her, Miranda shook hands to meet him wearing a robe for cover in Hacker's studio.

"Oh good evening Mr Waterhouse," Miranda said smiling as she extended a hand once again. "Welcome to the lady's dressing room if you've never been up here before."

"Unfortunately no," Nino said as he happily kissed Miranda's hand, "but I've been on the other side of the curtains in the audience many times."

"Muriel should be ready in a moment. Allison is finishing her hair . . . and Mr Waterhouse your young lady for the evening is ravishing."

"I've known since I met her that she's beautiful."

"But tonight sir, Muriel is more than that. She's gorgeous. She looks like a Cinderella princess, so hang on to her because she will turn heads in the theatre including the queen's and all the men."

"We're told the queen will attend tonight's performance and we're excited about it. She usually comes backstage after her first attendance to a new play to meet the cast . . . and wouldn't you know it Mr Waterhouse, I play Lady Clara, a royal. I'll be nervous of the queen watching."

"I'm sure you'll do just fine."

"But our play, *King Charles the Second*, is a spoof on royalty and I hope the queen isn't offended. Would you watch from your box and tell me if she laughs."

"Of course! But has the queen ever laughed?"

"I don't think so, but in anticipation of an introduction Allison and I are practicing curtsies."

"If no one was watching I would show you how."

"Never mind," Miranda laughed, "we know how, and men don't curtsy anyway. You would look funny doing one. And besides, if the stage hands see you curtsy to me they will think you're carrying on."

"Who me?" Nino grinned. "Perish the thought!"

"Well men try . . . and sometimes a handsome one succeeds," flirtatious Miranda said with a coy wink at Nino.

Nino blushed and stammered. "Well just look at you. I couldn't blame a man for trying."

"Why, thank you Mr Waterhouse," Miranda said as she returned his smile. "Please bring Muriel backstage as soon as the play is over. She wants to see the queen up close, so try to get her up front on centre stage.

"Its been fun for Muriel Mr Waterhouse. She likes dressing up and doing her hair . . . and she likes you I might add. You have done so much for her and she loves you for it, certainly in the ways she talks about you."

Nino's face reddened by the flattery, and pleased that Miranda noticed what Nino already suspected. "The feeling between us is mutual I can assure you. I'm very fond of Muriel."

"And she you. She's a sweetheart of a girl, and as funny as anyone can be. Allison and I loved her from the start but we've only known her for an afternoon and she's worn us out already.

You've known her for months. She must be a constant uphill chore for you to keep pace with her."

"Well now that you mention it," Nino chuckled.

"Well she's certainly worth the effort, and she'll certainly make some man happy someday. Muriel is very pretty and we've noticed all afternoon how men have looked."

"I know the looks and I'll envy any man in Muriel's life," Nino replied, disheartened by thoughts that she would someday be in the arms of another man.

"Now if you will excuse me Mr Waterhouse I'll tell Muriel you're here. Curtain time is in half an hour and I can't be late. I'm on first. Allison doesn't come on until Act Two."

Nino waited by the dressing room door only minutes more, happy to have seen Miranda again, when a beaming, ravishing, "Cinderella" appeared. Nino could hardly believe his eyes over Muriel's metamorphosis though forewarned by Miranda. Only hours before, Muriel was a barefoot faery-child on a canvas but now she was *La mademoiselle Muriélle la belle dame*; a stunning "princess of the ball" as if she had just stepped from a cover of *Le Journal des Modes*.

Nino took her gloved hands, held them out, and stepped back to admire her attire from hat and coiffured hair down to her slippers and back up again. He lingered for an instant on a sensually revealing neckline and bare shoulders, the most of her other than bare feet he had yet been so fortunate to see. Every inch of her was stunningly dressed. Nino stood mesmerized. "Oh my!" he exclaimed to himself.

"But your slippers aren't glass," he joked. Muriel looked puzzled for an instant then smiled, understanding his comment.

Muriel's evening dress was fashionable lavender satin trimmed with embroidered silk floral designs of miniature dark-red roses and dark-green leaves. The floor-length dress with an hourglass waist fit snugly over her rounded hips accentuated behind by a bustle. Most of her auburn hair was coiled atop her head and pinned beneath a hat of matching lavender satin and embroidered roses. Around her neck was a choker of opalescent pearls, and her lips were the most ruby of rose petals as if they were the source of her rose-water scent.

Ringlets of hair decorated her temples. The remainder hung in long, tightly-twisted curls down her pale-white back made bare from the fore and aft design of her off-the-shoulder dress. A plunging neckline revealed ample curvatures, and the way Muriel's auburn hair contrasted with the lavender of her dress and whiteness of her skin was stunning. Nino stood breathless admiring his exquisite lady for the evening.

"Oh my!" he exclaimed aloud. "You *are* the belle of the ball."

Heads turned even as Muriel descended the first flight of steps from the third floor dressing room. The three young stagehands who saw her earlier in the day nudged one another as they watched Muriel descend to stage-level holding up the front hem of her dress. They walked her direction.

Muriel saw them approach and whispered to Nino: "Whatever they might be rude enough to say, just play along with me."

"Of course! But what, pray tell, are they going to say?"

"Who knows! But I told them this afternoon you were the older man in my life. I said that so they would leave me alone. So go along with it . . . okay?"

"Okay!" Nino responded and beamed, proud to be seen with Muriel and to know he was "the man in her life."

"Hello, hello, hello," said the one young man who spoke in triplets as he gazed at Cinderella. Muriel diverted her eyes.

The young man who called her "Red" said, "We never did catch your name, Miss."

"My name is of no concern to you," sassy Muriel replied aloof, "and this is my distinguished well-mannered gentleman friend I mentioned . . . Mr Waterhouse, Esquire, which I'm sure you don't know means 'Gentleman.'"

"Glad to meet you mate," he said in a cockney brogue as he extended his hand to Nino to impress "Red" that he too was a gentleman. "I 'ope I didn't embarrass the lady this afternoon, mate but I didn't know she was spoken for already."

Nino was caught unaware of what "spoken for" meant, but to

cover all bases to play along as Muriel asked—and be a rascal when occasions for humour demands it—Nino commented tongue-in-cheek. "Yes . . . I've 'spoken' for the lady's hand in marriage." The comment caught Muriel by surprise. That wasn't how far she meant Nino to play along but, nevertheless, now that it was said, deadpan Muriel played the game further by nodding agreement as she placed a hand inside the crook of Nino's arm and moved in closer.

"Well sir . . . all I wanted was to make the lady's acquaintance. I only thought she was taking up 'abitation with Allison and Miranda."

"No . . . the young lady lives with me," Nino said nonchalantly placing his free hand on top of Muriel's. "My intended is staying tonight with her friends, but tomorrow she'll be back at home with me."

In a sense of Muriel and Nino living under the same roof, no truer words were spoken, but "back at home with me" led to implication of something less than upstanding, and Nino's devious comment was said to Muriel's satisfaction. She smiled to herself.

Muriel squeezed Nino's arm for going along with her chicanery, and to play the game further, said "I think we should go now, dear. The play starts soon and we should take our seats in Prince Edward's box before Queen Victoria arrives," Muriel said smugly, dropping the names and titles of royalty.

"Yes darling," Nino commented to continue the pretense as he turned away and walked arm in arm with Muriel. The three young men watched and scratched their heads.

Nino escorted Muriel up a flight of stairs to the Prince of Wales box where they were ushered to a pair of deeply cushioned red-velvet chairs trimmed in gold. The two seats for the Prince and Princess of Wales overlooked the stage opposite the royal box where Queen Victoria sits.

How many times, Muriel wondered, had the prince and princess sat in the very chairs she and Nino occupied. She couldn't believe her step up in life.

"What exactly is the play about?" Muriel asked as she laid a hand atop Nino's arm and leaned in close. "Allison only said it was a comedy about King Charles the Second who wanted to meet a tavern owner's daughter named Mary . . . the part Allison plays."

"That's essentially it. The King goes incognito to a tavern in Wapping called 'The Grand Admiral' to meet a pretty maiden he's heard about . . . that's Mary. But he gets too familiar with her and flees back to the palace chased by the maiden's angry uncle with a shotgun.

"The uncle goes through the palace looking for the scoundrel not knowing that it's King Charles he's after. That's the best of the comedy but the story isn't true. At least I don't think so," Nino chuckled, "but royals are known for tomfoolery outside the confines of bedroom doors and palace gates, and King Charles the Second had his share of *affaires d'amour*. I've read he had thirteen."

"Thirteen!" Muriel gasped. "I didn't know royals even had ONE."

"Oh definitely . . . as can anyone. Falling in love with someone one shouldn't is a common occurrence, and few are spared the temptation at least once in a lifetime. Many succumb to it," Nino commented, knowing he had fallen to Muriel's allure.

"How long do affairs last?"

"One night, days, weeks or months. Some last for years or a lifetime . . . but why are you asking?"

Muriel seemed overly curious about affairs. Earlier, Allison revealed in confidence that Nino was "in love" with her; a "woman's intuition" Allison said. Miranda passed the word in the lady's dressing room that Nino said he was "fond of her," but before Muriel could ask anything more about affairs they were distracted by an usher below walking briskly to the orchestra pit. He whispered a message to the conductor who immediately tapped his baton calling the orchestra to attention, and held it at the ready as the audience grew quiet. Then on a down beat of the baton the orchestra began the national anthem of fifty seconds.

The audience stood facing the royal box as Queen Victoria and her Lady in Waiting entered through a curtained portal followed immediately by Their Royal Highnesses Princess Helena, wife of Prince Christian of Schleswig-Holstein, and Princess Louise, the Marchioness of Lorne, to the applause of the audience. All the royalty stood dressed in black.

Muriel's heart raced as she tucked her hand inside Nino's arm again and watched Queen Victoria acknowledge the orchestra and audience with a nod of her head, and the cast standing on centre stage in front of the curtain.

Muriel glanced down to see Allison and Miranda, and caught Allison looking up at her. The two girls smiled then diverted their attention back to the queen. The royal party sat; the audience followed; and the cast facing the queen stepped backwards through the curtain that then closed.

At once the conductor tapped and raised his baton again to start the overture to the play. The audience grew quiet. The chandeliers high above in the vaulted ceiling dimmed to half intensity to give late arrivals illumination enough to take their seats. Muriel sat in the subdued lighting excited by her only time to see royalty, attend a play, wear such finery as draped her, hear an orchestra, or go out for an evening in the city. And she had a distinguished, handsome, gentleman in formal attire for an escort. Muriel glowed inside.

While the overture played, Muriel sat with hand on Nino's arm reflecting on her recent past as a ragamuffin flower girl living in a back-alley flat in the tenements of the Southbank. Now she resided in Primrose Hill in the studio home of one of London's distinguished painters—the far other side of the tracks leading into Waterloo Station.

Now she sat in a plush upholstered red-velvet chair, like a throne, in the gilded grandeur of the Prince of Wales Box of a magnificently tiered and ornately adorned theatre, dressed in finery and watching a play in the presence of the Queen of England.

Muriel sat in awe of the directions her young life had taken under Nino's care and tutelage since she first knocked on his door apprehensive of what was to become of her. And so much had happened to go her way in a new life coinciding with coming of age as a maturing young woman. Each and every day Muriel grew more comfortable to be around the man sitting quietly beside her and having him to herself for the evening; a man she admired so very much; a man who was so very attentive to her; who treated her so very well; and a man of maturity and reputation with whom she had fallen in love. "Yes," Muriel admitted to herself, she was in love with Nino Waterhouse.

With such ardent feelings, it happened that when the overture swelled to its soul-stirring finale, and chandeliers dimmed still more, Muriel didn't withdraw her hand in near darkness when Nino laid his atop hers. He squeezed gently, feeling the warmth and softness of it, testing her response to his bold attention. Muriel didn't object and she removed her glove allowing him to entwine his fingers with hers so gracefully long and slender.

Muriel sat receptive to Nino's affection, and in response gave him a gentle squeeze of assurance that holding her hand was permissible. And except for occasions of applause and when lights came up for intermission Nino held Muriel's hand the remainder of the evening, squeezing it often in a silent form of conversation with squeezes in return.

The curtains opened to Act One, Scene One, and to applause by the audience, the queen, and her entourage. Once again, the cast appeared and the men made bows left and right. Nino smiled watching Allison and Miranda hold their dresses, bend their knees, and lower their bodies in perfect curtsies to the queen.

The curtains closed then reopened to more applause as Lady Clara took centre stage with the rogue, Lord Rochester. Throughout Act One, the scoundrel Lord expressed his love for Lady Clara, wanting to marry her, but also desiring to meet and know maiden Mary.

Throughout Act Two, the story involved adventures of sweet Mary and her sour-tempered uncle, Captain Copp, caught up in the plots and escapades of Lord Rochester, King Charles the Second, and the King's page, Edward, who loved Mary.

Muriel daydreamed along with the plots and parts played by Allison and Miranda, imagining that *she* might act someday before the queen. What would that be like, she wondered, to have one's name in lights, one's photo on posters, and headlines to rave reviews in papers as a leading lady.

ACT TWO

Scene One

Captain Copp's tavern "The Grand Admiral." A view of the Thames and Wapping. Mary comes on stage for the first time and gives her opening monologue. (Voices within the tavern. Wine! Wine! Barmaid more wine!)

Mary: What noises drunken sailors make in the barroom. I should like to take a peep at them but my uncle forbids me to show myself in the public rooms. He brings me up more like a young lady than a niece of a tavern keeper.

What a tiresome long day! I wonder what can keep my singing teacher away? For three days he has not been here to give me a lesson . . . and he was just teaching me a pretty song, too . . . all about love. I'll try it (attempts to sing). No, I can't . . . its all out of my head . . . well so much the better!

Muriel watched and listened as Mary paced the stage emoting despairingly. How can anyone memorize so many lines and act so professional, she wondered? (Mary at last sings song.)

> Oh! not when other eyes may read
> My heart upon my sleeve,
> Oh! not when other ears can hear.
> Dare I speak of love.

The "heart upon her sleeve" gave Nino a romantic idea for Muriel's dress in *La Belle Dame*, and with the words "Dare I speak of love" Nino squeezed Muriel's hand and looked smiling into her big, blue-grey eyes. Muriel returned his smile.

"Dare I speak of love?" Nino asked himself, wary of admission by a married artist to an unmarried model, and by a man to a woman so much younger. May/December *affaires d'amour* happen, but would Muriel be receptive to his confessions with such a difference in their ages? Although Muriel sat unaware of Nino's thoughts, she sat quite aware of his timely squeeze to the question, "Dare I speak of love?"

Mary continued to sing in a beautiful, lyrical, soprano voice.

> But when the stars rise from the sea,
> Oh then I think of thee, dear love!
> Oh then I think of thee.

Nino squeezed again to the words "I think of thee, dear love," and with another timely squeeze Muriel suspected Nino was speaking to her in a language of love through squeezes synchronized with words of the song. Had he just told her he loved her? Had he just called her "dear love?" Dare she squeeze back?

> When o'er the olives of the dell
> The silent moonlight falls,
> And when upon the rose,
> Oh then I think of thee, dear love,
> Oh then I think of thee.

Nino squeezed again to "I think of thee, dear love." Muriel's heart raced at Nino's signal that she was "dear love." Yes! It had to be! Nino's squeezes coincident with certain words must mean he loves her. Muriel placed her disengaged hand across her neckline lest Nino see her glow. She tried to constrain mutual feelings but it was for naught. Muriel squeezed back in response.

Muriel found concentration on the play difficult when half-listening and half-dreaming. She sat absorbed in her own romantic thoughts of the man beside her, and by responsive squeezes said that she loved Nino too. He understood and squeezed back. "Words" through timely squeezes communicated messages of love between them though not one word was said aloud. The play continued.

Rochester: I must see this barmaid named Mary . . . I hear she is devilishly pretty.

Nino squeezed to tell Muriel that she, too, was "devilishly pretty." Muriel almost laughed, knowing that she could be "devilishly" impish when it amused her. Now she learned she was also "devilishly pretty." Muriel looked at Nino and wrinkled her nose, then diverted her eyes back to the play. King Charles entered.

Rochester (assuming a serious air): I must beg your majesty to excuse me early. I have an engagement of an important nature.
Charles: Wither does this engagement take place?
Rochester: At the tavern 'The Grand Admiral' in Wapping. I'll see there a girl I'm told is as beautiful as an angel.

Nino squeezed to say Muriel, too, is "as beautiful as an angel." His signals in lieu of words now went unquestionable. Muriel responded with a squeeze to acknowledge the compliment, then whispered "thank you." Nino knew his messages were getting through.

The comedic escapades of King Charles the Second escalated through the play for another hour to intermittent bursts of uproarious laughter and loud applause as actors entered, emoted lines, and exited. The play proved worthy of the raves by critics attested to on this particular evening by Queen Victoria laughing and applauding despite the naughty tenor of the spoof on royalty. The evening's performance drew to a close.

Captain Copp: So here we are all safe in port after last night's shenanigans . . . and with the betrothals this morning of Lady Clara to Lord Rochester and maiden Mary to the King's page, Edward.

King Charles (to the audience): Let me particularly enjoin all present the most profound secrecy in regard to our whimsical tomfoolery last night. The world is never to know the escapades of the monarchy. I ask for honour among you tonight to keep this secret quiet. Mum's the word from this night on.

The curtain fell then rose again, and the lights came up with all the cast on stage. The audience stood in a rousing ovation with seemingly endless curtain calls and shouts of "bravo." Actresses Allison Paige and Miranda Marie and the others in the cast made bows left and right, and the girls received bouquets from gentlemen admirers. Others near the stage threw flowers.

The cast with hands held, backed onto centre stage and took one last bow in unison as the final curtain fell. Muriel and Nino squeezed hands one last time. Muriel replaced her glove and the two vacated the Prince of Wales box anxious to go backstage to congratulate Miranda and Allison and see Queen Victoria up close.

Nino presented their Royal Box tickets as passes for entry on stage and joined a gathering crowd of theatre guests and patrons to congratulate the cast and see the queen. The crowd swelled in numbers with excited voices about the queen and her entourage expected on stage any minute. Muriel held to Nino's arm not to get separated in the milling crowd.

"Do you see Allison and Miranda?" she asked anxiously, standing lower than Nino and seeing only backs of people and hats.

"I see both. They are standing on the front of centre stage."

"Well I can't see anything . . . not with all the hats," Muriel fretted, "and if I don't get a vantage point I'll miss seeing the queen and princesses. I need a foot stool."

"I don't see one around here," Nino said, looking around.
"What about up in the dressing room?"
"Yes, of course! A vanity stool! Can you escort me?"
"I wouldn't leave you alone in this madhouse for a minute." As people crowded closer, Nino led Muriel through the throng and up the stairs to the lady's dressing room.
"Oh I hope the stools aren't taken," Muriel muttered to herself, and returned immediately with the same stool used to do her hair. "Can you get us back to front centre stage? That must be where the queen will be, and I do want to see her close."
Nino got them as close as he could through the crowd but then it happened they had only to stand in place to get closer. As ushers moved the crowd back to make room up front, Nino and Muriel stood fast while a determined Muriel fended off the backing crowd with the legs of her stool.
When the crowd settled amid excited whispers of "Here comes the queen," Muriel planted the legs of her wobbly three-legged stool, and with Nino's help got on her knees atop the cushioned seat. Now as tall as Nino with his top hat, Muriel looked over and around the line of others still in front.
"Nino . . . hold me!" Muriel whispered, concerned. "This stool is wobbledy."
Delighted to assist, Nino stood with a hand on the back of Muriel's waist and Muriel with an arm across Nino's shoulders whereupon, Nino found himself near eye level to Muriel's low-cut neckline. "Oh my!" he thought. But despite the best of his intentions not to look, Nino was unable not to notice the sensual curvatures of Muriel's shapely bosom. Moreover, the scent of Muriel's heady perfume was intoxicating. "Oh my!" he thought again to himself.
"The queen, the queen . . . she's here!" Muriel whispered excitedly to Nino as Queen Victoria walked on stage through a side entrance and was now but feet away. Not before the play had Muriel seen royalty and now she looked at Queen Victoria and two princesses almost face to face. Muriel squeezed Nino's shoulder to relay her excitement.

"Can you see Allison and Miranda?" Nino asked.

"I see them both. They just curtsied, and they are shaking hands with the queen . . . and the queen is talking to them. How exciting! Allison and Miranda are *speaking* with the queen of England. I wish I could hear." And as Muriel leaned forward hoping to hear something of the conversation, she lost her balance on the stool with wobbledy legs and gasped "catch me" to Nino as she toppled unceremoniously through the front line of people.

Heads turned in the direction of the commotion including the royal party amid a chorus of "What happeneds!" Nino tried catching Muriel but couldn't and both pitched forward from the momentum of her fall. People just in front were shoved aside, and a very embarrassed Muriel and Nino on hands and knees looked up at Queen Victoria looking down at them.

Nino uttered still another "Oh my!" as Muriel placed an open hand across her dipping neckline and the queen looked down at Nino squaring his top hat cocked askew.

"'Oh my' is correct Mr Waterhouse," the queen said. "You have no need to kneel. You aren't being knighted. And you, young lady, please stand," the queen said. "You are carrying a curtsy much too far."

A rare smile broke the queen's otherwise impassive expression as she extended a black-gloved hand to help an obviously embarrassed young subject to her feet. Muriel stood discomposed apologizing profusely while holding briefly to a hand of Queen Victoria.

"Your Highness . . . ma'am, I'm so embarrassed," Muriel apologized as she curtsied. "I lost my balance trying to hear you talk with my friends 'Mary' and 'Lady Clara,' and I fell off my stool."

"You aren't hurt are you?"

"No ma'am, Your Highness . . . I mean Your Majesty," Muriel stammered, still flushed with discomposure, "except for my dignity."

"You'll live through that I imagine. Most everybody survives indignities. So, you are a friend of maiden Mary and Lady Clara."

"Yes ma'am Your Majesty . . . I mean Your Highness ma'am." Allison and Miranda nodded agreement.

"Then stand with them while I finish greeting the others in the cast . . . and don't go away. I'll get back to you in a minute . . . and you Mr Waterhouse, don't you go away either."

"What, pray tell, happened?" Allison asked.

"Oh Allison," Muriel replied looking sheepishly also at Miranda, "I am so embarrassed to spoil your moment with the queen but I knelt atop that shaky stool from the dressing room. I was trying to hear you and the queen when I lost my balance and fell."

Nino nodded agreement. "I tried to stop her fall but I lost my balance too and both of us fell to our knees."

Allison whispered with a chuckle at what now was funny. "The passes, Nino, are for admittance backstage to *see* the queen . . . not for an audience *with* her."

"Believe me, an audience was the least of what I wanted. I'm not *that* close with the queen." Queen Victoria reappeared.

"Mr Waterhouse, will you introduce me to your charming companion? I noticed you two in the Prince of Wales box this evening."

"Your Majesty . . . I would like to present Miss Muriel Foster. She's the model for my new painting."

"And what painting is that?"

"It's of Keats's *La Belle Dame sans Merci*, Your Highness."

"I know the poem. It's one of my favourites. When do you plan to exhibit your painting?"

"At the autumn Academy exhibit . . . if it gets selected by the hanging committee."

"Your paintings always get selected and hung on line [The desired lower row of paintings at eye level.] And I'll look forward to seeing you in it Miss Foster. You'll surely be voted 'belle of the line.' Mr Waterhouse said your name is 'Muriel?'"

"Yes ma'am, Your Highness, it's 'Muriel.'"

"Do you have a middle name Miss Foster?"

"No ma'am Your Highness, Your Majesty I have no middle

name. I'm just plain old ordinary Muriel Foster." Muriel curtsied again.

"Well, 'plain' and 'ordinary' you are not, and you most certainly aren't 'old.'" The queen cracked another rare smile.

"Thank you Your Highness . . . ma'am." Muriel smiled back and curtsied again not knowing what else to say or do.

"For heaven's sake Miss Foster with no middle name, one curtsy in a conversation is quite enough . . . don't overdo it."

"Yes ma'am . . . I mean Your Highness . . . I mean Your Majesty," Muriel stammered still discomposed.

"A simple 'ma'am' is just fine."

"Yes ma'am."

"Your Highness," Nino spoke up, "if you will permit me, may I reintroduce you to Allison Paige . . . 'Mary' . . . who is another model of mine . . . and Miranda Marie . . . 'Lady Clara' . . . who models for Arthur Hacker, a Royal Academician."

"Yes . . . I know Mr Hacker. He came to my garden party last summer for Royal Academicians . . . but not everyone was there. One showed up a day late I seem to remember," the queen added, looking straight at Nino. Nino squirmed.

The queen then turned to Allison and Miranda. "I just met you two as actresses, and now I have the pleasure of meeting you as models. And you Miss Foster, do you plan to be an actress too? And please don't curtsy again."

"Yes ma'am Your Highness . . . I mean ma'am."

"If you want, then I'm satisfied you will be." Looking again at the three girls Queen Victoria said: "I hope we meet again someday. All three of you are beautiful and talented."

Queen Victoria ended her conversation as abruptly as it began when Muriel fell off her stool. The three girls curtsied. Nino bowed, and as the queen turned to leave she spoke briefly to her Lady in Waiting who walked immediately to the three girls chatting over the unbelievable events of what just happened.

"The queen asks that I take your names and addresses. It's her habit to have such information in her personal files to remember subjects with whom she had interesting encounters and conversations."

The lovely Lady in Waiting wrote down the information given, then smiled at the three girls and added: "The queen enjoyed meeting you, and she seemed amused with you Miss Foster in the novel way you gained her audience by falling off a stool. She said that never happened to her before." The Lady in Waiting couldn't help but smile. Muriel smiled back.

"But my audience was unintended," Muriel tried to explain. "I fell trying to hear the queen."

"I understand Miss Foster but that aside, Her Highness was most taken with you and I feel confident all three of you will hear from her someday."

The Lady thanked the three girls then returned to her position behind the queen as the entourage vacated onto the street and boarded royal carriages for the ride back to Buckingham.

"Oh my goodness!" Muriel exclaimed, "I can't believe what all happened."

"What happened will be headlines in tomorrow's newspapers if we don't get out of here. Look at those reporters coming this way."

The girls retreated to their upstairs dressing room and Nino slipped out a side door onto the street and hailed a double brougham with one blast on his carriage whistle, then waited patiently to take the girls home. Allison and Miranda changed into less formal wear but Allison dressed Muriel in a provocative off-the-shoulder evening dress with a low-cut neckline.

"Now that the play is over," Allison remarked, "Nino will want to take you out for the remainder of the evening, so look seductive for him."

"But he hasn't asked me."

"He will ask if I know men, and believe me I know men. Any man would like to go out with you dressed like this, so take this key to the flat in case you get in late ... and good luck in my dress. Men like *me* in it and it looks ravishing on you." Muriel stood eyeing the neckline in the mirror, turning first one way and then another.

"To say this dress looks ravishing on me is questionable . . . but no one will argue revealing, that's for sure," she said as she pulled the neckline up.

"My mother would have a fit if she saw me dressed like this," Muriel fussed, turning again from side to side eyeing herself critically. Allison pulled Muriel's neckline back down.

"Well your mother isn't here tonight, and Nino is. Men like dresses with low-cut necklines and you can be sure Nino isn't going to have a fit about this one. You're a woman now, so look and act like one. This dress has gotten lucky for *me* with men, and I've had some good times in it . . . and out of it," Allison grinned but Muriel blushed.

"Allison is right," Miranda piped in. "Dress the way you want. The fun of being a woman is dressing for a man, and cleavage drives them crackers."

"And being with men afterward I have to assume." Muriel laughed as she pulled her neckline back up.

Allison pulled it down again. "Now leave it there," she fussed. "Be yourself! Look feminine! If you show enough to get a man interested he will want to see more, and then a girl's evening gets very interesting. Believe me! Nino will be bewitched with you."

"He is already. He told me he loved me."

"I *thought* as much! When did he tell you?"

"During the play . . . but he didn't say a word." Muriel explained how Nino squeezed her hand to the words of Allison's song.

"Allison . . . you know Nino. Will he want to kiss me? Has he ever kissed *you*?"

"No, and he never tried, or anything else. He was always the perfect gentleman with me even when he painted me for *St. Eulalia* and messed with my hair. I lay nude in front of him with my arms outstretched. He did nothing but sketch me so I just went to sleep, but he had every opportunity to kiss and touch me."

"Would you have let him?"

"I would have let him *love* me had he wanted," Allison laughed. "Nino is a handsome man you know."

"I know, and especially tonight with his top hat and cape and cane and all . . . he's dashing . . . but if he wants to kiss me should I let him?"

"Let your heart be your guide. But Nino *is* married, and even if he's alone with you his propriety won't allow it, so don't hope for a kiss and not get one."

"But he told me in the theatre he loved me . . . well with the hand squeezes . . . but I knew what he was saying. Doesn't a man in love with a woman want to kiss her?"

"That's the way things usually work, but remember we're talking about Nino."

"Well he's romantic towards me in the way he's painting me for *La Belle Dame*. And if you want to know something, *I* think Nino is the knight hidden in his helmet, and I think he wants to kiss me. Did you notice how close he placed our faces in the study, and how he looks at me? Isn't that saying something?"

"That's probably true!" Allison replied. "I saw the study. Nino *is* no doubt the knight and you're his damsel desire. But if you remember, I said he would love you only from a distance, and the armour is his wall of propriety to do nothing more than kiss you, even if that. A man can't do much of anything else wearing a suit of armour?" Allison laughed.

"But what does Nino mean by the way the knight holds his lance?" Muriel asked, curiously. "He said the way the knight holds his lance is symbolic of something, but he wouldn't say what, and I don't get it."

"That's just as well, for now," Allison grinned. "You'll learn soon enough, but it may be symbolic of the knight wanting to make love to the faery-child, and that's all men think about anyway . . . making love." Allison grinned again. "That's what the knight and faery-child did in the poem when they 'slumbered on the moss.'"

"I read the poem but there was nothing written about a noose of hair, and nothing about a lance. And Keats said precious little about the 'moss' thing."

"Such things are symbolism and artistic license. An artist can paint a story any way he wants."

"Nino didn't even paint an 'elfin grot,' and that's a major thing in the poem! All he's painting are trees."

"Well making love out under trees can be just as fun," Miranda said with a giggle (knowing about her skinny-dipping escapades) "and be just as dark in the woods at night as the darkest room. But *if* Nino kisses you somewhere tonight, I know the 'somewhere' places men like to kiss . . . on girls that is," scampish Miranda added, then laughed.

"Oh hush!" Muriel fussed. "Don't talk like that! But what do I do if he doesn't kiss me, and I want him to? I mean *on* my mouth," Muriel hastened to add, dryly.

"Well again, we're talking about Nino here," Allison said, "so you may have to outright seduce him for a kiss. Put your face up close to his. Put all of you in close so he can smell your perfume and look down your dress." Allison pulled Muriel's neckline down again.

"Men are born to look down dresses. God makes them look by the time they start growing fuzz, and especially when women bend over." Muriel bent over in front of the mirror to see how much of her showed.

"Oh heaven!" she exclaimed, seeing down through her cleavage. "There is *no* way I'm going to bend over in *this* dress."

"What do you think God made cleavage for? It's for men to look at."

"Well there's a limit to how much of me I'm willing for a man to see," Muriel fussed and pulled her neckline back up. Miranda pulled it down again.

"If you want to get Nino romantic then keep it down, and if you bend over let him look. All men do. That's the nature of them."

"But too much of me shows!"

"Then don't bend over if that bothers you, and cover yourself with a hand if you do, but leave your neckline down. The more alluring you are tonight the more romantic Nino will get, and it may mean the difference of getting kissed or not."

"Dabs of perfume in strategic places also help," Miranda added. "So here . . . dab a little of this behind your ears and down inside your cleavage."

"And down anywhere else you want," Allison piped in to say. Allison and Miranda laughed at the suggestion but Muriel blushed at the thought of "down anywhere else."

"It's true," Allison added. "Men love the scents of a woman in feminine places."

"That's nothing I ever read!"

"Probably not! But another thing you probably never read . . . and your mother never told you . . . is to let your hair down in front of a man, and if you can get him to brush it out for you you've usually got it made . . . except for Nino maybe," Allison grinned. "But letting a man brush your hair and run his fingers through it is usually guaranteed. Kisses come next and then the 'whatever.'"

"Allison is right," Miranda agreed with a giggle. "But be careful with the kisses and the 'whatever.' Too many kisses can lead to more than what a girl might want."

With another "Oh hush!" the girls vacated the dressing room and the theatre to join Nino outside waiting with the carriage. During the short ride to their flat the girls remained excited and animated in talk about meeting the queen, but as the carriage pulled to a stop the topic turned to saying 'good night' to Nino. Muriel wanted to stay longer but he hadn't asked. Worried thoughts raced through her mind.

"Maybe Nino doesn't want to be alone with me," Muriel fretted to herself. "Maybe Allison is right. Maybe Nino's propriety won't allow him. But be seductive," Allison advised. Muriel eased down a bit on her neckline.

"Mind your step," Nino cautioned Allison and Miranda as they stepped from the carriage which was an anxious moment for

Muriel. She remained hesitant to leave, still hoping Nino would want her to stay, but when she ventured to step from the carriage Nino held her back. "Spend the rest of the evening with me," he asked.

Muriel's heart raced at the hoped for request. She glanced quickly at Allison and Miranda as if approval was necessary. They of course nodded, and Muriel replied "yes" to Nino.

Nino stepped back into the carriage to sit beside Muriel, and as the carriage pulled away both waved a last good-bye to Allison and Miranda watching from their doorway.

"The dress must have done it," Allison remarked to Miranda smugly. "It's been lucky for me with men."

"Yeah," Miranda laughed, "and it got lucky for Muriel when she bent over to step out of the carriage. Men are so predictable as to where they look."

"And what they think," Allison laughed.

"Would you like to see the lights?" Nino asked Muriel.

"Yes," she replied. "I've never seen the city at night."

"Drive us through central London," Nino called up to the driver, "then take us out Piccadilly to Hyde Park and The Serpentine."

"Yes sir," said a reply.

CHAPTER NINE

THE LAKE AND THE WILLOW

The remains of the night lay ahead and Muriel was a Cinderella princess without a curfew. For her, there would be no stroke of midnight to end her night and she hoped the night would never end.

Their Maythorn and Sons carriage with cushioned seats, curtained windows, and polished brass lamps was pulled by a Morgan mare. The carriage inched through the busier city crammed with a jumble of other horse-drawn vehicles, carts, barrows, bicycles, and throngs of people on foot more than Muriel had never seen at once. Gaslights on lampposts lined and lit the streets, and the whole population of central London seemed on the move at every turn and street crossing. Pubs, cafes, markets, and shops with plate glass windows occupied ground-floor levels with tiers of flats above. People up high on balconies with wrought-iron railings peered down.

"Look!" she said, pointing at first one thing and then another. Nino smiled to himself watching her every move and expression; the delight that she was.

In one place a hand-cranked hurdy-gurdy with a grinder and his capuchin monkey captured Muriel's attention. "See the monkey!" she exclaimed. "It's wearing a red cap and coat. And look! It's begging for pennies. Can I give it one?"

"Of course!" Nino replied smiling. Nino called up to the driver to stop by the kerb beside the grinder and smiled watching Muriel search the bottom of her purse for a penny down through a brush and comb, compact, lipstick, and an assortment of other items.

"Aha!" she exclaimed as she held one up. "Here's a penny for you, you pretty thing," Muriel cooed to the monkey as she held the coin at arm's length down through a window. The monkey on its leash took the penny with a furry little hand then dropped it into a cup with a clink.

"Isn't it adorable? It touched me when it took the penny." Nino smiled.

Another block away, a man with a barrel-organ played a lively tune. Street urchins danced about while a crowd of bystanders clapped to the music and laughed. Muriel had never danced, but something innate in her made her tap her foot.

Here and there through Covent Garden, jugglers, acrobats, and contortionists entertained crowds. Along Soho streets ladies of the night paraded in proximity of 'houses of accommodation' striking up conversations with passing men, or sitting advertised on brothel window ledges. Others stood on lamp-lit corners waiting on rides in carriages to dark and secluded back-street places.

At a busy intersection stop Muriel exchanged curious glances with a youthful trollop leaning against a lamppost. The young girl in a thread-bare velveteen gown advertised her profession with beads and bows; a floral hat with a feather; and her face layered with rouge and lipstick. But the young girl looked dispirited.

Muriel could only imagine she was no older than thirteen or fourteen, but how many times in a night, Muriel wondered, does so young a girl serve herself to hungry men from a menu of what kinds of services? Is it once, twice, thrice, or more? Muriel couldn't imagine.

"I feel sorry for her," Muriel lamented. "Isn't what she's doing unlawful? Won't she be arrested and go to gaol?"

"Likely not! Street soliciting *is* unlawful but constables here in Soho and Covent Garden seldom interfere unless complaints are made in cases where ladies of the night are visibly offensive. And even if the young girl there *is* arrested she will only be booked and released to go elsewhere. There aren't enough cells in all of Britain to hold just those of her here in London.

"In *The Times* some months ago an article gave estimates of one hundred thousand ladies just in London selling themselves a total of two and a half million times a week. Let's see now, if my math is correct, that's about twenty-five times a week on average, or about three or four times just tonight the young girl standing there will be available . . . and at this hour she has probably been with two or three men already. Prostitution by girls her age, and as young as nine or ten, is rife, and there are always men who prefer the youngest."

"I can't imagine such a thing. Do you think she enjoys what she does?"

"Probably not. Trollops don't involve themselves for love or pleasure . . . only for money . . . likely the only way the young girl there knows how to support herself and help her family."

"I could never do what she does."

As the carriage pulled away, Muriel and the young girl parted with lingering glances. Muriel looked back, feeling sorrowful for the girl, and the girl wondered, perhaps, if Muriel in fashionable attire with an older gentleman wasn't a courtesan one of them.

"Drive on to Hyde Park," Nino called up to the driver, "then go down Rotten Row and find a secluded spot along the lake."

"Yes sir," said the acknowledgment.

The request for a secluded spot sounded romantic but Muriel began to wonder what would be expected of her. Would Nino want to kiss her? That would be no problem as Muriel wanted to be kissed, but what if he wanted something more? There was a limit to how far she wanted to go beyond a kiss or two, but she couldn't help but wonder what might happen after three or four or more. Would he then want something else? Would he want to touch her? Muriel remembered the boy who tried one time to touch her breasts. She slapped him silly, but had she let him would he then have wanted something "more" than touching?

Allison said touching was much the fun of being with a man. "That's why God made fingers," she claimed.

Miranda cautioned Muriel to be careful—that kissing could lead to something "more" than what a girl might want. But how much "more" was "more?" With no experience, Muriel knew nothing of what "equipment" men have, except on statues like *David*, and nothing of how used. She once heard it called "outdoor plumbing" that can get "excited." Her mother once said that when girls are married and their nightgowns lifted, girls are to "turn their heads and grit their teeth." But her mother never said what happens under nightgowns, and the why of the grit. Did things hurt? Muriel read stories of willing or unwilling girls carried off by aggressive lovers, but none she remembered described what happens when doors get shut and clothes come off. And Miranda didn't say.

Allison dressed Muriel in a low-cut dress to show some cleavage. She said the more that showed the more a girl's night out could get exciting, though Allison doubted Nino would ever kiss her. He never tried with Allison though she would have let him had he wanted; even let him "love her" had he wanted, she said. And if Allison would have, should she? Muriel looked up to Allison, and to Miranda. They had already done "everything," and Muriel wanted to be "one of the girls." Should she, then, let Nino make love to her if that was what he wanted. But she didn't know the how of anything.

But Muriel knew she could never be a *femme fatale* and lead men down "primrose paths." But what if she let Nino kiss her, then said "no" to anything "more?" Would he think her a tease? "Oh dear!" Muriel fretted to herself with her hand to her bosom.

As the carriage rolled to its lakeside destination, an inadvertent glance caught Nino's gaze fixed upon her tempting ruby lips. But before Muriel could turn her head he caught her off guard by tracing the outline of her parted mouth with the tip of a gentle finger. He smiled when she looked surprised by such an intimate touch, but she didn't resist. Muriel's heart raced, and her breath quickened. She felt a warm feeling course down through her and she blushed, not only from the touch of her mouth but from a sensation new to her where something strange in an odd place seemed to come alive and stir about.

Muriel blushed all the more when she saw Nino gaze along her neckline. As if by that natural reflex girls seem born with, and with a soft intake of breath, she covered her bosom with an open hand then turned her head and looked out onto the passing world of stately brick homes with wrought-iron fences, and with ghostly moon-lit gables, towering chimneys, darkened doorways, and shadowed gardens. Now and then steeples of churches passed by, and the full moon high above raced on and on through tops of trees as the carriage now moved swiftly with rumbles of wheels, clops of hooves, and jingles of harness rings. A fleeting glance back to Nino confirmed where his gazes lingered, and thoughts raced through her mind again as she looked out into the night.

Allison and Miranda said women dress for men. They said women wear low-cut dresses purposefully to be alluring and exciting to men; or why wear such dresses? They said "show some cleavage." Allison said men were born to look, so let them. Muriel's hand slipped slowly into her lap and she sensed again where Nino looked.

An aura glowed about Muriel's head back-lit as it was by the moonlight through her window. Nino studied her profile again as during her interview, except now he admired Muriel as a man in love with the beauty of a woman, not with an eye for the artistry of her beauty. She looked all the more inviting in the soft glow of moonlight filtered through towering chestnut trees. Angelic Muriel was a creature so lovely to admire that any man tempted would yearn to hold, touch, and kiss her everywhere and forever.

Nino studied her coiffured hair coiled as it was on top her head pinned in place beneath a floral hat. Some hair hung in long, tightly twisted curls near to the middle of her back. Playfully, Nino pulled one forward, stretched it out and smiled to see it recoil; then took and inhaled its fragrance. Allison said scents of a woman were aphrodisiacs to men, and Miranda grinned when she said men know all the places. "Oh me!" Muriel gulped as Nino smelled again the hair on her head.

Her hair was scented with rose-water perfume, and like a rose herself Muriel had lips the colour of ruby petals. Nino paraphrased words to himself from *Romeo and Juliet*. "A rose by any other name is still a rose and just as sweet." Nino took the curl again to inhale its intoxicating fragrance and look again at her reddest of red lips.

Muriel lowered her eyes from Nino's welcomed familiarity. She was elated by it. Only moments earlier he traced the outline of her parted mouth, and now her heart raced from his fondling her hair. His pulling on it, playing with it, and inhaling its fragrance excited her all the more in primal ways alive and puzzling. She wished for a fan. Her face flushed and she glowed warm all through but she knew nothing of the why of where she seemed to melt.

Muriel glanced at Nino with a blushing smile self-conscious of her strange new feelings, inexperienced as she was of a woman's innate reaction to a man's caresses. Nino returned her smile and looked again at her ruby lips but resisted a compelling urge to pull her face hard to his and devour her parted mouth; unsure if Muriel wanted to be kissed. If only he knew.

"Stop somewhere along the water's edge away from lights," Nino asked the driver as the carriage turned up Rotten Row along the lake shore. The sounds of wheels and hooves softened in the soil of the track but the harness rings jingled on.

"Yes sir" said the reply, and within minutes the carriage stopped along a lonely expanse of sandy shore rimmed with grass and reeds and forested with chestnut, oak, weeping willows, and growths of flowering shrubs. Nino opened the carriage door, stepped out, took in a deep breath of warm, sweet, lake-scented air, then to Muriel's surprise swept her off the carriage step and spun with her before putting her down.

"When you sweep a girl off her feet you really do it, don't you," she laughed, elated to be in Nino's arms if only for a moment.

"It's pretty here," Muriel commented as she looked about with the moon on the water. "Can we walk along the lake?"

"If you want. And if you get chilled you may wear my cape."

"Maybe later, thank you . . . but I'm fine for now. It's warm tonight . . . and one might say balmy with the fragrant smells. I can smell roses and violets like the ones I used to sell," Muriel commented as she took in a deep breath of lake and flower-scented air and tucked a hand in the crook of Nino's arm.

"Please wait on us," Nino asked the driver. "We want to walk along the lake and we may be gone awhile."

"Yes sir . . . I understand. It's only midnight so the night's still early, and it's a right nice time for a stroll it is . . . a warm night, a full moon, and a pretty lady on your arm. So take your time. I won't leave without you, and if you're gone for awhile I may be napping when you return. My mare could use a rest as well." The driver stepped down and blew out his carriage lamps.

Muriel and Nino strolled leisurely arm in arm along the water's edge down a distance out of sight of the carriage to a large clump of head-high reeds at the water's edge adjacent to a magnificent weeping willow where they stopped to look. Its pendent branches draped the ground in a circular wall of leafy curtains.

"Have you ever been in under a weeping willow?" Nino asked. "They are like a room inside."

"No . . . never! Can we peek?"

Nino parted the leafy drapes and led Muriel inside into a dark, circular, room-like interior. Inner branches devoid of leaves hung part way down like stalactites in a little cave—rather like in an "elfin grot." A carpet of moss and leaves matted the floor, and a pleasing, earthy aroma rose from it as they walked around the trunk. Then lo and behold in the dappled light of the moon Muriel discovered a heart on the trunk with initials carved inside.

"Look Nino! Others have has been in here." Muriel fingered the faint outline of the initials. "Who were they?" she wondered to herself, and how long here? An hour, two hours, or for a night. Feeling now that she and Nino had intruded someone's private hideaway, Muriel led Nino back outside to stand along the water's edge.

Muriel took in another deep breath of lake-scented air and looked out across the water and up at the romantic moon. Then with lingering curiosity Muriel looked back at the weeping willow where others in under had a trysting place.

The noises of the city now gone were replaced by croaks of natterjack toads, common frogs, and choruses of male bush-crickets; the latter high in trees stridulating calls for mates like tiny serenading fiddlers.

"Just listen to them!" Muriel exclaimed as she looked up into the trees then stooped to swish a hand through the warm water. The disturbance alarmed a natterjack that hopped into the growth of reeds. "Blimey!" Muriel gasped as she stepped back, surprised, and grabbed ahold of Nino.

Nino took her into his arms "for protection" and reassured her it was only a natterjack.

"I know that now!" Muriel admitted sheepishly, "I've seen natterjacks before but when this one jumped it scared me. I didn't know it was there," Muriel said, then laughed at the now funny situation and emoted in pretense. "That little croaker coulda up and done me in."

Nino laughed with her, and at her. "But I really think it thought you were going to 'up and do *it* in,'" he said teasing. "It must have thought you wanted to catch and kiss it and turn it into a prince."

"Ha! ha! Ah would ye think that now?" Muriel emoted again, slapping Nino playfully on his arm, and retorting: "You are just an ever hopeless tease beyond all hope of any cure I do believe."

Nino laughed again, enjoying Muriel's humour in the amusing ways she often said things. He delighted in her verbal responses and facial expressions to his flirtatious clowning, and she in turn with him. Over weeks of knowing one another the two developed a playful repartee of witty remarks and snappy comebacks dampened in spirit only when Esther would look disapproving and frown.

But in studio privacy the two truly enjoyed the fun of one another's companionship. Nino treasured Muriel's youthful charm, articulate wit, and delightful prattle. She could go from light-hearted girlish chatter into intellectual conversation of an adult level committing no faults of speech or imperfections of accent. She neither dropped her "h's" nor broadened her "o's" and "a's." Beyond required education, Muriel was self-taught by an insatiable curiosity to learn, and a love for reading from which she learned more than an average amount of information and vocabulary.

Nino looked forward to their quiet, daily retreats in the privacy of his studio with the door closed. He enjoyed, as now, being alone with Muriel, and though he kept their friendship and conversation within bounds of propriety there were suppressed desires to speak to her of intimate things. He wanted to tell her he loved her but could never do it; thoughts best left unsaid he always decided. Nino was married and Muriel was much younger although girls in teenage years often married much older men.

Muriel was Nino's ideal vision of womanhood, model or not, and of the models he had painted, Muriel was by far his favourite. There was a bewitching aura about the charming young woman that fast eroded chinks in his armour of propriety not to pursue a sitter. But such things happened. Art history was littered with love affairs between older artists and younger models, and fantasy thoughts of intimacy and marriage to Muriel often plagued his mind. But marriage to her was an impossible dream.

Nino had to debate with himself over how far he was willing to go in pursuit of a love affair with his alluring sitter, if at all. There was wide latitude between chastity and intimacy; between friendly affection and romantic passion; and between innocent chatter and talk of love.

Nino stood behind Muriel at the water's edge with his arms around her waist and her back with a bustle drawn in pleasurably close. The two gazed quietly at the full moon shimmering on the water and playing hide-and-seek behind slowly drifting clouds. Somewhere out on the lake, clanks of oarlocks and muffled voices betrayed the presence of at least one other couple enjoying the warm summer night and moonlit water.

"I love it here," Muriel said. "It's so pretty and peaceful. Thank you for bringing me."

Mesmerized by it all, both stood close and content enjoying one another's company. Nino casually kissed her on the side of her neck as a show of fond affection, and though it was only casual Muriel felt elated by the kiss and by Nino's arms around her.

"Nino?" Muriel finally asked to break a long silence of solitude. "May I go wading? I've never waded, and the water looks so nice."

"You don't need permission to wade. You're of an age to do as you want."

"But would anyone mind?"

"Who's to mind, and who's to see you anyway? We're all alone . . . and besides, if people can swim in the lake there is nothing wrong with wading in it."

"Are you sure no one can see me? I will need to take off my shoes and stockings."

"No one can see you. We are too far from the carriage and there is no one else about, and besides I've already seen your feet so many times in the studio that yours are nothing to get excited about anymore," Nino said in jest, and grinning.

"Oh hush! Then I'll do it . . . and of course you're right. It's a free country and I'm old enough to do things I want. I'm a woman now!"

"A woman? Where?" Nino asked facetiously as he looked around, then laughed at Muriel's frowned expression.

"Just button your mouth," Muriel fussed as she slapped him playfully across his arm. "In case you haven't noticed, *I'm* a woman, and these are the 'nineties' you know. Times are changing for women these days to do as they want. That's what everybody says. Allison and Miranda do what *they* want, and would you believe they skinny-dip of all things, and sometimes with men."

"I wouldn't put it past them."

"Well they said skinny-dipping is fun, but wading will be fun enough for me." Muriel walked into the seclusion of the willow canopy to remove her shoes and stockings out of sight of anyone watching.

She hadn't been there long when she called out: "Can you help me unbutton my shoes? I can't by myself standing up."
"Then sit down!"
"I can't in here! Allison will surely be upset with me if I go home with moss stains on her dress . . . and I can hear the questions already."
"I guess questions *would* come to mind," Nino said, amused by her comment.
"I don't know why Allison wanted me in this dress anyway. She had another I wanted to wear but Allison insisted on this one. She says it is 'lucky' for her when she's out with men . . . whatever that means," Muriel said tongue-in-cheek.
"Allison must have reasons."
"I never had a dress I would think 'lucky' for any reason. That sounds dumb to me." Nino grinned to himself.
"Did you know that Allison stays out all night sometimes? [Muriel looks up to Allison.] She outright admitted it, and she wasn't embarrassed one iota in confessing it."
"Nothing much embarrasses Allison. Well, you know! She says what she wants and does what she wants, and if she wants to stay out all night and skinny-dip with men I imagine she does. She's old enough you know."
"I know. The both of them are already in her twenties and I'm getting there myself, but I have to admit I've never been out like this, and never with a man to go places like Allison and Miranda do, so tonight is something special for me. I liked your taking me to the play, and bringing me here. The carriage ride was fun, and the lake is pretty. I love the moon and all the trees.
"You know, if I lived a hermit's life I would want this very willow for a home," she said looking around inside. "I could be up at dawn to see the sunrise and be on my own all day. Without city smoke there would be lots of fresh air, and berries to pick, and fish in the lake to catch. Without city lights I could stay up late and see the stars, and stroll along the lake, like tonight, in the light of the moon or with a lantern. There wouldn't be any

bloomin' buggers around to bug me, and if I got lonely I could just talk to myself or to the animals. That would be the life."

"That *would* be the life, wouldn't it, what without your chocolates and ginger ales. And what would you do without soaps and perfumes?" Nino asked with tongue in cheek. "And what would you do without *The Times* to read over a decent cup of morning coffee?"

"I have to admit your Bourbon Santos is delicious. I would miss a daily cup or two."

"Well living here you'd have to boil leaves for coffee and flowers for tea, and eat mushrooms instead of crumpets. Just be sure you know differences between the ones good to eat and those that aren't . . . and toad stools. You'd have nothing much else to eat except roots, berries, and slugs and worms. Yum yum! Wouldn't *those* be tasty?

"As for talking to yourself, you'd drive your own self daft as much as *you* like to gab." Nino chuckled.

"Well say what you want," Muriel fussed. "You're just poking fun at me, but living in under this tree *would* be fun," Muriel said as she looked around some more. "It's like a little house in here. There's room enough to stand and walk around. There are limbs to hang one's clothes on, and there's room enough for a table and a chair . . . and a bed. That's really all one needs, except maybe a window or two to look out and let in some light. It's dark in here."

"That's all interesting to hear, but you may be right about sitting down in there. Don't just yet!"

Nino opened the canopy and walked in under, removed his cape and spread it out for Muriel to sit on as Sir Walter Raleigh might have done. "Now sit and I'll help remove your shoes," Nino ordered.

"But if I sit I won't need any help. I just can't take them off standing up."

"I'll help you anyway!"

With that said Nino sat and pulled Muriel down beside him then kissed her again with another casual peck on the side of her neck. Although Muriel knew nothing about kissing—real kissing that is—she didn't consider perfunctory busses on her neck the same as the passionate mouth-to-mouth kisses she had read about over and over on dog-eared pages in her romance novels. Nevertheless, Muriel sat elated by his show of affection, such as it was.

"I thought you were going to help take off my shoes."

"I am . . . and your hat! It pokes my face," and to Muriel's surprise Nino pulled the pins and removed it. She didn't object, but a thought raced through her mind. Was the hat his start to undress her?

That's not what Muriel had in mind. She thought back to Miranda's caution, and the hat cautioned her not to let a situation get out of hand. Removing her hat was romantic, she had to admit to that, but kissing her mouth, *if* it happened, was all the further she wanted to venture.

But Miranda had warned her that kissing could "lead to more" than what a girl might want to handle; that kisses lead to touches and then what? And where? Muriel wanted to be kissed but she hadn't yet—not really—and Nino was already taking off her clothes—well her hat—and he was preparing to take off her shoes. What comes off after hat and shoes? Muriel worried.

Allison had said she knew about men, and she talked like she did. She said all men think alike. Then Miranda said men have ideas about where on girls they like to kiss . . . "if you know where I mean." Miranda sniggered as though *she* knew, and likely she did from skinny-dipping with men and staying out all night. But Muriel didn't need to wonder where the "I mean" meant. With an "Oh me!" under her breath Muriel pulled her knees up close and wrapped her arms around them to hold them closer to her bosom. And then with a second thought she crossed her ankles.

Maybe things *were* getting out of hand, but Allison said that while Nino might be flirtatious he had too much propriety about him to be less than gentlemanly. But Allison's dress seemed to have a mind of its own with men. It wanted to dip and sag. Muriel pulled her neckline up again.

"I thought you liked my hat," she commented casually so as to seem unconcerned about her hat coming off.

"I love your hat . . . and everything under it all the way down to those sexy feet of yours the knight in *La Belle Dame* is so enthralled by."

"My feet? I thought you said it was my long hair and wild eyes that excited him."

"Well those too . . . but the knight is a 'foot man' in case you didn't know. His adventures in life are looking for damsels with pretty feet, like yours," Nino grinned.

"Oh hush!"

"Well women's feet are wondrous things when ballerinas can do a *pas de deux* on tiptoes. And otherwise, women of every temperament can stomp about and kick buckets and shins if so moved, but their feet aren't always things of beauty to see. Every now and then, however, Mother Nature turns out a pair of feet like yours seen in paintings and on statues pleasing to behold. And the world is full of men who enjoy the sights of women's feet with delicate toes and well-turned ankles."

"I never heard of such a dumb thing!"

"Well it's true! Most men in life are the 'foot men' of the world who enjoy sights of pretty feet. The medical field is full of podiatrists who enjoy their profession and the things they do with feet, and there are men in shops who are always happy to try shoes on ladies. And the world is full of men with fetishes other than feet, but not nice enough to mention at the moment," Nino grinned. "But for the 'foot men' of the world I sketched yours with all twelve, er uh ten toes . . . six on one foot and four on the other . . . lovely and dainty with manicured nails for men to see and enjoy."

"You did no such thing! You drew my feet with five toes each, just like normal. You're teasing me."

"Nevertheless, I drew your feet sensual to make it easier for you . . . I mean for *La Belle Dame* . . . to seduce the knight. Didn't you wonder why I spent so much time sketching them?"

"Aren't we just chock-full of revelations! What you really wanted was to see my feet, wasn't it? Well shame on you, and it's

a darned good thing you didn't try to touch them," Muriel giggled.
"And what else of me did you have in mind," Muriel fussed in pretense, "what with all your talk of nymphs and mermaids showing more of girls than feet?"
"No need to wonder. I'm an Italian-born Englishman which should be enough said on the subject I rather think. That takes in about everything a girl has from feet on up."
"Oh my God!" Muriel exclaimed in the humour of her hands to the sides of her face in a pretense of shock. "An Italian-born Englishman . . . and a figure painter at that wanting to paint my everything. I'm a goner for sure," she joked.
"You just *might* be with your perfumed hair," Nino bantered as he pulled a curl to his face and inhaled deeply. "You've heard it said, I think, that a full moon and perfumed hair drive werewolves mad, and you're driving me daft already."
"Don't you think we would have heard about werewolves and perfumed hair if that was true? All the stories I ever read say it's a full moon and the smell of *wolfsbane* that drive werewolves mad. Perfumed hair has nothing to do with it! Don't you know anything?"
"Well I know it's a full moon and *your* hair that's driving *me* daft. The werewolf in me is coming out already. 'Grrr,'" Nino growled and pulled up a sleeve to show a hairy arm. "See! And my fangs are getting longer" he said, feeling on a canine. Then with another "grrr" Nino bit Muriel gently on the side of her neck.
"Just stop that with my neck you beast!" Muriel said as she hunched up her shoulder. "You're starting to scare me, and I don't want rabies shots. And besides, it's vampires that bite people's necks . . . not werewolves. You still don't know anything!" But delighted by the nibble on her neck shivers went through her.
"Okay! But getting back to your feet for a___"
"There you go again with my feet."
"You little imp! I'm only suggesting that if you want to wade you need to get out of your shoes and stockings and into the water. We don't have all night and it's late already."

"Oh all right!"

"Then may I help with your shoes?"

"If you want, but shoes *only* mind you. I'll take my stockings off myself, and please don't tickle my feet. That would surely make me scream aloud and beg for mercy."

"Do you have secrets I can tickle out of you . . . and how loud will you scream? Will you wake the dead and scare the carriage mare?"

"Don't even think like that! I'm trusting you to behave. You're *supposed* to be a gentleman . . . at least that's what Allison says."

"Who, me?"

"Yes you! Biting my neck is ticklish enough but please don't tickle anyplace on me, and I do mean anyplace. I'm a woman in case you hadn't noticed."

"Well now that you mention it, I hadn't," Nino jested biting his lip. Muriel frowned.

"You don't notice much in life, do you?"

"Well now that I think about it, there must be *something* about you I should notice, but at the moment I can't quite put my fingers on anything," Nino grinned, gazing along her neckline.

"Just keep your fingers to yourself," Muriel fussed as she pulled her neckline up again, "and don't put them on *anything* anywhere if you know what I mean . . . and especially not on the bottoms of my feet."

"Does that include both feet, or just one or the other?"

"For heaven's sake, dummy! When I say 'feet' I mean both my 'foots.'"

"Oh I understand that, but do you mean all parts of one or both your 'foots,' or only bottoms?"

"For goodness sake, Nino, you're teasing me something dreadful."

"But I promise I won't tickle or touch you any place you don't want tickled or touched."

"Well all that too," Muriel fussed, pulling up on her neckline again and tightening her arms around her pulled-up knees, "but right now I'm concerned about tickles on the bottoms of my feet. Swear you won't tickle me."

"I swear I won't tickle your 'foots,'" Nino laughed.

"Get serious now. I mean really swear." Muriel looked Nino straight in his eyes. "Raise your right hand and repeat after me." Nino raised his left hand.

"No no no!" Muriel complained. "You're cheating! Raise your right hand just like in court." Nino raised his right hand.

"Now repeat after me. I, Nino Waterhouse, exalted member of the Royal Academy of Arts, do hereby on my honour swear not to tickle my favourite model on the bottoms of her feet under the penalty of a dunking in the lake."

Nino paused to think about the oath. "I can't swear to that," he said.

"What for heaven's sake don't you agree to?"

"The 'favourite model' part," Nino retorted, stifling a laugh. "What ever gave you the hare-brained idea you're my favourite? I never said that!"

"I thought you said you loved me."

"I did and I do . . . but when I said I___"

"No 'buts'," Muriel interrupted with a serious air. "Do you love Allison?"

"No!"

"Did you ever love Allison?"

"No . . . but I___"

"No 'buts' I said. Just answer with a simple 'yes' or 'no.' Did you ever love Allison?"

"No . . . but I___" Nino started to say again.

"I thought I said no 'buts.' Don't you ever listen?"

"Did you ever love *any* of your models?"

"Well one time there was this Italian girl who___"

"Never mind!" Muriel cut him short. "I don't want to hear about it."

"Well you asked, but I've had models prettier than___"

"Unh-unh-unh!" Muriel cut him short again. "Don't even say it. Am I or am I not your prettiest?"

"I refuse to answer on grounds my answer might incriminate me," Nino replied, trying to keep a straight face but Muriel's expressions would make the Sphinx and Mona Lisa laugh out loud.

"Please answer the question. Am I or am I not your prettiest model . . . and let me remind you that the penalty of this court for a refusal to answer or to perjure yourself is a dunking in the lake."

"Oh No!" Nino protested. "I got the dunkin' judge. I'm damned if I . . . I mean I'm dunked if I do or dunked if I don't. What kind of a crazy court is this?"

"This is my court. That's what kind it is, so answer the question please. Am I not your prettiest model ever?"

"Oh all right . . . yes!" Nino mumbled.

"Mr Waterhouse, I didn't quite hear you. Now speak up! Am I your prettiest model, or not?"

Nino feigned despair with the back of his hand to his forehead. "Yes! yes! I can't keep the secret any longer. You are the prettiest model I ever had." With that said Nino broke out laughing.

"Well fine Mr Waterhouse . . . just fine," Muriel grumbled, "but you don't need to laugh about it. I thought you said I was pretty, not funny looking. But we ARE getting to the case in point. I have but two more questions."

"Then be on with them. I can't take much more of this grueling." Nino bit his lip.

"Mr Waterhouse, did you not just say you are in love with me?"

"Yes, but I didn't quite mean what I___"

"Just answer the question with a 'yes' or 'no' and not with a lot of lip," Muriel interrupted. "Now let me rephrase it. Are you not in fact in love with your favourite model?"

Nino buried his face in his hands. "I confess," he emoted in another pretense of despair.

"Then let me summarize the facts established in this rather elementary case . . . and we don't need Holmes and Watson to deduce them do we?"

"I guess not."

"Then fact one . . . the model presently in this court is your prettiest . . . and let me remind you you said so under oath. Fact two . . . said prettiest model is your favourite. Again, you said so under oath. Isn't that true?"

"Okay! okay!"

"Then does it not stand to reason that if you are in love with your prettiest model, then said model must also be your favourite? And remember you're still under oath to tell the truth." Muriel felt smug to have argued her case to an indisputably successful conclusion.

"Oh all right!" Nino said with resignation, and then in monotone with admission said: "The said model is my favourite . . . she is the prettiest . . . and I'm in love with her."

"Then let me beg the jury to___"

"Wait a minute!" Nino exclaimed to interrupt the summation. "What jury . . . where? I don't see any jury," he said looking around.

"All those natterjacks out there . . . and like I said, this is my crazy court."

"Well that I can believe, and with a natterjack jury and you as the judge I don't stand a chance," Nino grumbled, trying hard not to laugh.

"Now let me see. Where was I? Oh yes! Let the jury and the court show leniency to the accused in sentencing . . . and such sentence is to help remove the shoes . . . shoes only mind you . . . of the favourite model so established without tickling said model's feet . . . specifically the bottoms. Does the defendant agree to abide by the sentence of the court?"

"Oh all right!" Nino fussed without admitting to a "yes."

"Then so be it Mr Waterhouse. You may now remove the shoes from your favourite model . . . but nothing more mind you, even if you love her . . . er me . . . and *don't* tickle."

Muriel presented her two 'foots' one at a time and to his honour Nino removed her shoes without so much as a tickle.

"That was very good! Mr Waterhouse. You obeyed the orders

of the court and you didn't tickle once. As your reward you don't get dunked." But devious Muriel plotted. Nothing was said about getting splashed, and technically there is a BIG difference between getting dunked IN water or getting splashed OUT of water.

"Oh thank you Your Honour. Now, are you ready to wade?"

"As soon as I take off my stockings, but turn your head please. It wouldn't be ladylike of me to let you watch."

"But I would be more than happy to help with my eyes closed."

"Never mind!" Muriel said with a giggle as she pulled them off with Nino's head turned, "but you may carry me to the water if you will. I don't want to step on anything between here and there that might poke or bite my feet . . . and the grass might tickle. And who can know in the dark where ducks or geese have been?"

"No telling, but is carrying you to the water something else ordered by the court?"

"You didn't hear me adjourn did you?"

"Oh all right," Nino grumbled, "but a word to the wise, 'Little-Miss-sitter-who-needs-her-job.' Don't push your luck."

Nino lifted Muriel, spun around to hear her shriek, then carried her from under the canopy to the water edge and put her down. Nino stepped back, sat on the grass, and leaned back on his elbows to watch the little imp wade. In the light of the moon Muriel swished a foot through the water and without hesitation and without concern of what of her showed, lifted her dress and petticoat to above her knees and stepped ankle deep into the water.

"Oh my!" Nino exclaimed. "I must say you have lovely knees."

"For heaven's sake! Haven't you ever seen a girl's knees before?"

"Yes, but not yours, and certainly none prettier, except I remember one time seeing knees like yours on a canary." Nino lay back laughing.

"Oh hush! That wasn't a nice thing to say. I thought you said you loved me?"

"I do . . . but I love canaries too," Nino laughed again. "They sing beautifully."

"Well don't ask *me* to sing, or you'll stop loving me for sure. I have no ear for it. I wouldn't know an 'A' from a 'K' and couldn't sing a single note in tune." Nino laughed.

"Well it's no wonder you can't sing if you can't sing a 'K.' Even the best of singers have trouble with that . . . even the 'Great Caruso.'" Nino laughed again.

"What's so funny?" Muriel fussed.

"Oh nothing, but I didn't really mean what I said about canaries and singing. Every canary and every bird in the world should be so lucky to have knees like yours."

"Well thank you for saying so . . . I think . . . but mine are plain old everyday ordinary knees like everyone else's."

"I'll argue with you on that," Nino said looking at them. "You have lovely knees . . . and your calves aren't bad either."

"Never mind! And anyway, there's no one here but you to see me. My knees and calves are for your eyes only, but don't get any funny ideas about seeing anything more."

. . .

Muriel seemed not to mind, now, lifting her dress above her knees to show her limbs, but would she ever lift it over her head to disrobe for sitting? That remained to be seen, but there had been changes already when weeks before Muriel wouldn't bare a toe.

Was she rebelling from the restraints of an overly strict and moral upbringing? Was she changing along with a new morality among young women of the time? Maybe!

Was she more daring, now, from the peer pressures of free-minded friends already in life styles of their own different from those of their mothers? Likely!

Was she starry-eyed from a romantic evening in the theatre and a carriage ride to the dreamy setting of a moonlit lake? Was being in love with Nino breaking down previous inhibitions? No doubt!

. . .

"You wouldn't say what you said about 'ordinary old knees' if you could see my knobby ones," Nino remarked with a laugh. "Yours and your calves are much the prettier."

"Oh hush!"

There was a long pause in the conversation as Muriel swished merrily through the water and after awhile, asked: "Nino, would you come in and wade with me? The water is so nice," and with a devilish grin Muriel kicked water in Nino's direction.

"Be careful there, or you might get me wet . . . and believe me you don't want to do that . . . but hey! I thought you said no 'dunking.'"

"That wasn't dunking dummy! That was splashing! Don't you know anything? And why not splash? Just what are you going to do about it anyway? Why nothing I would bet . . . just nothing. That's what I think. You're nothing but a big, lovable fluff-ball of a pussy cat."

"Well for starters, I'll get as mad as a wet hen if you splash me."

"Silly, you mean as mad as a wet rooster, don't you? You're not a hen are you? Or are you meaning to tell me something quirky?" Muriel laughed.

"Well be warned!" Nino retorted. "Don't splash me! Believe me, I'm no 'pussy cat' when it comes to getting wet, and cats don't like water you know. I can spit, scratch, arch my back, and bite with the meanest of them, and be warned that if you get me wet I'll chew you up and spit you out."

Nino paused momentarily thinking on the matter in humour, then added: "On second thought, with all that hair of yours, I'd probably get sick and cough up hair balls for a month. Yuck!" he said, pretending to gag.

"Well you can sit there and gag and grumble all you like, but do you want to know what I think?"

"Not especially," Nino answered nonchalantly.

"Well listen anyway! I think you're nothing but 'purr,'" Muriel said in singsong, "just purr, purr, purr, purr, purr. There's no spit and scratch to you," Muriel said, then daring to do it, kicked water again splashing Nino with several drops.

"Okay you little imp! You had sufficient warning."

Slowly and methodically Nino removed his coat and tie and carefully folded his coat. He set coat and tie down. Then he took his time rolling-up his shirt sleeves while with a frowned brow glared straight at Muriel. Muriel caught his glower, unsure if in pretense, and began to fidget just in case. But quick enough decided she must be in big trouble by the intensity of the glower.

Slowly and methodically, one by one, Nino removed his shoes and socks and set them aside while mumbling something under his breath probably not at all nice to hear. Then he rolled up his trouser legs and stood. Muriel squealed in anticipation of what was surely next to happen.

"Nino don't! I'm truly sorry I got you wet. I didn't mean to. Can't we forget what I did?"

"That's nothing *I'm* going to forget! You *meant* to get me wet you little imp, and now you're going to suffer the consequences. I hope for your sake you know how to swim."

"I don't know how," Muriel shrieked as Nino caught up with her. "Didn't you hear me say I was sorry?"

"All I heard was, 'and what are you going to do about it?'"

"Then you didn't hear everything."

"I heard enough!"

"Well then be nice to me you big, lovable pussy cat. Don't get me wet . . . I beg you. Allison will never forgive me if I go home with her dress soaked."

"You should have thought of that before you splashed me. Allison's dress isn't so lucky for you now, is it?"

Now Nino had no intention of getting Muriel wet, but fear he might heightened her uncertainty and volume to her squeals.

Nino grabbed her, pulled her close, picked her up with her dress still above her knees, and spun her around.

"Nino stop before you make us dizzy and make us fall. Please . . . I said I was sorry."

Nino stopped, but he didn't believe the little imp felt sorry enough about getting him wet; not to the extent she proclaimed. If an opportunity happened she would do the same thing all over again. And had they towels and changes of clothes Nino would have waded with Muriel out to her chin to experience the full repertoire of her gasps, shrieks, squeals and highest-octave screams.

When Nino stopped spinning, Muriel quieted, but for a long moment he held her tightly in his arms with hers around his neck. He reveled in the firmness of Muriel's nubile bosom buried hard into his chest; the undersides of her bare limbs over his bare arm; and the aphrodisiac scent of her perfumed hair against his face. The neckline of Muriel's dress in disarray concealed little under. Nino couldn't help but hold his look, and his armour of resolve not to make love to a sitter cracked. For some reason odd to her Nino seemed to breathe harder.

Moreover, Muriel's dress and petticoat were well above her knees but she no longer cared how much of her he saw; cleavage, limbs, and all of her if he wanted. Love changes things, and with romantic thoughts Muriel imagined Nino ripping off her clothes and doing with her whatever men do with girls. She felt stirring again down deep.

Muriel laid her head upon Nino's shoulder, enjoying to be held. Her scent, like a pheromone, urged him to kiss her anywhere that she would allow, and in anticipation Nino carried Muriel in under the willow where others before them had been for an hour or a night. For a long moment he held Muriel with his face to hers inhaling the sweetness of her exhalations.

"Aren't you going to put me down?" Muriel asked demurely, glancing down at the cape on a bed of moss.

"Not yet."

"Then what are you going to do? Just stand here and hold me all night?"

"That too . . . but also this," Nino said as he turned his face into Muriel's and kissed her never-tasted lips with passion, savouring the flavour of her wet mouth preliminary to the most delectable of her hoped yet to come.

Muriel gasped for breath but she didn't want him to stop. She hungered for more. Nino then moved up over her face and onto her eyelids closed as if sleeping, then down again to reclaim her mouth.

She laid back her head to let Nino kiss into the hollow of her throat, then up the side of her neck to consume an ear. Her heart raced and her breath quickened desirous now of that something "more" about which Miranda spoke, but which Muriel knew little.

Muriel knew nothing of how to kiss, but she returned Nino's kisses with reckless abandon hoping she was doing it right. But then Nino left her mouth and kissed out along her bare shoulder and down along her neckline into the cleavage of her bosom scented with perfume. Her scent and his desire made him dizzy and kiss deeper.

"Nino you must stop!" Muriel suddenly implored, pulling his face back to hers. "You mustn't kiss me like that anymore. You are getting me out of breath and making me feel funny. Something must be wrong with me."

Nino felt relieved that one of them had come to their senses. His means to take Muriel's virginity already stood ready, but as a gentleman it was *his* responsibility to safeguard her innocence. He lowered her bare feet onto the softness of the velvet cape and Muriel stood motionless a long moment with her forehead against Nino's chest catching her breath and collecting her thoughts. Then she spoke softly, looking up.

"You are the first man to hold and kiss me, and I don't know what I am supposed to do in return, or how I should or shouldn't be feeling. But my heart is pounding and you made me feel odd where girls can't talk about."

Nino kissed Muriel's forehead to acknowledge her concern knowingly, and was starting to say "I'm sorry" when Muriel shushed him.

"Before you say anything, every girl in love must want to be kissed. I wanted you to kiss me in the theatre and during the carriage ride and here on the lake. I think I must feel like *La Belle Dame* wanting her knight, but I don't really know what all of that is. Don't think of me as a big tease letting you kiss me then asking you to stop."

Nino realized the extent of Muriel's angelic innocence and vulnerability. Despite wanting her in every which way a man can desire a woman he knew it was best, now, to take her home.

CHAPTER TEN

ON WANDERING KNIGHTS
OUR SPELLS WE CAST

Now that she felt more at ease that the kissing and the feelings from it had stopped, Muriel stood close on Nino's cape with her head against his chest listening to his heart thump a message. "I-love-you I-love-you I-love-you," it seemed to say in its rhythmic beats. "Do not expressions of love come from the heart?" she mused.

Nino stood pulling on Muriel's curls while gathering thoughts on how best to discuss intimate matters, if at all, but in the doing he hoped to establish familiarity with Muriel more personal than their usual but casual and everyday light-hearted raillery.

By establishing a more intimate rapport with Muriel, Nino hoped eventually to break down her modesty and reluctance to pose nude for him and, perhaps, cultivate an intimacy between them dreamed of since the day they met. For it was during her interview when with her hair down and eyes closed that he fell in love with the young goddess so mature but innocent. It concerned her that day to be alone with a man without a chaperone, and to see a nude sketch on a wall.

Muriel's insistence that day, even to this day, she would never pose nude now seemed weakening. When so modest at first that she thought it sinful of a woman to show her feet, Muriel did, in time, walk about the studio unconcerned that Nino saw her barefooted. Just *that* was a hurdle to get over to get her out of her shoes and stockings.

And as of today Muriel waded with her dress above her knees though it was immodest for a woman to show any part of her lower limbs. Muriel seemed unconcerned about that except, she said, they were for "his eyes only." The coy comment made with lowered eyes and a flirtatious smile suggested her shyness was breaking down. Muriel seemed to take delight in her new role as a minx knowing that Nino looked at her more now as a man than a painter.

Moreover, Muriel didn't object this day to being carried, held, and have her hair fondled. In fact, she enjoyed it even though she experienced the feelings so naïvely mentioned; unaware that experienced men already know of such things. But now was an opportunity to keep her talking of intimate concerns.

"It is unfortunate girls don't come with instructions on how their parts work, but yours reacted to the pleasures of being held and kissed. That's normal for women, and believe me it is normal with men."

"Then you liked kissing me too?"

"Of course!"

"Do I get an 'A' for a grade?"

"More than that! You get a gold star for a stellar performance."

"Well good for me, but I must admit I've never had practice. Boys tried to kiss me in school, and men tried in the station sometimes, but I never let them. I didn't know until tonight that being held by a man and kissed could make a girl dizzy and feel funny."

"God willed it that way when He created Adam and Eve as man and woman and told them to be fruitful. God said 'Unite as one and have children.' It was His command. Since Adam and Eve had no prior experience, and no urge to procreate without stimulation, God created the biological phenomenon known today as arousal that makes people *want* to procreate . . . or at least go through the motions.

"Arousal is the urge God created that says 'reproduce me.' It's akin to hunger that says 'feed me,' and arousal to obey the command of God happens when people hug and kiss, hold hands, sit close and look at one another, or do nothing more than fantasize about making love. Looking at suggestive pictures will do it," Nino grinned.

"All of that?"

"And perfume I should add. The scent of a woman is aphrodisiacal to a man."

"I'm wearing perfume," Muriel giggled, amused by the idea of something that caught her fancy. "Am I 'aphrodisiacal?'" she asked innocently.

"As a matter of fact, yes!" Nino chuckled, "what with you and your perfume together. Perfumes on women and colognes on men stimulate love-making, but there is nothing more stimulating than passionate kissing. But whatever the cause, arousal is difficult to stop once the urge starts. It helps, though, to bite one's lip."

"Or grit one's teeth I suppose."

"That too," Nino smiled, amused she knew of the alternative.

"Do men get strange feelings like women . . . I mean like something down in an odd place comes alive?" Muriel asked, now out of curiosity. Her modesty began breaking down.

"Men have reactions that make lovemaking possible . . . if that's what you mean," Nino replied, casually.

"I see!" Muriel mumbled to herself, held as close as Nino held her with contours "married."

"See what?"

"Oh nothing! It's just that a man never held me close, or held me at all for that matter."

"Didn't your mother ever tell you anything about the birds and bees . . . or anything at all about men, and about what goes where and how used?"

"Nothing such as that, except that I wasn't to let a man kiss or touch me before marriage, and after that I was to grit my teeth and do my duty when my husband lifts my nightgown. But she never said what men do, except that marriage between a man and a woman is for procreation, not recreation, and that any measure of pleasure is sinful. But Nino, I didn't want to grit my teeth when you kissed me, or bite my lip as you say. Anyway, I couldn't," Muriel giggled. "I was too busy kissing to even think about it."

"Haven't you read of sexual pleasure, or heard talk from girls?"

"I've read romance novels. Some are rather steamy I have to say . . . and I've heard girls talk in school, and in the station, but nothing I've read or heard described the why of feelings or gave instructions on the how of anything."

"I would have thought you already knew about such things."

"Well I don't!"

"Well someday you will. The knowing will come soon enough, but not tonight. It's time I take you home."

"Can't we stay a little longer now that we're here?" Muriel fussed. "If you didn't want me here then why did you bring me?"

"Because the lake here is a favourite place of mine and I wanted to share it with you."

"Is that the only reason you brought me?"

"And to be alone with you I have to admit . . . but it's best now we don't stay any longer."

"Shush!" Muriel argued with a finger to his lips. "Being here didn't stop me from coming with you did it?"

"No."

"It didn't stop you from bringing me did it?"

"No."

"I could have said 'no' when you asked but I didn't."

"That may be. But still, I need to get you back to Allison's for tonight."

"But tonight is too much fun to leave right now with the water and the moon and all. Can't we wade some more before we leave?"

"Not now . . . it's getting late."

"But we've got all night for heaven's sake. You don't need to go home early to an empty house, do you?"

"I guess not, but that doesn't mean staying out all night."

"Well Allison does when she goes out with men. She told me she does, and she gave me a key in case I . . . we . . . stay late."

"But there is the carriage driver to think about."

"You heard him say he would wait on us, and for us take our time. He said he wanted to rest his mare, and you saw him blow out his lamps. He is probably asleep himself already so why wake him now? And it's pretty here on the lake. It's warm and nice, and all around us love is going on."

"Where? I don't see anyone," Nino remarked, looking around to lighten up the conversation.

"Not people, silly! I mean all the toads and frogs, and all the crickets. Just listen to them serenade their lady friends."

"I guess you know, then, that it's the males of a species that make the noise. Females know to keep their mouths shut," Nino laughed.

"Ha! ha! But it stands to reason that males of anything would be the loud mouths," Muriel laughed in turn. "But see!" she said as she fingered the heart on the willow. "Some male of the human species once had a lady friend in here, and I'll bet *he* didn't fuss about staying late."

"That may have been true for them! Nevertheless, it's not a good idea for us."

"Not because of some silly old kisses, I hope," Muriel hastened to interject. "The reason I said you mustn't kiss me the way you did at first was because you made me feel funny. I thought there was something wrong with me."

"There was nothing wrong with you. Feeling how you felt was for a reason, and it's to be expected."

"I know that now since you told me, but otherwise I don't think you understand about tonight . . . I mean about me."

"What about you?"

"I'd rather not say!"

"Just say it!" Nino urged to keep her talking.

"It's just that . . . it's just that when you kissed along my neckline I wanted you to . . ." Muriel paused, hesitant to continue. "I can't say anything more."

"Why not?"

"Because what I wanted wasn't ladylike."

"Why?" Nino asked to urge her more.

"Oh Nino! It's just that . . ." Muriel paused again, but her reluctance to speak of things intimate finally broke down.

"It's just that when you kissed along my neckline I wanted to pull it down so you could kiss me lower. So there! I said it, and now you know. But to let you kiss me where I wanted seemed shameful."

"But where you wanted to be kissed is where women the world over want. It's a craving women have to experience the pleasure of a man."

"Maybe so, but that's why I asked you to stop. It seemed unladylike to *me*. I had never been kissed before tonight, and certainly not where we're talking about. Ladies don't do that sort of thing."

"But they do! Being kissed where we're talking is a pleasure to women and to men as well despite what the holiest of clerics and most pious of purists will argue."

"My mother wouldn't think so."

"Well, despite what your mother and the queen might think, virtues and inhibitions break down behind closed doors. Queens relieve their boredom with stable grooms, and kings romp with chambermaids. And beneath their habits priests and nuns are still human with all the urges, and if they don't want to gratify their own selves then they seek help from others of the cloth, or sympathetic parishioners. And widows and spinsters have gentlemen friends more than willing."

"And who do artists have . . . huh? They have models, and you have me, but the reason I asked you not to kiss me anymore was because I didn't want you to think me shameless."

"There's no need to think that, or even talk about such things. Some of the most fun two people can have is when nothing is said or asked."

"Then I won't say another word, or ask for anything more tonight except that we stay a while longer."

"That's not a good idea, not now anyway, and tonight only tells me we need to limit time alone just to the studio. I have paintings in mind for you long after *La Belle Dame* is finished."

"I know. I know you want to paint me next as a naiad and a hamadryad. Allison told me, but that means posing with everything of me showing. I can't do that!"

"Sure you can! You're making good progress already . . . to everything showing I mean," Nino grinned.

"How so?"

"I mean that in the studio I've seen your feet already, and I have to say yours are as lovely as an artist could ever hope to see and paint."

"Oh hush!"

"And tonight already I've seen your lower limbs and lovely knees, so we're . . . you're . . . making progress in the direction up to what's next of a woman lovely to see . . . er I mean paint." Nino grinned.

"Well shame on you for talking like that! How gross! And for goodness sake how can that part of a woman be thought as 'lovely?' I never heard of such a thing, and certainly nothing *I* would ever think." Nino had Muriel talking.

"'Lovely' is all a matter of opinion . . . certainly a man's versus a woman's and has been since Creation. One day when out of idle curiosity with nothing else to do . . . a case of *Far Niente* [doing nothing]" Nino said in Italian, "Adam peaked under Eve's fig leaf and saw in awe . . . to be poetic about it . . . what men today consider the loveliest of God's creations." Nino grinned but Muriel frowned.

"Shame on you!" she sputtered. "That's sacrilegious."

"It's just complimentary to God! It was Milton who once said of Eve, 'Oh fairest of creation, last and best of all God's works.' And Blake described a woman's nakedness as a 'Work of God.' That's why Adam remarked 'lovely' when he saw Eve beneath her leaf. He was awestruck by her lovely beauty."

"Oh rubbish! What can possibly be lovely and beautiful about where you are talking?"

"And pleasurable I have to add . . . ever since Adam discovered by trial and error the purpose and joy of what God created for the pleasure of all mankind. From his first time and every time thereafter Adam knew the pleasure, but he didn't put two and two together to know its purpose until Cain and Abel came along." Nino chuckled.

"What cockamamie things to say! The Bible doesn't say anything like that . . . not that I ever read . . . I mean about the 'lovely' thing you say Adam said, or anything 'pleasurable' about it. You need another version of the Bible to learn what's true."

"But what I said *is* true! It's written! It's in the book! It's in Genesis Two of my King James Version where it's said that God gave Adam the responsibility of naming all things created, and that 'whatever Adam called them would be their name.' Now *that* was God's command. So Adam being the dutiful man that he was obeyed. He named lions and tigers, and elephants. He gave the name of 'Eve' to Eve, and he named her parts. He named her arms 'arms' and her limbs 'limbs,' and hands and feet and everything else just like we still call them today. That's where the name 'breasts' came from." Muriel blushed.

"I guess you never knew, then, that Adam gave the name 'Lovely' to what he found beneath Eve's leaf." Nino squelched a grin with a bite on his lower lip.

"Balderdash!" Muriel fussed.

"But there is more to the story. After everything was created, God looked back on all His work and said 'all is good.' And when He looked Eve up and down God said 'VERY good.' Now that's the truth, also in Chapter Two. And remember, Blake described a woman's nakedness as a 'Work of God,' and Milton said Eve was the 'last and best of all God's works.' And men today the world over voice unanimous opinion with an 'Oh God yes!' whenever a naked woman is seen and/or enjoyed." Muriel frowned again.

"That's poppycock!"

"Well think what you want, but God *must* have been especially pleased with His Eve, and Adam with Eve because when Adam discovered the pleasure of her he moaned God's name in ecstasy. And to this day, would you believe, that every night in every city, town, and village, and on every farm in every hay loft, and on back seats of carriages, and under trees like this willow here all across the land, men cry out 'Oh God!' in thanks for God's gift of women." Nino chuckled.

"You're just full of it! The Bible I know doesn't say anything about 'moans,' and about 'Oh Gods.' And for all you know, Adam said 'ugh!' when he looked down at Eve at where you are talking, and likely said another 'ugh' when he discovered the why of it."

"I doubt that, knowing men as I do . . . and women . . . but I *will* admit that chest-beating Neanderthals may have groaned 'ugh' since 'ugh' was likely the only word they knew for anything. And while Adam simply called 'lovely' what Eve possessed, men today call it all sorts of things though most, I'm afraid, aren't mentionable in mixed company."

"What sorts of things?" Muriel asked in all her naïvety.

"Never mind. You wouldn't want to know."

"Why not?"

"Well if you *insist* to know, now that the word is mentioned, I suppose it is innocent enough to tell you that women smile among themselves over talk of 'things.' That's the common word used and one even royalty would use. But you asked how that part of a woman can be considered 'lovely,' so now you know. It's a 'lovely thing.'"

"I'm sorry I asked!"

"Well, knowing what men talk about other than the weather, sports, business, the monarchy and politics, what I told you is part of your worldly education. Men talk about women more than anything else, and when the subject gets around to virgins, as it always does, men speak fondly of them as 'fields unplowed' or 'flowers unplucked,' . . . and not to forget 'fruits untasted.'"

"Oh yuck! Shame on you for talking like that! Wash your mouth out with soap!" Nino couldn't help but grin at Muriel's frown, but to keep her *really* going he continued.

"Well think what you want, but with regards to 'fruits untasted,' Shakespeare said those of a woman are the 'dearest morsels on earth.'"

"That's disgusting! How could a man think that?"

"Well most men do, and Shakespeare did. Much of his writing can't be read with propriety in a family but I'm only telling you what one of the great literary minds of England once wrote. People love to read the works of Shakespeare from the way he writes such bawdy things just like I'm telling you, and a Dutch moralist of Shakespeare's time said something similar. He said 'infertile land must be plowed, planted with seed, and kept watered before it can bear fruit.' You can interpret that however you want!"

"More shame on you."

"And Keats, still another romantic, put a religious spin on 'lovely' when he described a woman's 'land' as a 'Holy See of love,' and Keats is one of the most popular of the Romanticist poets. Some of his poetry was said to be 'unfit for ladies' but that only made women want all the more to read it. In fact, some of the most read by women of *any* writing is that titillating enough to make girls and Satan blush and make girls dog-ear pages to read and re-read the most arousing passages. It's why girls pour over Penny Romances, tabloids, and paperback novelettes in the privacy of their bedrooms, and any woman so naïve to admit that something titillating embarrasses them is an 'old maid' and should stick to nothing but things religious. But even the Bible has some of the most licentious passages ever written. Read about Lot and his daughters sometime."

"Well I still don't get the 'Holy See' and 'land'" part.'

"'See' is spelled s-e-e, not s-e-a, and a 'S-e-e' in religion is a 'holy domain.'"

"I still don't get it!"

"A 'Holy *See* of love' as described by Keats means the pleasures of a woman are 'godly and holy' and belong to the domain of men. That's where her 'land' comes in 'owned' and 'ruled-over' by men."

"I still don't get it!"

"Oh never mind! Giovanni Boccaccio, still another literary great, called a woman's 'thing' a 'cage.'"

"For what?" Muriel asked, again in all her innocence.

"For 'nightingales.'"

"Nobody I ever heard of keep nightingales in cages."
"Well you don't know the story. It's about a girl of your age I would guess," Nino grinned, "who caught a 'nightingale' one night then played with it for awhile before putting it in her 'cage' to 'hear it sing.' I have Boccaccio's book at home if you want to read the story. It's a classic full of titillating stories you should read. Now *those* will make girls blush."
"Is the book vulgar?"
"Just funny."
"Then tell me!"
"If you insist," Nino grinned. "You see, Boccaccio wrote a story about a young girl named Caterina and her boyfriend Ricciardo who shared fun in bed, much as Shakespeare wrote about Romeo and Juliet. Being euphemistic about it, Boccaccio said Caterina had a 'cage' for Ricciardo's 'nightingale' . . . those being pet names for their 'things' you have to understand to get the humour of the story . . . and every time Caterina caught the 'nightingale' and put it in her 'cage' they heard birds 'sing.'"
"That *is* vulgar!"
"No, just funny!"
"Moreover, Caterina held Ricciardo's 'nightingale' even when out of its cage . . . much to both their liking . . . but they enjoyed the pleasure of it more when in than out. And Boccaccio said the 'nightingale' was in and out of its cage so much of the time that Ricciardo and Caterina heard 'singing' night and day.
"It must have been a cheerful bird, one has to imagine," Nino chuckled, "and had it been a cat, Boccaccio would surely have said it 'purred.'"
"That's vulgar! I thought you said the story was funny," Muriel fussed.
"It is! And Shakespeare wrote that after Romeo climbed to Juliet's balcony they heard nightingales through the night and larks when daybreak came."
"How dumb!"
"And in another story Boccaccio told of a crafty cleric who convinced a young virgin that there was only one way into heaven.

And after seven times in as many hours to help her get there, his 'devil' . . . as the cleric called *his* "thing" . . . couldn't perform anymore and was content to rest until another night of trying. The cleric's effort to help the young girl get into heaven must have gone on seven times a night for days."

"That's even dumber!" Muriel complained, but she couldn't suppress a smile.

"And Keats once wrote that when a young lover entered his lady's 'dream' they 'blended like the fragrance of a rose with a violet.' And you can interpret a lady's 'dream' anyway you want."

"More shame on you! Why do you tease me like you do with all your dumb stories?"

"Because it's fun to see you fluster and blush."

"You do it just to bedevil me."

"Well that too!" Nino grinned.

Muriel tried to look and sound fussed befitting to a naïve young virgin over manly subjects new to her as 'fields unplowed,' 'flowers unplucked,' and 'fruits untasted;' and about 'things,' 'dreams,' 'devils,' 'nightingales' and 'cages.' Such nonsense! But despite her demure demeanour of purity and modesty—until tonight that is—Muriel couldn't help but smile—even laugh—at Nino's nutty humour. And had she read such stories she would have dog-eared the pages.

"You're a mental case, Nino Waterhouse. Someone must have dropped you on your head when you were little, and if you need help these days wonderful things are being done for patients in Institutions."

"Say what?"

"You heard me! You've been out in the sun too much, and if you ever want to donate your half-baked brain to science . . . well don't bother. Science would give it back. They'd find it good for nothing but thinking about women."

"Well I admit to thoughts about pretty ones like you with red hair and long limbs," Nino grinned, "but if you want to know the truth of it, poets, writers, philosophers, artists . . . us deep thinkers . . . and the common man all think about women . . .

and certainly sculptors of nudes and those of us who paint them, like me. It's in our nature to contemplate the female form as we chisel and paint the parts."

"What parts, pray tell, do you contemplate of me? There's nothing of me in *La Belle Dame* to ponder like Allison in *St. Eulalia*."

"Your feet show, and footmen of the world will thank me when they see the painting."

"Oh hush! But there's nothing more of me showing than one ankle and my two 'foots.'"

"That's enough for your first painting. Two ankles would be too much of a good thing for now," Nino chuckled, "but we can decide later on how much more of you I need to show when I paint you for nymphs."

"You mean *if* you paint me."

"Well whatever, but for now it's time to take you home before you decide to kick more water on me," Nino said facetiously to change the subject.

"Then I've decided."

"Decided what? To pose for a water nymph?" Nino hoped Muriel would say.

"No silly! To kick more water on you." And with that said, Muriel broke laughing from Nino's arms and ran from under the willow to the water's edge. "If you want me for a water nymph you'll have to come in and get me," she called back, and with a giggle Muriel lifted her dress and petticoat to higher than before and stepped deeper into the water. "Oh my!" Nino muttered, seeing Muriel's long and slender limbs well above her knees; up to the hems of her leggy drawers trimmed with frilly lace and satin bows. His armour of propriety not to love a sitter began to crack.

In the light of the moon dancing in ripples all around her, and with an auburn aura glowing about her head, Muriel was in the words of Wordsworth a "phantom of delight." She was Sir Walter Scott's *The Lady of the Lake* where "danced the moon" over Loch Katrine in the Perthshire Highlands. She was Scott's maiden fair "With locks flung back and lips apart / Like some monument of Grecian art / But ne'er did Grecian chisel trace / A Nymph, A Naiad, or a Grace / Of finer form or lovelier face."

Muriel *was* a Grace, tall and slender and of no "finer form or lovelier face" than the nymphs he wanted to paint of her. She was Luna and Aphrodite rolled into one goddess, and she was Diana the virgin. She was the enchantress *Muriélle La Belle Dame* down from off her easel and into the water, and as Nino watched her splash about "with locks flung back and lips apart" he became so absorbed in his fantasies of her that had he been pricked with a pin he wouldn't have felt it.

Nino was torn all the more between keeping his relationship with Muriel chaste, or letting nature take its course. Every day since her interview he dreamed of holding her in his arms. During the hours Muriel sat draped for sketches he dreamed of her undraped. During their ride to the lake he traced her parted mouth with fantasies in mind of the most erotic of pleasures. And then there were kisses all over her face and neck and along her neckline with fantasies of the wonders in under. And now as Muriel waded with dress and petticoat lifted, Nino dreamed of the wonder up under, and doubted his resolve to keep Muriel chaste should they stay at the lake any longer.

Now *was* the time to take Muriel home before she lost her innocence, but the little tease and enchantress wasn't making decisions easy. She was both an angel and a Lorelei, and Nino took Muriel's tempting beckon of "come and get me" to be a siren's song luring him to "destruction." Was her challenge a dare that he wouldn't? And how innocent was the "get me?"

"I'll show you you little minx," Nino grumbled to himself as he rolled his trousers higher and splashed in after her."

Nino lifted Muriel into his arms enjoying again the bare undersides of her slender limbs over his hairy arm; her bosom buried into his chest; and the aphrodisiacal scent of her perfumed hair against his face. With Muriel's longest of long limbs kicking in a coy pretense of protest, Nino carried the little pixie back in under the willow so nothing in the grass would poke, bite, or tickle her feet.

"I need to take you home," Nino said as he sat with Muriel on the cape, realizing that his urge to lay her flat was overwhelming his resolve to keep her upright.

"Put your shoes and stockings back on so we can leave," he ordered.

"But my feet are wet!"

"Then dry them!" Nino argued, handing Muriel a handkerchief, "or do you want me to dry them for you?" he said half-kidding.

"Never mind! I can dry them myself. You would just tickle them now for meanness," Muriel muttered with a frown.

"Then get on with it! I need to take you home."

"You don't need to be so snippy about it, and be in such a hurry!" Muriel protested. "All I said was, I don't want to go home *yet*, so don't be such an old Scrooge and spoil my fun. I think Mr Dickens had you in mind when he wrote the part. You never told me Mr Dickens knew you."

"Don't be funny! Dickens wrote about Scrooge long before I was born."

"Well, whenever . . . but you know exactly what I mean. You're a grumpy old Scrooge of a man. There's no fun in you!"

"Bah humbug!" Nino retorted, trying hard not to laugh.

"Well don't 'humbug' me. Be nice! And why can't we wade some more? We've got the rest of tonight for goodness sake . . . and despite what I said earlier you can kiss me again if you want . . . the way you did the first time. Isn't it a woman's prerogative to change her mind? That's what everybody says."

"Not for you! Not tonight anyway! I need to take you home before the sun comes up without a smidgen of innocence left in you." Nino said what he said in jest but Muriel's heart raced at the inference.

"Then let the sun come up! And what's with innocence anyway? Allison and Miranda lost theirs years ago when skinny-dipping . . . and with older men and when younger than I am I might add."

"That doesn't mean *you* have to."

"I'm just telling you that Allison and Miranda seem happy in life with smiles on their faces, and they aren't wasted or feeble-minded, or are their complexions any the worse for it. And here I am only tonight kissed for the first time. You're the only man I've ever let hold my hand, or me, or play with my hair."

"Well, it couldn't have been more enjoyable had there been two of you with twice your hair to run one's fingers through."

Nino's comment excited Muriel because Allison believed a good way to seduce a man was to lure him into brushing one's hair; to let him get his fingers in it. And Muriel remembered Nino once said she had hair men "would sell their souls to tangle in." In fact, Nino once "played" with hers—so it seemed—when making her noose for a sitting. He didn't mind about that. At least he didn't fuss about it. And, she knew what Allison knew; that Nino was obsessed with long red hair.

"If we have to go," Muriel fussed in pretense to sound disgruntled about the whole affair, "then would you brush out my curls for me before we leave? You can at least do that, can't you? You're the one who made the mess of them."

"Oh I suppose!" Nino grumbled as if the task would be a chore. But in anticipation of the pleasure his armour cracked wider.

Muriel removed pins holding up her hair and let it fall long and loose. She handed Nino a brush from her purse then stood with her back to him. "Brush down full length," she ordered, "at least a hundred times or more until the curls are gone." ["On wandering knights our spells we cast, said the Lady of the Lake." (Scott 1810)]

The wandering artist/knight in pursuit of adventure fell to his Lady's spell. He knelt, sat back on his heels, and pulled down on Muriel's curls to play with as he pleased; to watch them recoil and twist around his fingers. He pulled handfuls of curls to his face for the sensual feel of them and to inhale their intoxicating scent. Then in long strokes, Nino brushed Muriel's soft, silken hair down full length to her knees. With every stroke down over her bustle and the shapely backsides of her slender limbs, Nino's armour of resolve not to make love to a sitter cracked ever wider.

The Lady of Lake Serpentine "with locks flung back and lips apart" reveled in the pleasure. With every stroke Muriel's heart raced, and her breath quickened. With every stroke down over her bustle she wanted that "something more" about which Miranda spoke, and that something that comes from the urges of arousal that Nino explained was the "Will of God."

Muriel had no wish to defy the Creator, or bite her lip or grit her teeth to suppress the warmth of desire. She felt herself melting, and despite restraints by everything moral and virtuous, Muriel and her knight errant succumbed to impatient longings. If sin existed, theirs was the longing between an artist and a model so common in the history of art. If sin existed theirs was surrendering to forbidden desires so common in the history of everyday life.

The barefoot enchantress with a perfect face and hypnotic eyes turned and sat fawn-like in front of her knight. She gazed into his eyes with a longing look, a sigh, and a whispered "I love you," then looped a noose of hair around his neck for an invited kiss.

With a spell upon him, and his senses reeling, the bewitched artist/knight accepted his Lady's offer and held her kiss while sliding his hands out over Muriel's bare shoulders and down her arms taking the neckline of her dress down with them. Muriel gasped softly when her dress slipped down to her waist and off her arms revealing a nymphet bosom as lovely as any artist could ever hope to see, touch, hold, paint, and savour.

Nino's armour of propriety clattered around him in shattered pieces. Free at last of long self-imposed restraints not to make love to a sitter, the knight errant lay down on a bed of moss cloaked in the knee-length tresses of a faery-child enchantress. And when in time he "entered her dream and melted as the rose blendeth with the violet" (Keats 1819) it was then the "nightingale sang" (Boccaccio 1350).

. . .

On a warm, moonlit, late-summer night in 1893 on the banks of The Serpentine curtained in under the canopy of a weeping willow, her elfin grot, the Lady of the Lake spread her nuptial wings like a virgin bee and soared into the heavenly heights of ecstasy to mate with the male of her choosing.

In a near-silent metamorphosis, *Muriélle La Belle Dame* came of age and emerged from maidenhood into womanhood. No questions were asked and no words were spoken except for frequent "I love yous." No other sounds were made except sighs of contentment. And those "instructions" Muriel was born without—the ones on how girls and their parts work—well, they weren't necessary. She learned lesson by lesson, step by step, everything needed to know by "hands-on" demonstrations.

Muriel lay blissful in the ways Nino had loved her in ways she could never have imagined. And after climbing walls and teetering on the very ragged edge of fulfillment, points of no return came for them both when by the good grace of God, euphoria pulsed through them in concert with the singing of birds.

Muriel pulled her dress up loosely and for long moments lay rapt in reveries basking in an afterglow of bliss as though off in paradise somewhere reveling in the pleasures of hearing birds sing. Spring had sprung all over again in the bloom of summer with courtship songs of willow warblers, skylarks, and nightingales, the sweetest of voices, and with the sweet smells of honeysuckles and wild roses amid fields of violets, poppies, and foxgloves. It was true as Keats had written that "roses blendeth with the fragrance of violets."

Maybe, Muriel thought, she should write a best selling book on heaven and men with chapters on knights and ladies, moonlit nights and willow trees, and about nightingales, roses and violets. Those would be the kinds of stories women would thirst for. She could give her book an eye-catching title with something like *Rapturous Rapture* or *Ecstatic Ecstasy*, and Nino could paint a cover that would sell books by cartloads. Maybe she should start up a diary with a lock and key, but then Muriel snapped back from her reveries with a whispered, "Nino? Are you awake?"

"Yes," he replied, stifling a long yawn.

"Did you like me?"

"Need you ask? You couldn't have been more enjoyable had there had been two of you with twice your hair. But you alone were one above and beyond any number of others, and had I a Union Jack I would have waved it . . . or rung church bells. I could have done cartwheels."

"Don't be funny! But did I do anything wrong?"

"Nothing was wrong but everything was right."

"But didn't you think I was . . . well . . . somewhat unimpressive? I mean there is probably nothing in life worse than being ordinary or humdrum. I wanted to be something special for you and I . . . well . . . wanted to be breathtaking."

"Believe me you took my breath when the last of your clothes came off. What I saw was incredible!"

"Oh hush! But I didn't know how to do anything, just in case you wondered why I wasn't . . . well . . . any better."

"You couldn't have been any better," Nino said with another long yawn.

"But through it all you didn't say anything one way or another except for that 'Oh God thank you!' you muttered when you really lost your breath."

"That was from the breathtaking experience of losing ourselves together. That doesn't always happen, but every now and then the good Lord in all His benevolence smiles down on someone. Tonight was our turn, so God got a 'thank you' and you earned another gold star for performance beyond the call of duty."

"Nino?" There was a long pause.

"What?"

"Oh nothing!" Muriel paused again.

"Well there *is* something. It's just that a woman shouldn't ask a man about marriage, so I'm not asking, mind you, I'm just wondering. But could we get ever get married somehow?"

"That would be another of God's blessings, but a married man can't divorce in this empire, and even if a man could, a man can't remarry. That's the law!"

"But it doesn't sound fair. I mean if a man and another woman are in love then why shouldn't they be able to marry if they want? People only have one life to live you know, so why waste it? And shouldn't having the right partner in life mean more than anything else? What if a man and his wife don't get along? What if they hate all the little things the other one does, like the way the other one slurps his soup? What if all they do is squabble, and what if they have separate bedrooms?"

"It still doesn't matter. Even if two people initially marry with good reason, people change, and when a marriage turns sour with no chance for a divorce it's like . . . well . . . like 'hell on earth.' Simply, when wrong people marry divorces can't be had to end mistakes, and you can thank the queen for that."

"It's still not fair. We've already done what married people do."

Muriel paused another long moment while twisting a lock of hair and thinking on another matter. "You know," she said, "you've seen me now without my clothes . . . so what do you think?"

"Breathtaking!" Nino grinned. "And as I said, 'incredible.' You are exactly the model I want for nymphs and goddesses."

"But you'll have to agree I'm not like those pictures in your books. I've noticed how you look at *Venus de Milo* with more than idle curiosity."

"For your information, Miss Nosy, I study the shapes, dimensions, and proportions of female figures to know how best to paint them."

"Sure you do!" Muriel grumbled in pretense of disapproval.

"In case you don't know it, *my dear*, Venus and others like her have the classical Greco-Roman beauty of human forms that artists like to study. That's why I look at statue pictures."

"Yeah! yeah!" Muriel fussed, dryly.

"Do you want to hear this or not?"

"Oh all right!" Muriel conceded.

"If you remember, I told you that artists and sculptors contemplate female parts to paint and chisel them. Take a foot for example. To look good . . . to look proportional to body size . . . the length of a foot needs to be fifteen percent of a person's height. No one wants to see a stubby foot in a painting or a big long one, now do they?" Muriel laughed.

"And the distance between finger tips of outstretched arms is equal to a person's height. It's all scientific, just like the height of a woman's head needs to be the same distance between her chin down to the level of her breasts, then another down to her navel and still another to the intersection between her limbs. So it's important to know that four head-lengths measure from the top of a woman's head down to her . . . well what Eve covered with a fig leaf." Nino grinned.

"It's obvious you know the 'what' and where on women. You found mine straight off with nary a problem."

"That was because after studying statue pictures I knew where to look," Nino laughed, "and yours was exactly where God put it."

"Fiddle-dee-dee! But is all of this going somewhere?"

"Well, yeah, to your education. You need to know, too, that one head-length is the distance between a woman's . . . well . . . where babies suckle. And measurements for models with desirable long limbs like yours are four head-lengths more from intersections to the tips of toes. That's a total of eight from tops of heads to tips of toes, and four is exactly halfway up or down.

"And halfway down to his or her intersection is where evolution conveniently designed arms and hands to reach for a number of reasons. Now that's important to know because how far down a person can reach tells artists how long to paint arms. Now think about that. If hands in a painting reach only to one's navel, then arms are much too short. And if hands reach all the way down to one's knees___"

"Then arms are much too long!" Muriel piped in with a giggle. "Even I can figure that out."

"Well there you are! You see! It's like I told you. Artists and sculptors need to ponder female parts to get them in perspective.

When you get back to Allison's tonight, measure Miranda's sketch of *Syrinx*. You'll likely find her a perfect four-four up or down to her . . . her fig leaf. And while you're at it, measure between her . . . well her nipples." Muriel blushed on hearing the word said.

"And notice on *Syrinx* what happened when Miranda posed with one arm lifted. That breast lifted, but with the other arm down, that breast hung natural. It's amazing how things work like that . . . up down up down up down." Nino smiled.

"I already know that, dummy!" Muriel fussed. "So does any woman who bathes with an arm lifted, but not on your life am I going to measure *Syrinx* anywhere you are talking about, and get caught with a ruler in my hand. I can see the looks already."

"I see your point!"

"Well, since you already know the ups and downs of women, and the wheres of whats, then you don't need Allison any more, or me. Sketch Venus instead!" Muriel grumbled. "Prop up *her* picture and you won't owe sitter wages."

"But Venus has no arms to pose, and she has the look of cold hard marble. There's no joy in that when you have arms and the look of a warm soft you. And besides, you have longer hair." Nino put a fist to his mouth to stifle another grin and another long yawn.

"Do you still want me for a nude model?"

"Of course! You have a torso as heavenly as Venus."

"But what about my ribs? Venus doesn't show hers."

"It doesn't matter. I love your ribs just as they are," Nino said as he counted up along them. "One, two, three, four___"

"Stop!" Muriel cried out before he could count to five beneath a breast. She couldn't stand the tickles.

"What about my hip bones? They protrude you know . . . and what about my collar bones? Miranda and Allison aren't bony by any stretch of imagination."

"Well quit worrying about it! If need be I can fatten you up on canvas to look as chubby as a butter ball. And beside, I love your bones just the way they are. Yours will make a lovely skeleton someday for study in the Royal Academy anatomy class. Men will come from far and wide to gather around. But you would be beautiful even if you had no bones." Nino yawned again.

"Don't be silly! If I didn't have bones to hold me up I'd be nothing but a lump on the floor and I'd evaporate to nothing when I die. And anyway, without bones I couldn't sit for you. All I could do was wiggle around like a wobbledy glob of something."

"There wouldn't be anything wrong with that," Nino laughed.

"I like the way you wiggle and wobble."

"Oh hush!" Muriel fussed. "Don't talk about things like that! But do you still want me for a nymph?"

"Of course! You're as lovely and as flexible a long-limbed four-five nymph as I could ever want for a sitter. You bend and twist every which way possible, and then some. You could pose for a corkscrew if need be," Nino said with a chuckle to Muriel's frown.

"Don't be funny! But if I sit for you will you promise never to reveal my identity? I don't want men see me in your paintings and know who I am . . . and fantasize about me like Pygmalion with his statue."

"I promise," Nino said with another long yawn. "I don't put names of models on paintings anyway, but I can't stop the fantasizing. Men will always do that . . . like with Lady Godiva for example, no matter who the model. By the way, did you know that the expression 'Hooray for our side' came from men peeking through windows on the side of the street facing the Lady riding sidesaddle."

"Oh hush!" Muriel said to sound fussed by the story, but couldn't help but laugh. "But still, won't people recognize me in your paintings?"

"If I paint you to look like you then they will of course. I could, I suppose, give *your* body the face of the queen so men would fantasize about Victoria."

"Ha! ha! Get serious now!"

"Well it's not uncommon that models don't want recognition, and in such cases it's embarrassing when a painting bears too strong a resemblance. If a painting is not a portrait to show someone at their best then I suppose it doesn't matter how a model looks, so long as she looks her best as someone else."

"Well I don't want to be recognized, especially by my mother. She already disapproves of me sitting as a model. She will blow her top."

"We'll have to think more on that, but an artist *can* use one model for form and another for face. And it happens that artists use two or more for composites . . . the bodies, hands, and feet of one or more, and faces of others. There *are* models who pose for nothing but hands or feet, and some only for faces.

"Take for example a painting of Cleopatra or Lady Godiva. No one knows what either looked like, so artists paint them beautiful with any face. And who has ever seen a nymph or a mermaid? It doesn't matter what face is used, but however I paint you, you'll have a beautiful face and body, and men will fall in love with your image no matter how you look."

"Can I keep the colour of my hair?"

"Of course! Auburn is my favourite colour."

"And when you paint me will you never let anyone watch? I couldn't pose wearing nothing to be seen by anyone but you!"

"Never! I only paint behind closed doors." Muriel's heretofore reluctance to pose nude finally broke down. It was a big concession after weeks of saying she never would.

"Then I'll do it! Now that you've seen me wearing nothing I'll sit like that for your paintings . . . so long as you keep the studio warm," Muriel giggled, "and you can paint me for as many nymphs and mermaids as you want. And I'll be available for you whenever you want to love me."

"Don't promise that. You're very desirable, and I see how men look at you. You may fall in love with someone else someday;" a thought that troubled him.

"I would never marry anyone but you. You already have my heart, and in my mind we're already married anyway." Nino didn't say anything, but Muriel prattled on.

"You know, if you think about it, I gave you the most valuable thing of me I have to give a man . . . I mean I had," Muriel giggled.

"A girl could never give away her innocence a second time, now could she? It wouldn't make sense to think it possible, now would it? I mean once a girl loses her virginity from where she kept it, it's lost forever, and it's not something a girl could find some day and stuff back in. Can't you just picture a girl trying?" Muriel laughed at the scene and her own humour, but Nino didn't answer.

"And anyway Nino I would never want someone other than you . . . never! The thought of another man would repulse me, and I could never give another man what he wished . . . at least nothing more than brotherly regard."

Muriel paused for a reply of some kind not in the coming, then sighed and prattled on in typical Muriel fashion. "Nino tonight must be my fate. If I couldn't be with you again like tonight I would rather do without. I'll be a chaste old maid when I die. And Nino . . . I could never sit for another artist no matter how much the wages." There was another pause waiting for Nino to reply.

"Nino? Nino?" Muriel asked softly. There was no response. Nino's eyes were closed. "Nino?" Muriel asked again. There was no response. Nino was asleep with his head upon her shoulder and an arm across her.

But Muriel lay wide awake in dreamy thought reliving moment by moment all the manners Nino had loved her sparing nothing of the ways. And after she climbed walls and teetered on the very ragged edge of that something euphoric yet to happen of which she knew nothing—not even to anticipate—it did happen when at the end of everything Muriel "lost" herself to the rapture of release.

"Oh God!" she muttered under her breath in response to the surprise of something even more pleasurable than the hour before that racked her body and made her gasp. How could her mother be so wrong to say "grit your teeth" to quell such joy? How could anything else be more euphoric than what just happened?

Before the night was over, or in days to come, Muriel hoped to be loved again for more of the pleasure. Once a night wouldn't seem enough, but "yes" or "no," to kiss and tell was not her way, or Nino's.

Muriel eased her shoulder from under Nino's head to sit upright against the willow and comb out her tangled hair, the big job that it was. Off in the distance oarlocks clanked again. Must be night fishermen, she thought, to be out so late.

Moonlight in under the willow wasn't bright enough to read her watch but the moon above had moved across the sky by another hour or two. Muriel sighed. She hoped the moon would cease its endless journey and the night would never end. But while still dark, and while Nino slept, Muriel had a hare-brained idea to skinny-dip like Allison and Miranda had said was fun to do. The water was warm, and there was no one else about, and should Nino see her in her birthday suit it wouldn't matter, not now.

But Muriel couldn't swim, float, paddle, or tread water, and the only girl she ever knew who could got drowned. Maybe it would be safer to stand in shallow water the way Miranda posed for *Syrinx*. And since Nino wanted Muriel for similar poses maybe she should practice some of the same.

But then she had worried thoughts. What if someone really out there lurked about and saw her standing posed with arms uplifted. "What the devil!" they would surely exclaim, and how embarrassing that would be. But when Muriel heard rustling outside the willow canopy she forgot the idea of posing. She inched nearer to Nino and pulled her dress up closer.

Muriel peeked through the willow drapes looking for someone or something, but saw nothing in the early morn except myriads of dewdrops now sparkling like little diamonds in the light of the silvery moon. Soon enough, however, the first rays of dawn would chase the dark away and the stars would disappear. Soon enough the sun of a new day would dry the dew. Never had she been out so late or up so early to see such things happen.

A smile broke across Muriel's face thinking more about the past hour. She had just slept with a man, the first in her life, and Nino proved, she concluded, that men are a half-man and half-something-else kind of creature. The full moon along with her pheromonal scents, like wolfsbanes, brought on the werewolf in Nino hungry enough to spend an hour satiating ravenous appetites. She never knew anything of the feeding behaviour of a half-something-else kind of creature, but what if she got rabies? A single bite anywhere on her would surely do it. And what if her mother saw a satiated man-type animal asleep beside her with her hair down, no makeup on, and unmentionables strewn about? "I warned you about men!" her mother would surely say. "Did you turn your head and grit your teeth?" her mother would surely ask. "I didn't want to!" Muriel would surely reply.

The balmy night outside the willow stood still, but all was not. Occasional "churring" calls of feeding nightjars; long drawn-out hoots and "ke-wick ke-wick" calls of tawny owls; and a background of late-night sounds punctuated with natterjack croaks and chirring crickets interrupted the quiet. Now and then a bream, a perch, or a carp slapped the surface of the lake, and foraging water voles rustled among the reeds; the mysterious noises heard. Maybe it was an otter. And sure enough, befitting to the occasion, a nightingale sang; that melodious bird of song up for the summer from out of Africa.

[For its quality and versatility from throaty chuckles to whistles and to the purest of treble-like trills the voice of the nightingale heard solo in the still of the night is one of the most beautiful of birds. Beethoven immortalized the singing by flute-like sounds in the "Pastoral" of his *Symphony No. 6*, and Milton said nightingales "warbl'st their sweet notes at night when all the woods are still, for it is then they tune sweetest their love-laboured songs." And Keats said "nightingales pour forth their souls in full-throated ease."]

Muriel smiled again remembering Boccaccio's tale. How inane the story when Nino told it, but now that she, like Caterina, had caught, held, and caged a "nightingale" the tale made sense. Now she knew why "caged birds" sing.

In the near distance the carriage mare snorted, but the distant sounds of oarlocks stopped. Muriel listened to Nino breathe, deep in sleep, and then on an otherwise windless night the most gentle of winds blew in from off the lake caressing the willow and Muriel's face as Flora kissed by zephyrs.

Muriel gathered her clothing strewn about when Nino removed it piece by piece with single-minded purpose, but for some odd reason he seemed to become shorter of breath and more anxious as each piece came off. The dress and petticoat were easy enough. Hat, shoes, and stockings were already off from earlier doings. The corset was more a chore with all its snaps and hooks, and with such a slender figure Nino grumbled about why she even needed one.

But when at last the last of what she wore came down and off it was then that Nino really lost his breath. Muriel lay before him half-cloaked in knee-length tresses pulled partially over her in some show of modesty, but her luxuriant mantle hid little. "Oh heaven!" Muriel muttered when he raked it out of the way.

It was an "Oh God!" that Nino muttered, time and again, while gazing up and down the full length of Muriel's lovely five foot eight inch form; up and over and along and around every curve and contour. And had anyone ever wondered about the natural colour of Muriel's head of hair, there was no need now. Auburn was the true colour the good Lord gave her, and the length of her lengthy limbs was at least another head-length more than normal. Had he a ruler, Muriel's would surely be a "five." "Phenomenal!" he exclaimed.

Muriel was truly the Creator's Eve; every inch of her a "Work of God" and superb in every way for the nymphs he dreamed of her since the day of her interview. As he gazed upon Muriel's lovely face with eyes closed, and her shapely form with long and slender limbs and knee-length hair, he could pose her for any nymph, mermaid, siren, or goddess that he imagined to paint. She would be the perfect model for Echo or Ariadne, and for any pose of Psyche. She was perfect for a naiad and a long-limbed hamadryad.

Muriel dressed, smiling, thinking that in the theatre and carriage and while strolling, Nino took care not to wrinkle her clothing or muss her hair. In under the willow, however, and in his anxiety, he seemed unconcerned. He rumpled her clothes when taking them off, and he tangled her hair while cloaked and rolling in it. It couldn't have been more tangled had she faced into the fury of a howling hurricane.

Muriel mused of that, and of other things while combing out the knots. In nuzzling where he seemed most eager Nino carried on with her as a cat with catnip, and surely what Shakespeare once said about "dearest morsels on earth" must have been said in truth. Muriel smiled.

But now that Nino knew her more intimately than she could ever know her own self, Muriel thought about her decision to sit nude for him. He wanted her for nymphs, first as a naiad and then a hamadryad, but there are ocean, sea, mountain, and cave nymphs, and forest, orchard, and fern nymphs. There are meadow, lake, river, swamp, and storm nymphs. Heavens! What other kinds could there possibly be?

Then Muriel exclaimed wide-eyed from sudden realization. "Oh heaven! Maniac nymphs!" Nino once told her how nymphs and nymphets lust after men, and that "nymphomania" is an insatiable female desire for sexual pleasure—a bottomless pit she had to imagine—but could a woman, a girl, could *she*, become afflicted from only one experience?

How in painting could Nino portray a "nympho-nymph" cursed with lust? How could he depict a state of mind? Maybe he could paint a coy glance from the corner of an eye, or a flirtatious smile with lowered eyes. Or maybe paint a glassy countenance like a crazed Ophelia or a Lady of Shalott. That was how Nino painted his Lady in the Tate maddened by lust.

But dare she be so bold, Muriel mused, to awaken Nino for another go before they left. And a third time again during the long ride home with the curtains drawn? After all, doesn't a girl need to know if she's afflicted? And three times in as many hours could surely be construed as proof.

Muriel could think of nothing against the idea, and with the clops of hooves, the rumbles of wheels, and with the carriage already rocking, the driver topside would never know of her affliction down inside on the back seat of his double brougham.

But how many times in a night can a person indulge in the pleasures of sex before being wearied out? Once, twice, thrice, or more? Being new to it all Muriel had no idea except that another time or two seemed not a problem. Boccaccio told of a cleric who did seven times in a night. "Good heavens! Could *that* be possible? Hmmm," she wondered.

"Such nonsense thoughts!" Muriel finally reprimanded herself as being too unladylike to dwell upon, but she had to smile thinking that loss of innocence was finding the way to heaven. Loss of innocence *was* heaven, and the cleric who helped a virgin explained that loss of virginity was "God's only way." Nino explained why God invented arousal, and that "union" between a man and a woman was God's command. Moreover, hers and Nino's that night was blessed because of the way it ended in "unison."

Was obeying the Lord's commands a nightly holy duty? Muriel wondered. And is once a night with but a single "Oh God thank you" enough to praise the Lord for all His benevolence? Even if only once a night was enough, once a night would still be going to heaven.

Muriel sat thinking of other things; about the day of her interview when she feared Nino wanted to see her nude; of how she fought with herself just to bare her feet for sketches; and now tonight she had bared her everything and agreed to let him paint the all of her for nymphs and mermaids.

Muriel remembered when Nino purchased her flowers at the Waterloo station so she could spend the day with him. He made her laugh with a caricature. She remembered his confrontation with her mother to let her be a sitter, and when he carried her through his door the day she grew faint. All of that now seemed ages ago.

Muriel recalled the fun of riding bicycles with Nino, and the camaraderie in Primrose Hill when sketches were made and the study painted. It seemed he teased her about everything, but she enjoyed his attention. Allison said that if Nino teased her, then he liked her. Muriel knew that Nino liked her from their second day on when he teased her in the Waterloo station. Muriel sat gazing upon Nino's sleeping face, remembering the evening. In the theatre he held her hand and with squeezes said he loved her. She squeezed back. During the ride to the lake he played with a curl; something she would never allow another man. And what was Nino thinking when he traced her parted mouth with the tip of a finger? Now she knew of the things men think.

Muriel remembered their bantering repartee during the mock trial to make Nino swear he wouldn't tickle her "foots," and to his honour he didn't. And to draw out of him she was his favourite, and to admit he was in love with her as she was with him. Nino was an older man but that didn't matter. She fell in love with him for his gentle voice and caring. She liked the idea that she was his favourite model, and because of that she was his muse and inspiration, and in that respect she was his "possession." She liked the idea of being his, about everything.

She fell in love with Nino because of his talents, his art, his romanticism, and his nutty humour. He chuckled when telling her wicked things in devilish ways to make her fluster and blush. Yet, he made her laugh despite herself and he laughed with her and at himself. He smiled with only an occasional frown. Nino was not a man of a single mood or character but of many, and because no other man could mean so much to her she gave him her innocence; his to keep for the rest of his life.

On a balmy summer night in 1893 on a moonlit bank of The Serpentine in under a weeping willow—her elfin grot—*Muriélle La Belle Dame*, the Lady of the Lake, cast spells upon her errant knight soon shed of armour but cloaked in tresses. She gave him her most precious one-time gift, and in return he gave her the womanhood she wanted from the man she wanted. For Muriel that night, a nightingale sang amid roses and violets.

Not long thereafter another one sang and in honour of the night in lover's tradition she and Nino carved their initials on the willow inside a heart of their own. Muriel beamed. Nino carved the initials and she carved the heart like the one upon her sleeve.

. . .

After a long and romantic ride home in a rocking carriage with rumbling wheels and with curtains drawn, Muriel eased her latchkey into the door of Allison's and Miranda's flat hoping not to disturb them. She had been with Nino long into the early morning and surely her two friends would be asleep.

Muriel chose to sleep on the parlour sofa to not disturb the girls in the bedroom. She was weary from a long night, and achy, but she had no more than sat to remove her shoes and stockings when the girls awakened by her return entered the parlour. They stretched and yawned. One asked, yawning, "Why were you out so late?" And the other asked, "What could you have been doing until this wee hour of the morning?" Muriel smiled to herself.

Allison peeked through the parlour drapes and exclaimed, "My Lord Muriel! The sun is coming up already. And look at you! Your hat's askew, your hair is down, you haven't on a smidgen of makeup, and why in heaven's name is my dress so rumpled?"

"Nino and I went strolling in the moonlight . . . and we listened to birds sing," Muriel remarked nonchalantly.

"Strolling! Up on one's feet all night! I could never just stroll all night, and it's rolling around in dresses that rumple them like that, not strolling, and believe me I know about that one. And what's with the birds?"

"Yeah!" Miranda piped in. "When Allison and I come in at dawn with dresses rumpled, hair down, no lipstick on, and with smiles on our faces we know what *we* did all night, and it wasn't strolling. You laid down in Allison's dress, didn't you? You rolled around in it, didn't you? It got lucky for you, didn't it? You let Nino make love to you, didn't you? Confess it all! Tell us all of everything after your hair came down."

"Well, we *did* sit," Muriel responded nonchalantly. "Nino spread out his cape for us and we sat under a willow tree. We looked up at the moon over The Serpentine, and we talked all night," Muriel said, hoping to be believed. She put her hand to her mouth to stifle a long yawn.

"The Serpentine!" Allison exclaimed, "Sitting and talking and looking all night! And if it was a weeping willow I know for a fact you don't see out too much from under one of them. You did more than sit and look. My guess is you were flat on your back not looking up at much of anything except Nino looking back down at you. So what did you do flat on your back as if we don't know? But spare us no details!"

Taking time to decide how to reply to such personal questions, if at all, Muriel removed her shoes and stockings and leaned back into the sofa with her hands behind her head. She gazed up at the ceiling for a long moment remembering the night, then closed her eyes for another long moment weary from lack of sleep, leaving her two friends waiting anxiously for answers and details— especially details—but Muriel never told. Her night with Nino was much too personal to confess, but the smile across her face said it all.

It all happened as Nino predicted. They stayed at The Serpentine and the sun *did* arise without so much as a "smidgen of innocence" left in her. It was true all right. She lost her innocence but found a path into heaven.

. . .

There are no diaries or letters to speak of Muriel's *affaire d'amour* that summer night long ago as *La Mademoiselle Muriélle La Belle Dame "avec compassion."* There is nothing to say they ever returned to the willow on the lake. But maybe they did, and maybe they knew of others. Weeping willows with branches to the ground are common in England.

It's said, however, there's an age-old willow on the banks of The Serpentine with initials inside hearts carved up and down its gnarled trunk; records of long-ago love-affairs. Some initials are hard to read—worn by the passage of time—but those in one heart appear to be a "NW" and a "MF."

There hangs today in a far away museum a painting named *La Belle Dame sans Merci* that's viewed by millions. It's of a knight in armour kneeling before a barefoot lady. Her hair is long and it's looped around the knight in an act of seduction. And as the story goes, the lady "sighed deep" and said "I love thee true." It was then that they "slumbered on the moss." [See following "La Belle Dame sans Merci" Commentaries.]

The painting was created by a "NW" and modeled for by a "MF." One can read into the coincidence of initials with those on the tree whatever story one wishes.

The End

"LA BELLE DAME SANS MERCI"

COMMENTARIES ON THE POEM, THE POET, AND THE PAINTER

THE POEM AND THE POET

Recurrent themes in the poetry of John Keats (1795-1821) are often melancholy preoccupation with art, love, mythology, sorrow, human suffering, and the natural and supernatural world; all of which except art are condensed into the brief 48 lines of Keats's 1819 and 1820 versions of *La Belle Dame sans Merci* ("The Lovely Lady without Pity"). The story was taken from a medieval poem of the same name by Frenchman Alain Chartier in 1425.

Keats's narrative in two versions based on Chartier tells of a mortal man enamored with an immortal lady. Keats used sights, sounds, touches, and tastes, and the painful emotions of desire, love, abandonment, and anxiety to tell his story; one that mirrored, perhaps, Keats's own despair, fear of death, and turmoil over a tormented love affair.

The narrative is composed of questions and answers in simple though somewhat archaic language. The story is brief, leaving details to curious readers to "fill in blanks" although clues to missing narrative are found in other of Keats's poems discussed herein.

A lack of details also made Keats's story challenging to painters fascinated by the story who visualized the knight and his lady in a variety of sensually depicted scenes. Noteworthy are those by Waterhouse (1893), Dicksee (1902), and Cowper (1926).

Literary interpretations of the poem vary as well. Some scholars interpret *La Belle Dame sans Merci* as Keats's personal rebellion to the heartaches and frustrations of love reflective at the time on conflicting passions for the young and coquettish Fanny Brawne. Keats felt his love for Fanny—and the time eaten with jealousies over her attentions to other men—took time from his writing; a loss of freedom he resented. "I find I cannot do without poetry," he wrote a friend.

In his poem *Lines to Fanny* Keats asked: "What can I do to drive away / Remembrance [of you] from my eyes. / What can I do to kill it and be free / In my old liberty?"

Yet, in his subsequent *Ode to Fanny* Keats changed his mind and begged: "Keep me free from torturing jealousy. / Let none [other men] profane my Holy See [domain] of love / Or with a rude hand break / The sacramental cake [hymen]. / Let none else touch the just new-budded flower."

Keats was clearly in turmoil with obsession and jealousy. Also, without gainful employment, he worried that if married to Fanny he couldn't support her, and he didn't want to give up his time and freedom to write poetry.

Moreover, Keats feared his time to live was limited. His brother died of tuberculosis in 1818, and Keats became ill that same year with a throat condition causing chronic coughing, pain, and fear that he, too, would die of tuberculosis which he did three years later.

In the year his brother died, Keats wrote: "When I have fears that I may cease to be / Before my pen has gleaned my teeming brain." And in a poem a year later he wrote [while] "This living hand is now [still] warm and capable."

[It's been said that tuberculosis stimulates creative minds to become more creative as victims get sicker. It's believed that some of the most imaginative works of intellectuals who died from tuberculosis, such as Keats, Chekhov, Chopin, and D. H.

Lawrence, were written in the last years of their lives. Literary creativity may have been heightened by use of laudanum; a tincture of opium commonly used to alleviate pain that, like heroin, creates euphoric highs. Addiction to heroin may have inspired the vivid colors in paintings by Paul Gauguin and Vincent van Gogh, and the creative writing by Edgar Allan Poe and Arthur Conan Doyle. Doyle's Sherlock Holmes was a heroin user, and it's believed there was something of Doyle in Holmes.]

A disappointing love experience previous to Fanny Brawne occurred in 1814 when Keats was nineteen. He saw a beautiful young woman only briefly but was so infatuated by the "fair creature" he became "tangled in her beauty's web." [As written in Keats's sonnet *To a Lady Seen for a Few Moments at Vauxhall.*] Even the "ungloving" of her hand was erotic to him, and though Keats never saw the young woman again his memories lasted.

Four years later, Keats wrote: "And when I feel fair creature of an hour / That I shall never look upon thee more," Keats feared lasting love was unobtainable. First is the joy of discovering love and then the anguish of losing it, if ever possessed.

The tale of *La Belle Dame sans Merci* is just that—a story of love found and love lost. As originally written by Chartier, the story is of an abandoned lover who died when rejected by his lady. It represented ideal but unobtainable perfect love; the moral of Keats's poem.

Some scholars believe his story is not specifically of Keats or of Fanny. It may be of tormented love in general; a theme that inspired Keats from the works of Boccaccio, Chaucer, Chartier, Spencer, Shakespearean tragedies and Greco-Roman mythology. And there are scholars who feel the poem should be read only as a fable and nothing more.

Whatever Keats's inspiration, and intent, he set the haunting narrative of love and its woeful aftermath in a bleak and wintry landscape in medieval times when and where "sedges have withered from the lake and no birds sing." That the "squirrel's granary is full" and "the harvest is done" suggests the end of fall and the start of winter. The knight, loitering alone on a cold hill side, is pale, feverish, haggard, and "woe-begone." Some scholars believe the knight is dying as in Chartier [and as was Keats when his poem was written.] An unidentified person puzzled by the knight's deathly appearance asked: "Ah, what can ail thee, wretched wight?" ("knight at arms" in one version). The knight answered that he met a lady "full beautiful," a "faery's child," who sang to him a "faery's song" and "made sweet moan." The lady looked at him as though she loved him and said in "language strange" [what the knight interpreted to mean] "I love thee true." In smitten response he wooed her with flowers and gave to her all of his attention so that he saw "nothing else all day long."

The lady fed him roots, honey, and manna dew [an alcohol made from fermented fungi (mushrooms and lichens) and other plants], then took him to her "elfin grot" where the poem—lacking details—only implies a consummation of their liaison for it was there they "slumbered on the moss." But when asleep, the knight had nightmarish dreams. [These may have been induced from the honey—if fermented in the form of "mead"—and from "roots and manna dew" suitable for a faery's diet but strange, intolerant, and, perhaps, intoxicating and hallucinogenic for a mortal.] Upon awakening, the knight found himself abandoned.

A similar story was told a year earlier in Keats's versions of Greek myths published as *Endymion: A Poetic Romance*. In one story Endymion, a shepherd living in a cavern, awakened one morning and found that he was abandoned by his moon goddess lover, Selene, of the night before. It's written that while they slept in each other's arms, his "fair visitant unwound her gentle limbs from around him and vanished." In grief, Endymion "pressed his empty arms together." "How lone he was." "Love's madness he had known," for he "swooned drunken from his lady's nipple."

"I sought her arms and lips . . . but she was gone." "Disappointment struck me so sore I ran out and searched the forest o'er." When Endymion realized his moon goddess was truly gone he walked about in "slow, languid paces with face hidden [buried] in muffling hands;" suggesting he wept aloud from a broken heart.

With that aftermath in mind, Keats said the knight in *La Belle Dame sans Merci* loitered about [believed to mean] hoping the faery-lady would return. There seemed little reason for him to believe her love was anything but real, while it lasted, but the brief affair may have been Keats's point—that love found is as quickly lost, and that joy and sorrow are entwined.

To fill in blanks to the story, one wonders. Was the knight in *La Belle Dame sans Merci*, like Endymion, "struck so sore he searched the forest o'er?" And when he realized that she was truly gone, was the knight so stricken with grief that he buried his face in "muffling hands?" He was as Keats said: "woe-begone."

There are those who interpret the faery-child as a heartless *femme fatale* who had no desire other than the story's "one night stand." That she took the knight to her "elfin grot" and there seduced him with her "wild [mesmeric] eyes, songs, foods, drinks, and sweet moans," to then leave him *sans merci* [without pity] suggests that their brief affair was only to satisfy her own lust; something of her "love them, leave them" attitude as with other men ("kings and princes too").

In *Endymion*, Keats wrote: "There never lived a mortal man who bent / His appetite beyond his natural sphere / But starved and died." In *La Belle Dame sans Merci* Keats wrote of "starvèd lips," "pale kings, and princes too, / Pale warriors, death-pale were they all." In Chartier's story the mortal died. In other of Keats's poems the mortal dies. So, there is another blank to fill. Did the knight in Keats's story die? Keats didn't say, but some scholars believe he did.

That the "wretched wight" in Keats's version is dying is suggested by: "I see a lily on thy brow / With anguish moist and fever dew / And on thy cheek a fading rose / Fast withereth too." ["Lily" is the color of a pale-white brow, and "fading rose" is loss of color giving rise to "death-pale" cheeks. "Fever dew" is perspiration.]

Faery-lands, cave homes, songs, sighs and moans, loves consummated, manna and honey foods, narcotic-induced dreams, and death occur in other of Keats's poems. His 1819 *Lamia* [a *femme fatale* based on Greek mythology painted twice by Waterhouse in 1905 and 1909] is the tale of another mortal/immortal pairing ending in abandonment similar to the story in *La Belle Dame sans Merci*. However, the longer *Lamia* of 707 lines vs. 48 is rich in detail, and as a more involved story the poem is lengthened with dialogue between the lovers, Lycius and Lamia, and other characters absent in *La Belle Dame sans Merci*. Since the faery-child in the latter spoke "in language strange," there was no verbal communication between the knight and lady to lengthen the poem.

And while the lovers in *Lamia* lived for awhile "in sweet sin" prior to a planned marriage (unlike in *La Belle Dame sans Merci*), love in both stories ended in failure. In *Lamia*, the immortal serpent-woman vanished and the mortal, Lycius, died. Perhaps in that, Keats's story of the abandoned knight in *La Belle Dame sans Merci* is only a theme repeated from his own poems, and from folklore tales, mythology, and the dark sides of love, dreams, and nightmares.

The debate, however, over the meaning(s) of *La Belle Dame sans Merci* remains unending. One scholar said that in literature "A great work takes on a life of its own as soon as it has left the hand of the writer who can do nothing to prevent readers from interpreting it freely."

In *La Belle Dame sans Merci* the knight and his faery-child "slumber on the moss." How can that be interpreted? With a lack of details to help, how much more is there to the story? Keats embellished the scene by quoting the knight in one version: "And there I shut her wild wild eyes with kisses, / And there she lullèd me asleep." In the other version: "So kissed to sleep / And there we slumbered on the moss;" thus adding intimate variations. Anything more, however, is left to the imagination of curious readers.

To some scholars, the knight and lady *were* lovers as those in other of Keats's pairings. Certainly, love and lust and loss of love were parts of Keats's poetry as in his life.

Keats once confided to a friend that in the company of women he had immoral thoughts, and lust may have been fantasy in his poetry. In 1819 he wrote *The Eve of St. Agnes* as an engagement gift for Fanny Brawne. Basically, the story concerns a belief that on the eve of the Feast of St. Agnes a virgin might dream of her future husband and learn his identity. She must, however, follow specific rites; one of which is to retire for the night in a supine position with eyes to heaven. The bedroom scene of the sleeping virgin [Madeline] in Keats's poem was too sexually explicit, and was criticized by reviewers as "unfit for ladies." Keats was required to rewrite objectionable lines before publication of his poem.

Excerpted herein from the edited version—and what might be imagined from the original "unfit" version—young Porphyro (Keats?) with his "heart on fire for Madeline" (Fanny?) hid in her bedchamber closet watching the young maiden undress. Madeline freed a wreath of pearls from her hair; unclasped jewels one by one warmed by her bosom; and when at last she "loosened her bodice and let drop her dress" Porphyro grew faint to see nude "so pure a thing so free from mortal taint" [a virgin].

After Madeline fell asleep, "he from forth the closet crept and over the hushed carpet, silent, stepped." Porphyro "gazed entranced" upon Madeline's empty dress, then "tween the curtains of her bed he peeped, where lo!—how fast she slept." [To reader imagination, sleeping nude with breasts also "looking" to heaven.]

[Madeline may have "drugged" herself into a deep sleep with laudanum—the tincture of opium derived from poppies used not only as a pain killer but a sedative leaving a sleeper in drowsy euphoria. She wanted to be sure that she slept without danger of awakening during a dream. In *Ode to a Nightingale*, Keats wrote: "A numbness pains my sense as though I emptied some dull (dulling) opiate to the drains." Keats, no doubt, used laudanum as a pain killer—and was likely addicted to it—to dull daily the chronic pain of his throat.]

Keats wrote of Madeline: "In [a] sort of wakeful swoon she lay / Until the poppied [laudanum induced] warmth of sleep oppressed / Her soothèd limbs and [her] soul [mind] fatigued away; / Flown like a thought until the morrow day / Blissfully havenèd from [senseless to] both joy and pain."

[One has to wonder what kind of "pain" Keats thought Madeline might suffer during her sleep? Deep sleep in itself is not painful. It can be assumed that Keats thought Madeline—a virgin—-would be "out of it" for any sexual pain the remainder of the night feeling nothing afterward "until the morrow day." Likewise, she would feel no "joy."]

Porphyro looked down at Madeline and mused, "entoiled in [lustful] fantasies." Then he whispered: "My love awake / Thou art my heaven." But Madeline didn't awake. "Wherewith disturbed," however, in her sleep Madeline "moaned and mumbled witless words," and though her "frightened blue eyes wide open shone," Madeline remained trance-like seeing Porphyro only as a vision in her dream. Then, "Ah, Porphyro!" she mumbled [talking in her sleep] realizing in her dream he would be her husband.

Some scholars believe Porphyro then took advantage of Madeline's comatose condition said to be "senseless to both joy and pain." "My Madeline! sweet dreamer! lovely bride!" Porphyro murmured in his (their) consummation whether fantasized or real. [There is some ambiguity in interpretation, but "sweet dreamer" verifies Madeline was comatose, and while deep in sleep "lovely bride" suggests Porphyro considered them wed and consummated their marriage; at least day dreamed of it. "Into her dream [in her sleep] he melted as the rose blendeth with the violet / Solution sweet." Did Porphyro unite with Madeline only in fantasy or in reality while Madeline slept comatose supine with eyes to heaven?]

Later, when awake and no longer numbed with laudanum, and aware that Porphyro had loved her [dreamed of or in reality], Madeline bemoaned that he might now leave her—a "love her leave her" fear. "I curse [you] not for my heart is lost in thine / Though thou forsakest [me] a deceivèd thing; / A dove forlorn and lost."

But Madeline forgave Porphyro and Porphyro proposed. The engaged couple then fled her castle for fear her father would kill Porphyro if discovered with Madeline. [They may have fled to an unhappy fate, however, based upon unhappy endings in other of Keats's poems. That Madeline and Porphyro "fled into a storm" suggests it.]

Was Keats, through *The Eve of St. Agnes* written especially for Fanny, making known his desires for her? She was the tiny, lovely, five-foot blue-eyed teen-ager who lived in a flat on the other side of his sitting room wall? Fanny was surely on his mind with immoral thoughts.

Day after day Keats heard Fanny move about. He saw her daily inside their two "houses" under a common roof. They shared a bathroom and had side by side kitchens. Keats visited and dined with Fanny. He watched her walk in the garden below from an upstairs window and "caught her beauty" as Lorenzo did of Isabella in Keats's 1820 poem *The Pot of Basil*, based upon a fourteenth century Boccaccio tale. [No doubt influenced by both Boccaccio and Keats, Waterhouse painted his *Isabella and the Pot of Basil* in 1907.]

Lines in Keats's poem, paraphrased, are reflective in part of the time from 1818 on when Fanny and Keats were engaged to be married and lived under the same roof. Long-time engaged couples living wall to wall cannot help but have romantic desire, and talk of love if not act upon it.

In the poem "They [Isabella and Lorenzo (Fanny and Keats)] could not dwell in the same mansion without stir of heart." "They could not sit at meals but feel soothed with the other by." "They could not beneath the same roof sleep but dream of one another."

Keats wrote that Isabella secretly visited Lorenzo in the room where he slept, and every day their "love grew deeper." [Did Fanny slip secretly out of *her* side of the house to visit Keats where he slept? One wonders. Was that the basis in part for Keats's version of the Boccaccio tale? And in *The Eve of St. Agnes* Porphryo (Keats) slipped into Madeline's (Fanny's) room.]

In a letter to his brother George, Keats described Fanny's

shape, countenance, movements, language and demeanor. She "wasn't yet seventeen," Keats wrote. He called her a "minx" [a pert, sly, and playful girl] and said she had "a penchant for being stylish." Keats obviously knew Fanny well. An 1825 acquaintance (four years after Keats died) described Fanny as a "beautiful young creature," and an 1833 portrait in the year of her marriage, twelve years after Keats died, showed Fanny blue-eyed and elegantly dressed.

Was it more than coincidence, then, in *The Eve of St. Agnes* that Keats created Madeline blue-eyed, virginal, stylish, beautiful, and sexually desirable? Since the poem was written *for* Fanny, curious readers have to wonder. Was blue-eyed Fanny the same blue-eyed Madeline in fiction? Keats made a point of Madeline's blue eyes, and only in *The Eve of St. Agnes*, and in other poems about Fanny, did Keats write with such passion and intimacy.

In his 1819 *Bright Star*, a year after his engagement, Keats feared he might "swoon to death pillowed upon [his head upon] his love's ripening breast [suggesting Fanny's adolescence] to feel forever its fall and swell." Keats no doubt had breasts in mind when in the company of women he had "immoral thoughts" for he wrote a year earlier in Book II of his epic poem that Endymion "swooned drunken from pleasure's nipple." In Book III, Keats wrote, in first person, of Glaucus who said the sea-nymph Scylla "took me like a child of suckling time."

Both stories are highly sexual and explicit. The second had still another tragic ending when the witch, Circe, killed Scylla in jealousy. [Waterhouse painted the story in his 1892 *Circe Invidiosa* based in part on Keats's poem and in part on Greek mythology.]

Perhaps Keats knew the pleasures of women—of Fanny— for in *Lines to Fanny* (ca 1820) he wrote: "O let me once more [suggesting he had already] rest / My soul [pillowed head] upon that dazzling breast." [Curious readers wonder how he knew that it "dazzled." In another poem Keats said her breasts were "warm, white, and lucid," said as if he knew.]

But in the same ambivalent poem, Keats also said: "Enough!

It is enough for me / [just] To dream of thee." Or was he dreaming? [Some scholars believe *The Eve of St. Agnes was* a revelation of Keats's true-life pleasures.] The fictional Porphyro [Keats] had his way with Madeline [Fanny], but Keats was contradictory in his poem saying Porphyro was not a "rude infidel;" that he would "save Madeline's sweet self" [her innocence]. Moreover, Porphyro promised a reluctant maidservant who led him secretly to Madeline's bedchamber that he would not "harm" Madeline. "By all saints" he swore not even to "displace a ringlet [?] of Madeline's hair," or "look upon her face with ruffian passion." Yet, what Porphyro promised the maidservant was not in truth what happened in the privacy of Madeline's bedchamber, unless only in fantasy.

In his 1819 poem, *To Fanny*, the year before *St. Agnes*, Keats wrote [looking forward to marrying Fanny] "O! let me have the whole [not yet lost her virginity], all, all, be mine / That shape, that fairness, your kiss, those hands, those eyes divine / That warm, white, lucid, million-pleasured breast [again, how did he know that?] / In pity give me all / Withhold no atom's atom or I die." More daydreams?

In the same poem, his line "the palate [mental relish] of my mind" suggests Keats was fantasizing about Fanny. He said in a letter to Fanny that her lips "grow sweet to his fancies." But fantasizing or not about Fanny, Keats was a romantic, and in his 1818 *A Song about Myself*, a whimsical poem written for his sister, also named Fanny, Keats admitted that he was a "naughty boy."

Keats could, however, get too sexually explicit in his poetry. Publishers Taylor and Hessy asked him to rewrite the lines considered "unfit for ladies" in the bedchamber scene of his *The Eve of St. Agnes*. What the publishers wanted deleted as "unfit" is unknown as to how graphic, but the published version was titillating enough.

Keats argued that his poem was written for men only although it was an engagement gift for Fanny, and was certainly, as today, read then by ladies. [If such a poem was "unfit for ladies," then the graphic poem written especially for Fanny's perusal suggests familiarity between them more than casual.] But Keats lost his appeal, and while the edited story remained risqué, how could *The Eve of St. Agnes* been more "unfit" than *Endymion* published two years earlier about "limbs around him," and "swoons on nipples." What could have been "unfit" in *La Belle Dame sans Merci* wasn't written. Perhaps Keats feared more censure after *The Eve of St. Agnes* three months earlier.

All of the above establishes the "mind set" of the young and virile Keats prior to the time of his first version of *La Belle Dame sans Merci*, and what thoughts influenced the man in any of his romantic poetry.

The sexual encounter in Endymion's cave two years previously is believed basis for the faery-child's tryst in her "elfin grot" where she and the knight "slumbered" together like Endymion and his moon goddess. And with the faery-child's "faery song," "sweet moans," "looks of love," and the "I love thee true," the poem was clearly meant to imply seduction. For what reason other than consummation of a love affair, one has to ask, would the faery-child seduce a virile knight?

Based on simiar intimacies in Keats's other poetry, a reader of *La Belle Dame sans Merci* should have little reason to question blanks in the story. Did the faery-child—as the moon goddess in Endymion—wrap her "gentle limbs" around the knight? It's likely! Did the knight "swoon drunken" from his lady's nipples? It's likely! Did the two of them experience "love's madness" on the moss? It's likely." It wasn't beyond Keats's mind-set, therefore, to think and imply intimacy between the knight and his faery-child seductress.

THE POEM AND THE PAINTER

What was the mind-set of John William Waterhouse when with artistic license he painted a re-creation of Keats's *La Belle*

Dame sans Merci? Waterhouse often put stories on canvas adding imaginative details with strong senses of narration rich in symbolism. What blanks are to be filled, if any, when viewers study his painting? Was it for Waterhouse as for Keats: "Enough! Enough! It is enough for me / Just To dream of thee" [of the model], or did the painting tell a story of intimacy true to life? Waterhouse was strongly influenced by the passionate poetry of Keats that may have influenced Waterhouse in his romantic personal life as well as that of a Romanticist and Symbolist artist.

One biographer believed the knight in the painting *was* Waterhouse himself. Another believed the romantic painting *was* based on "realism." Still another believed Waterhouse was "obsessed" with his model, and that his desire for her, "strongly present" in the painting, is betrayed symbolically by the "rigidity of the lance," and the way he grips it.

With a fertile imagination equal to that of the poet Waterhouse used the freedom of his brush to picture on canvas what couldn't be said in print. While on first glance the story of the knight and the maiden goes no further than an initial seduction, what follows is left to viewer imagination.

With Waterhouse symbolized as the knight, his "lance" suggests that Waterhouse, like Keats, had "immoral thoughts." The symbolism of a heart upon the model's sleeve suggests mutual desires as the maiden pulls the knight down to her in invitation to a kiss and an embrace.

Knight-errantry, medievalism, chivalry, and courtship, became common themes among nineteenth century poets and artists, and Waterhouse was influenced by the playwrights and poets. From Keats's *La Belle Dame sans Merci*, Waterhouse took license to change the setting from a bleak and wintry scene where "sedges have withered from the lake and no birds sing" into the warmth of a woodland landscape with summer flowers and a barefoot maiden in a light and airy dress. There's no winter cold in Waterhouse's version and if birds could be heard, wrens and warblers would surely be singing courtship songs. And while there is no noose of hair in Keats's tale, Waterhouse added it to imply impending intimacy.

The object of an artist is to tell a story that captures interest and makes viewers ask questions. Curious viewers of Waterhouse's *La Belle Dame sans Merci* feel plunged into the center of some story, and the longer that viewers study the painting, and get caught up in the narrative, questions arise. What's the significance of the heart upon the maiden's sleeve, and the many pearls on her dress and in her hair? What's the significance, if any, of the background stream? Why isn't there an "elfin grot" in Waterhouse's version of the story so major a part in Keats's tale?

A sketch made by Waterhouse preliminary to the painting depicted the maiden wearing a lily pad for a hat; the same as the amorous nymph in Waterhouse's subsequent "A Naiad." The nymph standing in a stream eyes a young shepherd asleep on the bank.

According to Greek mythology water nymphs, or Naiads, are born from water-lilies, and as blossoms take on forms of human females who cavort about in water or out on land either draped or undraped. [Artists always depict them youthful, seductive, and beautiful (see opposite).] Slow moving streams and ponds full of water lilies are homes for water nymphs, and as sources of pearls from clams. Lily pads, blossoms, streams, and pearls appear in numerous Waterhouse paintings that were favorites of his props to paint.

A necklace of pearls is painted in *A Mermaid* and in *Vanity*. A nymph holds a handful of pearls in *Hylas and the Nymphs*. Pearls adorn the ornate dress of Waterhouse's 1894 *Ophelia*, and the neckline of the maiden in *The Shrine*. A maiden wears pearls in *Maidens Picking Flowers by a Stream*. Pearls are depicted in *Veronica*, *The Necklace*, *The Soul of the Rose*, *The Charmer*, *The Magic Circle*, Waterhouse's 1888 and 1894 *The Lady of Shalott*, and his two versions of *Lamia*.

Water-lilies and a stream are painted in *Nymphs Finding the Head of Orpheus*, and in *Echo and Narcissus*. Echo is a nymph,

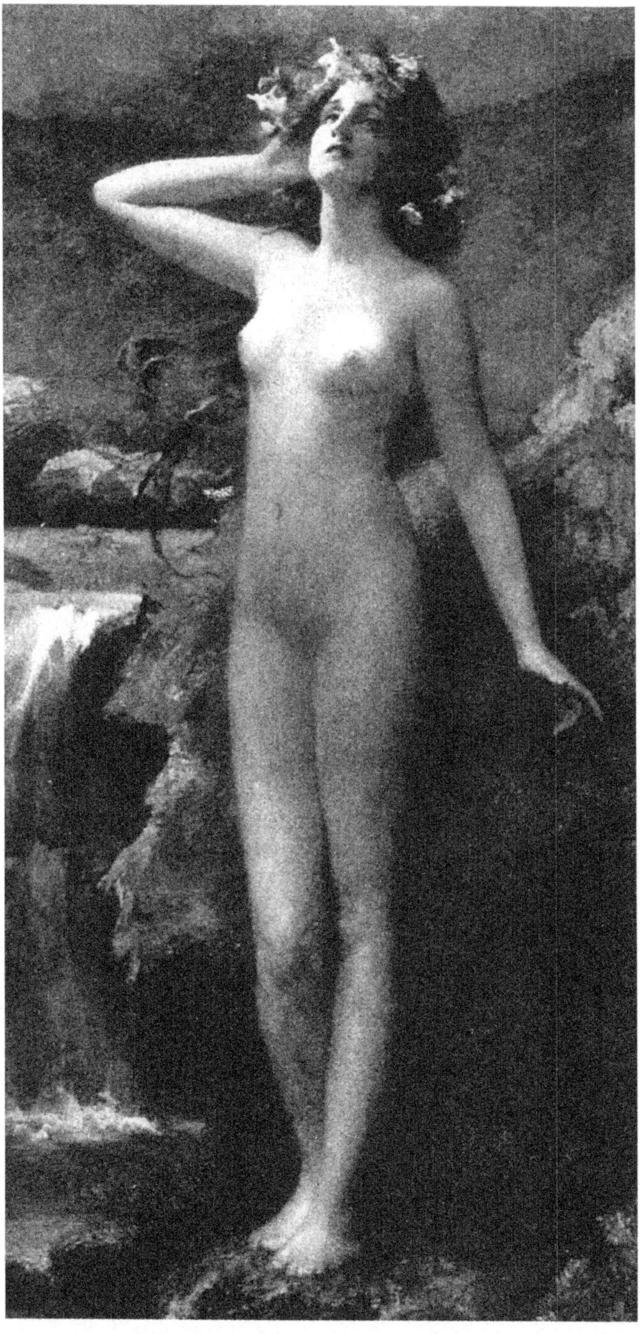

and the stream in *Windflowers* suggests the maiden picking flowers is another.

Clearly, Waterhouse was fascinated with nymphs, lilies, streams, and pearls. In his re-creation of *La Belle Dame sans Merci*, Waterhouse made the maiden a nymph adorned with pearls, and not a faery-child with a "garland on her head" as written by Keats. The maiden's source of her pearls is the background stream, and her home is the surrounding forest; the domain of water nymphs. [The preliminary sketch showing the maiden wearing lily pads suggests that Waterhouse intended her to be thought of as a water nymph in his re-creation and not a faery-child. Hobson, 1980, believes the knight "kneels before a nymph."]

Although little of Waterhouse's interpretation is written in Keats's poem, the artist took ideas such as a "lady full beautiful," and "her hair was long" which Waterhouse looped around the knight in an obvious seduction. Titillated viewers imagine what comes after.

The same scholar who commented about great works of literature said the same about great works of art; that "Everyone has a right to interpret them as he or she likes." Can the Waterhouse painting be viewed as a love affair between the artist and his model? Likely! Was it a narration on canvas to confess to a true story? Likely! Curious viewers imagine the rest of the story.

Readers puzzle over the meaning(s) of the poem, *La Belle Dame sans Merci*, considered one of the most popular ever written; being eighth in the top five hundred listed in *The Columbia Granger's Index to Poetry*, Tenth Edition (1994), and ninth in *The Top 500 Poems, A Columbia Anthology*, (1992)

THE POEM
"LA BELLE DAME SANS MERCI"

John Keats

Original Version in a letter to his brother George
April 21, 1819.

I

O what can ail thee, knight at arms,
    Alone and palely loitering?
The sedge has withered from the lake,
    And no birds sing.

II

O what can ail thee, knight at arms,
    So haggard and so woe-begone?
The squirrel's granary is full,
    And the harvest's done.

III

I see a lily on thy brow,
    With anguish moist and fever-dew,
And on thy cheeks a fading rose
    Fast withereth too.

IV

I met a lady in the meads,
    Full beautiful—a faery's child,
Her hair was long, her foot was light,
    And her eyes were wild.

V

I made a garland for her head,
    And bracelets too, and fragrant zone;
She looked at me as she did love,
    And made sweet moan.

VI

I set her on my pacing steed,
    And nothing else saw all day long,
For sidelong would she bend, and sing
    A faery's song.

VII

She found me roots of relish sweet,
    And honey wild, and manna-dew,
And sure in language strange she said—
    'I love thee true'.

VIII

She took me to her elfin grot,
    And there she wept and sighed full sore,
And there I shut her wild wild eyes
    With kisses four.

IX

And there she lullèd me asleep
    And there I dreamed—Ah! woe betide!—
The latest dream I ever dreamt
    On the cold hill side.

X

I saw pale kings and princes too,
    Pale warriors, death-pale were they all;
They cried—'La Belle Dame sans Merci
    Thee hath in thrall!'

XI

I saw their starved lips in the gloam,
    With horrid warning gapèd wide,
And I awoke and found me here,
    On the cold hill's side.

XII

And this is why I sojourn here
Alone and palely loitering,
Though the sedge is withered from the lake,
And no birds sing.

"LA BELLE DAME SANS MERCI"

Revised version published in "The Indicator"
May 10, 1820

I

Ah, what can ail thee, wretched wight,
　　Alone and palely loitering?
The sedge is wither'd from the lake,
　　And no birds sing.

II

Ah, what can ail thee, wretched wight,
　　So haggard and so woe-begone?
The squirrel's granary is full,
　　And the harvest's done.

III

I see a lily on thy brow,
　　With anguish moist and fever dew;
And on thy cheek a fading rose
　　Fast withereth too.

IV

I met a lady in the meads
　　Full beautiful, a faery's child;
Her hair was long, her foot was light,
　　And her eyes were wild.

V

I set her on my pacing steed,
    And nothing else saw all day long;
For sideways would she lean, and sing
    A faery's song.

VI

I made a garland for her head,
    And bracelets too, and fragrant zone;
She look'd at me as she did love,
    And made sweet moan.

VII

She found me roots of relish sweet,
    And honey wild, and manna dew;
And sure in language strange she said,
    I love thee true.

VIII

She took me to her elfin grot,
    And there she gaz'd and sighed deep,
And there I shut her wild sad eyes—
    So kissed to sleep.

IX

And there we slumber'd on the moss,
    And there I dream'd ah woe betide,
The latest dream I ever dream'd
    On the cold hill side.

X

I saw pale kings, and princes too,
    Pale warriors, death-pale were they all;
Who cry'd—"La belle Dame sans Merci
    Hath thee in thrall!"

XI
I saw their starv'd lips in the gloam
    With horrid warning gaped wide,
And I awoke, and found me here
    On the cold hill side.

XII
And this is why I sojourn here
    Alone and palely loitering,
Though the sedge is wither'd from the lake,
    And no birds sing

"SHE FOUND ME ROOTS"

(Undated parody on Verse VII)

She found me roots of relish sweet,
Doughnuts with jam and cream replete,
Dozens of oysters, pints of prawns,
Hams and tongues, terrines and brawns.

And honey wild and manna dew,
Syllabub and Irish stew,
Dover sole and lemon mousse,
Lobster, crab, and Charlotte Russe.

And sure in language strange she said
'Coq au vin, quiche aux courgettes,
Oeufs en cocotte, blanquette de veau,'
And then in husky murmur low

'I love thee true.
Come nearer do . . . '
But I cried 'Stuff!
I've had enough.

REFERENCES

Baker, James K, and Cathy L. Baker
    1999. "Miss Muriel Foster: The John William Waterhouse Model." *Jour. of Pre-Raphaelite Studies*, New Series 8: (Fall 1999) pp 70-82.

Barnard, John (Editor)
    1988. *John Keats; Selected Poetry*. Penguin Books, London, 233pp.

Bate, Walter Jackson
    1963. *John Keats*. Belknap Press, Harvard, Cambridge. 732pp.
    1965. *Keats; A Collection of Critical Essays*. Prentice-Hall, Englewood Cliffs, NJ. 177pp.

Finney, Claude Lee
    1936. *The Evolution of Keats's Poetry*. Two volumes bound as one. Russell & Russell, NY. 804pp.

Gurney, Stephen
    1993. *British Poetry of the Nineteenth Century*. Twayne Publishers, New York. 341pp.

Harmon, William (Editor)
    1992. *The Top 500 Poems*. Columbia Univ. Press, NY. 1132pp.

Hazen, Edith P. (Editor)
    1994. *The Columbia Granger's Index to Poetry*. Tenth Edition. Columbia Univ. Press, NY. 2150pp.

Hobson, Anthony
    1980. *The Art and Life of J.W. Waterhouse, RA 1849-1917*. Studio Vista/Christie's Book, London. 208pp.

1989. *J.W. Waterhouse*. Phaidon Press Limited, London. 128pp.
Inglis, Fred
   1969. *Keats*. Arco Publishing, NY. 159pp.
MacEachen, Dougald B.
   1971. *Keats and Shelly; Notes*. Cliffs Notes, Lincoln Nebraska. 75pp.
Marvick, Andrew Bolton
   1996. "Herself a Psyche: Feminine Identities in the Art of John William Waterhouse." *Jour. of Pre-Raphaelite Studies*, 5 (Spring 1996) pp 81-94.
Modern (The) Library
   (undated) *John Keats and Percy Bysshe Shelley*. The Modern Library, New York. 914pp.
Moore, Christopher (Editor)
   1993. *John Keats; Selected Poems*. Gramercy Books, NY, 192pp.
Perkins, David
   1959. *The Quest for Permanence; The Symbolism of Wordsworth Shelly and Keats*. Harvard Univ. Press, Cambridge. 305pp.
Trippi, Peter
   2002. *J.W. Waterhouse*. Phaidon Press Limited, London. 240pp.
Zaranka, William (Editor)
   1981. *The Brand-X Anthology of Poetry*. Apple-Wood Books, Inc. Cambridge. 357pp.

EPILOGUE

Muriélle is a work of fiction based on a Waterhouse model, "Miss Muriel Foster," whose name was found inscribed on a profile sketch of Waterhouse's 1905 *Lamia*. It is the only known reference to her identity as there are no known diaries, journals, letters, or other notations that might reveal anything more about her. Her true identity may never be known.

John William Waterhouse R.A. painted more than two hundred paintings of considerable value that hang in galleries, museums, and in private collections around the world. And more reproductions of his works are sold today in books, on cards and calendars, and as posters than of any other British artist. He was born on January 16, 1849, in Rome and died at age sixty-eight February 10, 1917, in London where he is buried in Kensal Green Cemetery. He remains one of England's most popular artists although one of the most enigmatic and least known.

The name "Allison Paige" is fictional in this story but whose character is based on another Waterhouse model who appeared in several of his paintings from the latter 1880s until after the turn of the century. "Allison Paige" is believed to be the model for *St. Eulalia* (1886); Waterhouse's "Circe" paintings of 1891 and 1892 and his 1894 version of *The Lady of Shalott*.

"Miranda Marie" is also a fictional name in this story but

whose character is based on a model who sat for Arthur A. Hacker (1858-1919) for numerous paintings through the 1890s including *Syrinx* (1892); *Circe* (1893); *The Temptation of Sir Perceval* (1894); *The Sea-Maiden* (1897); *Memories* (1898); and *The Drone* (1899).

Waterhouse and Hacker were friends as fellow students in the Royal Academy Schools, and later as Academicians. Still later, they lived as neighbors in St. John's Wood; an artist community. The two Waterhouse models in this story and the one Hacker model likely knew each other as friends.

Esther Maria Waterhouse (1858-1944), wife of John William, painted flowers displayed at the Royal Academy of Arts though she was not an Academician. In 1882, the year before her marriage, she displayed "Wallflowers" under her maiden name, Esther Kenworthy. Then under her married name of Mrs. John William Waterhouse, she displayed *Azaleas* in 1885; *Pink Roses* in 1887; *Violets* in 1888; then *Carnations* and another painting of *Violets* in 1889.

John Seymour Lucas R.A. (1849-1923), also a fellow Academician and close friend of Waterhouse, was a portraitist and a period painter and costume designer of seventeenth-century subjects. Lucas was also an antiquary of medieval armor that decorated walls of his studio home on Woodchurch Road in West Hampstead not far from Primrose Hill.

Frederick Richard Pickersgill R.A. (1820-1900) was a teacher, mentor, and sponsor for Waterhouse when Waterhouse enrolled in the Royal Academy Schools in 1870. Pickersgill exhibited mythological, Shakespearean, Scriptural, and historical paintings in the Academy between 1839 and 1875. After a long and successful career, Pickersgill retired to a country life on the Isle of Wight off the southern coast of England.

ACKNOWLEDGMENTS

For their help I am grateful to the following:

My wife for her loving help and companionship.

Robert L. Plunkett of California, an attorney, author, professor of creative writing, and an admirer of Waterhouse art, for reviews and comments.

Pauline Caulfield of Primrose Hill Studios, London, for her hospitality and help with information on the 1893-1901 home of John William Waterhouse where *La Belle Dame sans Merci* was painted in 1893.

Dr. Klaus-D Pohl of the Hessisches Landesmuseum Darmstadt, Germany, where *La Belle Dame sans Merci* is on permanent display, for his kind permission to use an illustration of the painting for a cover.

Julia Kerr of ArtMagick (*www.artmagick.com* & *www.johnwilliamwaterhouse.com*) foremost internet source for information on John William Waterhouse for continuing interest and cooperation with studies on the artist and his models.

The late Dr. Anthony Hobson, an artist, professor, and premier Waterhouse biographer who knew the identity of the model long considered "unknown," and for his generosity to share

253

that and other information with me on a visit to his cottage home in England.

And finally, much appreciation to Major Edward (Teddy) Waterhouse Foster DSO, MC, who provided much information on his aunt Muriel who is the inspiration for the heroine of this story.

PROVENANCE

(After Anthony Hobson)

La Belle Dame sans Merci (Cover)
44x32in (112x81cm) Signed lower left "JW Waterhouse 1893."
Coll: Hessisches Landesmuseum Darmstadt.
Exh: Royal Academy 1893 (149).
Guildhall 1894 (122), by permission Geo. Woodiwiss, Esq.
Liverpool Autumn Exhibition 1898 (1069).
Irish International Exhibition 1907.
Bristol.
Hessisches Landesmuseum Darmstadt 1964, "New Acquisitions" 1960-64.
Staatliche Kunsthalle, Baden-Baden, 23 Nov 1973-24 Feb 1974, *Präraffaelitin*.
Prov: Christie's 16 April 1920 (154) for George Woodiwiss to Mitchell, 190gns.
Christie's 16 June 1922 (183) for A H Wild to Mitchell, 200gns.
Christie's 31 Jan 1947 (10) for W J Sharp to Mitchell, 58gns.
Sotheby's 26 Feb 1964 (138) to W Mela, £70.
Mela 17 Mar 1964 to Hessisches Landesmuseum Darmstadt, £320 [Value year 2002, priceless].
Repr: *The Magazine of Art* 1894, facing p 118: etched by H MacBeth-Raeburn.
The Studio Vol. IV, No 22, 1895, p 108, by permission of 'the Owner Of the Copyright, G Woodiwiss, Esq, J P of Bath.'

The Art Journal, 1909, Christmas issue, p 17.
[Worldwide at present as cards, posters, and pictured on calendars and in books.]

Printed in Great Britain
by Amazon